CLOSE TO THE EDGE

CLOSE TO THE EDGE

RICK HOLT

Rick Holt

Copyright © 2017 Rick Holt

Follow him on Twitter@Holt_Rickster

This book is a work of fiction and any references to actual persons, living or dead, is purely coincidental. All references to drugs and any places where they are taken are fictional.

The moral right of the author has been asserted.

All rights reserved.
No part of this publication may be reproduced, stored in a retrieval system, or transmitted, in any form or by any means, without the prior permission in writing of the publisher, nor be otherwise circulated in any form of binding or cover other than that in which it is published and without a similar condition including this condition being imposed on the subsequent purchaser.

Published by Rick Holt

ISBN: 978-1-9794-3294-8

Typesetting services by BOOKOW.COM

This book is dedicated to my father who tragically passed away prior to publication

Acknowledgments

I would like to express my thanks to my partner, Caroline Higgins, for her inspiration and for putting up with the incessant noise of my clumsy typing. I could not have written this book without the expert guidance of Paul Smith in matters of national security and the editing skills of Jemima Forrester. Finally, I would like to thank Tommy, Spock and all of my friends for listening to my ramblings about writing my first book; I could not have done it without their support.

Prologue

Jack Reynolds stood still: cold, lonely and deep in thought, wondering who had tucked them up.

Chalked on the black identification board was a note identifying the corpse lying in front of him as Luke Grainger. Jack knew him as Lanky, but the corpse was no more lanky than the yellow piss streak on the floor of the mortuary, a facility that also reeked of Trigene disinfectant. Lanky was dead, very dead according to the young male pathologist whose body language suggested he would be good at irritatingly weaving between pedestrians on a skateboard as they walked down the busy pavement of a high street.

The pathologist had introduced himself as Eddie. He looked about twenty-two, with the remnants of a stubborn case of acne dotted all over his face. Straggly blond hair dangled over the collar of his starched white medical coat. He clutched a sandwich in his left hand whilst shaking Jack's hand with his empty right one.

What was it with people who worked in morgues, Jack wondered somberly and only just soberly. They all seemed to eat non-stop, unlike their unfortunate customers.

Eddie approached the pale corpse laid out on the metallic storage tray. The pathologist's sterile expression hinted at a complete lack of compassion for the man who had once been Jack's best friend.

Jack could barely hear Eddie describing how Lanky had come to such a horrific end in between the rustling of the out-of-date tuna and salad sandwich which Eddie loudly chomped on with his uneven nicotine-stained teeth.

He quietly swore to himself that he would make the murderer pay for Lanky's death when his mobile phone suddenly bleeped. He opened the picture message he'd received and froze. Staring up at him from the screen was a photograph of a terrified young girl sitting on a filthy urine soaked mattress, in her mouth was a gag and she was handcuffed to a radiator.

The deafening sound of his own fear overpowered the pathologist's monotone as the frightening situation facing Jack began to sink in; his best friend was dead but even more frightening than that - Jack recognised the young girl in the photograph.

CHAPTER 1

It had all started a long time ago when they were kids, spotty and feral. Jack and Lanky had met when Jack's parents moved to Effingham in Surrey. Jack and Lanky both lived at the top of the road, a *cul-de-sac* Jack's mum used to call it. A dead end was what Jack would have called it, but when you're young you can always find ways to escape and the cleverly disguised hole he had made in the fence at the bottom of the garden leading to the woods was his route to freedom.

At fourteen, Lanky was a year older than Jack. He was tall, good looking in a rugged way, but already someone the other kids at their school knew not to mess with.

They used to go play shooting in the local woods, killing blackbirds and the like. They pretended to shoot each other, just kids' stuff. Of course it was probably inevitable that one day Lanky actually did shoot Jack in the face with the imitation Luger air pistol stolen for the day from his dad's secret cupboard. A cupboard that also held an impressive porn stash and the odd can of Stella that they used to nick.

Lanky, the cheeky bugger, had just laughed it off saying, 'Accidents happen if you're stupid enough to stand in front of a gun.' Jack still had a small scar on the top of his left cheek.

Jack should have realised then that there was something different about Lanky compared to the rest of his mates. But he knew it was cool to hang around with him and it made him feel good, even though Lanky could be ruthless and had a way of always making Jack feel inadequate and childish.

They did everything together – they often drank litres of warm cheap cider on long summer days in the school holidays. They usually spent the mornings outside the local off licence asking any posh Henry that walked past if he would buy them a bottle of cider with their pocket money, claiming that Jack's dad would beat them up if they didn't come back home with a drink for him. Jack soon learnt at a young age how easy it was to fool people and play to their naivety.

Lanky had taught him to smoke. They smoked those little cigarettes you could buy in singles until they were violently sick. Well poncy, but they thought they looked cool and would impress the girls. They were going to go places and knew it.

CHAPTER 2

Thirty years later, Jack found himself wondering how the fuck he had let life give him such a shit deal. He was in his local pub, the Kings Arms in Dorking, a small market town in leafy Surrey suburbia which at one time had thirty-two pubs in the surrounding area. Maybe this was what had attracted him to live there when his life had initially started to fall apart at the age of forty-three.

The pub was very old, darkly lit inside and cluttered with worm-eaten old oak beams and pockmarked tables. It was rumoured that King Charles II had once stayed there, and the pub was firmly on the local tourist trail for anyone with an interest in English history.

For the last three hours, Jack had been soaking his brain in alcohol. The drinks were bought on the weekly tab that Jim, the young barman, let him have as he felt sorry for him. Jim was young and, despite his profession, he always wore a smart suit. Jack knew he had chosen to be a barman so he could cop off with as many of the female customers as possible. 'It's a dream job – beautiful women and plenty of booze,' Jim had once said. Jim liked to think he was Tom Cruise in *Cocktail*, mixing all sorts of bizarre and potent concoctions for him and Jack to taste. On the house of course.

Jack greedily finished his sixth lonely pint of Oranjeboom whilst his mind wandered. His doctor said he was an alcoholic and that was what his wife Sarah reckoned. Bullshit. He just liked to drink away all the nightmare memories of Bosnia and the hassle that other people gave him – especially in his latest line of undercover work with the NCA.

Jack was still very much in love with Sarah but his drinking and escalating drug use had put too much pressure on their relationship. After twenty-three years of marriage Sarah had finally kicked him out of the family home, telling him to straighten himself out. Jack still spoke to her every day, he didn't blame her for kicking him out and was hopeful she would relent and let him back home soon.

As Jack's mind pulled up images of Sarah – younger, happier, laughing at something he'd said – he heard the sound of Rihanna's song 'Diamonds'. His daughter Amy had set it as the ring tone on his mobile phone the last time she'd been home from university. He kept meaning to change it, but he liked that it reminded him of her. He missed her a lot since she had gone off to university, they had been close whilst she'd been growing up but lately they'd slowly drifted apart.

Who'd be calling at this time of night and on this number? He'd made sure this mobile number was not common knowledge so it must be something to do with the job he'd been assigned to.

'Jack Reynolds?'

The voice had an accent that Jack couldn't quite place. It sounded northern, quiet but with an air of confident authority. Jack guessed by the voice that the man was the sort of person who was used to others listening to him and so he waited for what the man had to say.

The phone went quiet for a few seconds and all he could hear was his own labored breathing. He needed to quit smoking.

Jack thought he recognised the voice from earlier surveillance phone-taps and felt a cold sweat run down the back of his neck. It trickled down to the small of his back like a drowning tadpole trying to escape.

'Who wants to know?' he asked.

CHAPTER 3

'It's Riordan.'

Mick Riordan.

The name hit Jack like a thunder-bolt. Riordan was the head of a large crime gang. Jack had spent the last three years working undercover trying to get close to Riordan and the chase had nearly cost him his family.

'Hello, Mr Riordan,' Jack replied, playing it much cooler than he was feeling. They'd not spoken before, but he knew exactly what the man behind the quiet northern voice stood for. Perhaps this call meant that after all of his hard graft he'd finally gained Riordan's trust.

'You've worked for me for a while now and I think it's time you stepped up the ladder a bit. Someone's taking me for a muppet and scamming some gear off me. I want you to find out who the scumbag is that's stealing from me and ensure they understand who they've crossed – if word gets around every James Blunt will be having a go, know what I mean?'

Jack didn't answer immediately, he found listening to a northerner speaking rhyming slang quite strange. Riordan coughed harshly down the phone, loudly swallowing his phlegm. Jack welcomed the chance to take a few seconds to think of how to respond.

'Crystal clear, Mr Riordan. What do I have to do?' Jack said slowly.

'Normally I would give the job to Skeggsy but I need a fresh pair of eyes. You've worked with Skeggsy before haven't you?'

'Yes,' Jack answered. Skeggsy was Riordan's right-hand man and a complete nutter. 'We've worked on various jobs together.'

Riordan continued, 'I'm not saying I don't trust Skeggsy but I want you to meet him and get the keys for Cavendish Road off him. I'll get Skeggsy to call you. You've been there before haven't you?'

'Yeah, a few times.' Cavendish Road was a safe-house the gang used for storing drugs.

'Right, well I want you to do the usual monthly drop in Southall instead of Skeggsy. Big V and his boys want to take my business so if you see anything funny you get straight back to me, don't say a fucking word to Skeggsy. I'll WhatsApp you a different number to get me on if you need to.'

'Skeggsy won't like it, me muscling in on his jobs,' Jack said buzzing with excitement that Riordan was finally trusting him. He'd never been trusted to do the Southall drug delivery without Skeggsy.

'Yeah, well, he's my dog and I'll control him. You just make sure the delivery in Southall goes off without any trouble.'

'Sure thing, Mr Riordan, but I'm sure it isn't Skeggsy trying to stiff you.' Jack was trying to defuse the situation and his involvement in any retribution that would follow.

'He probably doesn't have the brains but I can't be too careful. If you prove yourself I might get you to oversee the next delivery of gear in Wandsworth as well.' Riordan hung up, leaving just a dead tone ringing in Jack's ear.

Jack put the mobile phone down on the beer-splattered oak bar and thought about what the last few seconds had meant. He couldn't believe his luck; not only did Riordan want him to take over the drug delivery in Southall from Skeggsy but he'd mentioned that he might include him in the next large delivery of drugs being moved to the safe-house in Wandsworth.

'Hey, Jim, top us up, will you?' Jack shouted at the barman who was busy chatting up the latest young blond barmaid on her university break. Jim regretfully tore himself away from the blonde and poured Jack another pint.

One more, no more, he thought to himself. He really needed time to clear his head and think.

Riordan was rattled about something and Skeggsy might be the weak link to Jack gaining Riordan's trust and finally bringing him to justice.

The worst thing about working undercover was having to associate with the likes of Skeggsy. The guy was in his early thirties and, from what he knew of him, he was a total psycho. He had cropped red hair and he thought that everyone hated gingers. He had an excessively violent chip on his shoulder, which he used to hurt anyone with a pulse in his vicinity, whenever he felt like it. Skeggsy swallowed steroids like they were Smarties and Jack was damn sure he was also sticking needles in himself like a pincushion – speed, smack or probably both. The man was built like a Sherman Tank but with the brains of a monkey that had been experimented on by the people in white coats.

Jack knew the story on Skeggsy. He was born in Mile End and his mother had been a whore, getting money for them by lying on her back for numerous punters each day in a pokey third floor flat on their estate. Skeggsy's dad was supposedly a punter, but his mum was too dosed up on smack and crack to be sure so Skeggsy never knew his real dad at all. He never even had a step-father who lasted more than a week.

The Social Services had taken him off his mum when he was six and he had spent his youth absconding from every home they had put him in, picking fights with the other kids he came across.

When Skeggsy came out of prison after his first stretch of hard time as an adult, he heard that one punter had gone to town on his mum and had beaten her to a pulp. The pervert had strangled her with her own lacy black knickers and the Coroner's report said the punter had repeatedly raped her and beaten her with a claw hammer. Her defence injuries proved this. Her killer had then forced the bedside lamp stand into her anally, and left her to die a slow and painful death.

Jack wondered if Skeggsy was avenging the violent death of his mum every time he broke someone's arms or legs. He had a weird crazy smile which quickly spread maniacally across his scarred face. Others confirmed that Skeggsy seemed to revel with enjoyment when he inflicted as much pain on someone as he could without actually killing them.

And now Riordan wanted Jack to spy on Skeggsy and find out if it was him or someone else who'd been ripping off his gear.

Mick Riordan was the reason Jack was undercover. He was the biggest and most ruthless drug dealer in the south east of England with strong ties to the north where he came from. He was a real tough arsehole from a real tough shithole and Jack had been working for the last three years to take him down. Finally, this was his shot at nailing the bastard and there was no way he was going to mess it up.

CHAPTER 4

Jack thought back to when he had left the Army with an honourable medical discharge due to his injuries and his fragile mental state. He didn't think he could have got through those early days of his recovery without the support of Sarah. It wouldn't have taken a lot to get a gun off one of his army mates and blown his own head off. Nowadays there were so many guns on the streets of London. Most of them had been smuggled back into Britain from Bosnia in the bergens of soldiers who were looking to make some extra cash or for souvenirs. Nearly every weapon recovered by the police or secret services such as MI5 originally came from Eastern European war zones.

Jack had decided to join the police once he had felt fit enough from his injuries. He missed the buzz and adrenalin rush that came from being in armed service. Power and vulnerability in equal measure. He was desperate to experience danger again, even the pain and uncertainty it bought with it. Without danger he didn't feel alive. He revelled in living life close to the edge.

On joining the police he had quickly worked his way through various divisions. Most sections moved him on quickly anyway as he was a loner and had a knack of pissing off practically anyone who worked with him. There was no way he was going to be just the average beat bobby. He pushed the rules very close to the legal limit and his superiors didn't like it. But he got the results one way or another.

He had finally found his niche working on special operations as a Detective Constable for the National Crime Agency, primarily doing all the dirty work no one else wanted. Undercover work was his area of expertise and it meant he could work virtually alone, which was just the way he liked it. Even though the pay was not all it was cracked up to be – his beat bobby colleagues thought he was well paid – Jack loved the job and got real satisfaction breaking the balls of career criminals and putting them inside for a long stretch.

For the last three years he had been working on infiltrating the complicated crime network that the NCA believed was headed by Mick Riordan, a hard northern bastard with a reputation for ruthlessness that few dared to speak about. Jack had slowly climbed up the ranks of Riordan's organisation and had finally gained his trust. Jack was going to take Riordan down and it would be sooner rather later.

Mick Riordan was fifty-two. He had a bald bullet-shaped shaven head and had grown up in a tough family involved in all sorts of crime. He and his brother had run Manchester for a number of years now, but his brother, Big Dougie, had died a couple of years ago.

Big Dougie had come out of a snooker hall the brothers owned which was just behind Gorton railway station when a motorbike appeared out of nowhere and the pillion passenger had pulled a Glock 19 from under his coat and shot him repeatedly.

It was rumoured that Riordan had put out a contract worth a hundred grand to find his brother's killers, dead or alive. He had found them and he personally nailed the two killers to the floor by their hands and feet in a perverse cross shape and then tortured them for hours. Rumour had it that he had broken nearly all of their bones with a hammer and used an oxy-acetylene torch on their testicles. After satisfying his desire for revenge he poured weed killer down their throats and watched calmly, whilst sitting on a stool smoking one of his fat Cuban cigars, as they died a slow agonising death. The twisted mess that had been human bodies at one time had been found by the police after they had received an anonymous telephone call, but a huge unbreakable wall of silence amongst the criminal fraternity and the scared general public had led to no arrests being made.

Drugs, prostitution, people trafficking and loan sharking – you name it and Riordan's gang network had their fingers in it. So far the NCA couldn't find a money or paper trail to connect the gang to any crime.

Riordan calling Jack was a big surprise and possibly could just be the lucky breakthrough that he had been looking for. The last three years of nerve-wracking dangerous undercover work had so far resulted in wrecking his marriage and damaging his already sensitive daughter, Amy.

The gradual breakdown of Jack's marriage had a profound impact on Amy and she had taken to hanging around with the wrong crowd and using drugs. He blamed himself and his job for Amy going off the rails. Either way he was going to make Riordan pay for his personal suffering.

CHAPTER 5

The water was hammering into the back of her head as the steam rose, slowly swirling around her. She reached out of the shower for the shampoo bottle balanced carefully on the corner of the bath and began to rub the bright blue gel that claimed to be full of 'refreshing sea minerals' into her shoulder-length brown hair.

Sarah Reynolds still thought of herself as an attractive woman even though she was rapidly approaching her forties. This was when your body really started to go down south according to the depressing glossy magazines in her doctor's waiting room.

Stepping out of the shower and grabbing a cream-coloured towel from the heated towel rail, she gazed at her reflection in the mirror. She might be thirty-nine, but she knew she looked good and, if she wanted it, she could have almost any man she wanted. So why had it all gone so wrong with Jack?

Sarah had met Jack shortly after her nineteenth birthday when she'd been a trainee physiotherapist in her first year doing quite traumatic work experience at Headley Court Military Rehabilitation Centre.

It had been a Friday afternoon and she had been walking down the seemingly never-ending corridor towards the hydrotherapy pool to her last physio session after an exhausting day. That day had always stuck in her memory as her younger sister, Jane, had bought them gig tickets to see Elton John at Wembley Stadium. Sarah couldn't stand Elton John but felt she had to go as it was Jane's sixteenth birthday and she was paying. She'd spent months saving up money from her babysitting job and Sarah couldn't let her down. Sarah adored her younger sister and the feeling was reciprocated.

The hydrotherapy pool was used by the wounded military personnel to strengthen their muscles. There were resistance jets and an underwater treadmill which was used for building upper thigh strength and increasing stamina. The pool was kept at a constant thirty-four degrees Celsius.

Arriving at the pool, Sarah had noticed a good-looking man in a horrible old green-and-yellow striped dressing gown leaning heavily on a Zimmer frame just inside the entrance. He was blocking the sign saying *Please use the shower before entering the pool* and she didn't think she'd seen him before.

The new patient was quite tall and still muscular considering the apparent severity of his injuries. He had brown hair in a short crew cut, early twenties, definitely over six foot tall and very cute, Sarah thought to herself, pleasantly surprised that he was looking purposefully straight at her. As she walked past she could feel his watchful eyes following her, darting to her hips and the visible pantie line showing through her thin cotton uniform.

'Excuse me?' the man said to her as she walked past. 'I know I shouldn't really smoke but I can't seem to give up my only enjoyment in life at the moment. Have you got a cigarette I can pinch off you?'

Sarah looked into his penetrating brown eyes.

'Here, you can have mine there's only a couple left,' she offered. 'I've been meaning to give up the coffin sticks for ages.'

She handed him her packet.

'Cheers, love, I'll pay you back I promise.'

With that he shuffled off, propelling the Zimmer frame at a considerable speed, probably accelerated by his urgent need for a quick burst of nicotine.

Over the coming months, she'd got to know the good-looking man in the striped dressing gown quite well. He was funny and self-deprecating and Sarah enjoyed talking to him, though he rarely brought up the subject of his time in active duty.

She tried to spend as much time as possible with him and found herself daydreaming about him when he wasn't around or it was her day off.

From his file she knew that Jack Reynolds had been a Lieutenant attached to 2 Para and had been on special operations when he was injured by a rocket propelled grenade in Vitez in Bosnia. He had been out on a four-day patrol as part of a Pathfinder Platoon when their Land Rover got a near direct hit and only Jack and his best mate survived. Two of his comrades had been blown to smithereens. Jack had been thrown from the vehicle by the force of the exploding RPG and was badly injured with third-degree blast burns scarring all the way down his left leg, along with a broken right leg and fractured sternum, multiple broken ribs and tinnitus from the blast.

During his time at Headley, whilst Sarah and Jack talked and flirted, Jack recovered from his injuries and they quickly fell in love. Sarah never pressed Jack to talk about his time in Bosnia. She knew he had worked deep behind enemy lines and had probably experienced the worst atrocities that war could possibly throw at a human being. She'd heard stories of heads being impaled on spikes, testicles removed with a knife then stuffed into soldiers' mouths to stop them screaming.

After suffering Post Traumatic Stress Disorder, most of the mentally damaged soldiers quickly left the services and shortly afterwards were forced into civvie street, which sometimes led to homelessness, prison and often a sad lonely suicide. It was disgusting the no one cared or consciously looked after these war-damaged men, she thought to herself, but she had made herself a promise to look after this one curious individual who smoked too much and wore an awful old striped dressing gown.

Within a year of Jack being discharged, Sarah had fallen pregnant with Amy. They'd quickly got married at Leatherhead Registry Office. It had felt a bit like a shot gun wedding but also they were truthfully very much in love.

Sarah sighed to think of that happy day. How much things had changed in the intervening years.

Suddenly a loud barking and scratching at the newly wood stained bathroom door bought Sarah back from her dreams of the past. The dog should have gone out hours ago when she had first got out of bed and his barking signaled that he was probably bursting for his morning pee.

'Yes, H, I know, give me a minute to get dressed or I'll catch my death out there,' she said to the six-year-old black Labrador looking up at her with his expectant eyes and his long tongue which was dribbling as she opened the door. The dog was really Jack's and he had named him 'H' after Lieutenant-Colonel H Jones who fell at the battle of Goose Green whilst commanding 2 Para during the Falklands War.

Stepping out into the morning chill Sarah thought back to happier times when she used to take H for a walk with Jack. They used to do everything together – how things had changed.

Chapter 6

Amy Reynolds sat looking out of the window of her university halls of residence overlooking Dublin. She was attracted to the friendliness of the Irish people and their way of life, even though this was in contrast to the loneliness that she felt inside her own heart.

She thought back to when she was a little girl growing up. She'd been a real daddy's girl, following her father around everywhere. She had memories of holding onto his shirt or leg and never letting go until he gently shook free of her, the subtle feeling of rejection always made her cry.

Her parents used to take her on holiday to Cornwall every summer. There were fond memories of playing on the beach with her father and catching shrimps from the small pools of water formed between the rocks at the sea's edge. After a morning of shrimping they would return to where her mother was sunbathing and they would cook a small barbecue on the beach. There was nothing on earth quite like the smell of outside cooking and Amy could almost smell the burning sausages as she remembered.

Whilst growing up she had been a happy little girl but her father's job in the army and then the police meant moving around a lot. Amy had been too young back then to remember her father's army days when they lived abroad but she could vividly remember his early police days when they were constantly on the move around England.

Amy found it hard to make friends at school as her father's job meant that she was repeatedly taken out of one school and dumped in a different one in a new area. The older she got the more introverted she became.

The constant moving home had a damaging influence on Amy and her parents' marriage suffered as a consequence. In the early days her parents were so much in love but over the last few years their marriage had slowly crumbled in front of her eyes.

In the last three years the situation at home worsened considerably. Amy knew that her father was working on the hardest case he'd ever had to tackle and she knew he was working undercover again. However, he had fallen into the policeman's trap of *taking his work home with him*. He was drunk almost every day and she knew that he'd developed an increasing dependancy on drugs. All of this had a knock on effect and her mum and dad argued constantly; her father never hit her mother as far as she knew but she suspected he'd come close to it.

The constant rows at home had meant that Amy became isolated and withdrawn. She craved the love and attention that she used to get as a little girl. She still loved her father but missed his caring nature.

A year before Amy went to university she fell in with the druggie crowd from college and started smoking weed. She progressed from the odd spliff to smoking crack and moved quickly onto heroin. She had got herself into such a fragile mental state that one day she tried to kill herself with sleeping pills but her mother found her and rushed her to hospital.

Amy then spent six months having psychiatric treatment and her parents hoped that her going to university would break the cycle of drug taking and she would make new friends. Unfortunately, quite the opposite had happened.

Amy took the silver foil wrap on the table and poured the brown contents into a spoon, she then heated the spoon using a lighter. Once the spoon had heated enough she filled a new syringe with the contents. Amy always used new needles, she was a 'clean' junkie.

She hated herself for what she was doing but she had become so withdrawn from normal life that only drugs gave her solace. She wished that she was back at home with her parents but blamed herself for their constant arguing. She injected herself in the arm with the warm brown fluid; just before she passed out she managed to send her father one last text message: *I'm really sorry Dad.*

Chapter 7

The noise of the cheap bedside radio woke Jack from his drunken slumber. At least he'd made it into bed this time he thought compared to the last few nights. All week he had arrived back home so pissed that he had slept on the leather sofa without a clue as to how he had got there. He knew, but didn't care, that his drinking was spiralling out of control. The alcohol and drugs were part and parcel of undercover work, but they became increasingly more and more difficult to control the closer he got to busting Riordan's arse.

His mouth was dry and his nose was blocked from the cheap forty quid wrap of crap coke he had snorted in the pub toilet last night. Why he had bought the wrap when he was meant to be selling better shit himself was beyond him, he must have been more pissed than he thought.

The studio flat Jack rented on the outskirts of Dorking cost him nine hundred quid a month without council tax. It was daylight robbery, but what could he do; landlords were like legalised criminals in his book.

He got out of the creaking old Ikea bed and stumbled over his discarded clothes across the stained carpet to the 'cooking area'. He picked up the dirty grey kettle which had, at one time, been white and filled it up with fresh water from the tap. The cluttered Formica kitchen top displayed last night's Domino box containing a half-eaten pepperoni pizza. Jack couldn't even remember ordering pizza last night and why had it got pepperoni on it when he hated the stuff? He thought it was like eating rubber buttons.

He went to the bathroom and turned on the shower, persuading himself it would bring him some relief from the violent hangover that was beginning to make him feel dizzy. The jets of hot water burnt into him like shooting asteroids as the bathroom quickly steamed up.

The shower water sprayed all over the badly tiled floor as he had torn the shower curtain a few weeks ago, grabbing it and ripping it off its rails one drunken night. He remembered waking up the following morning with his head wedged between the toilet and the bathroom wall, thinking no more Jagermeister, never again. It hadn't even been on a Friday night.

He knew why he'd got so drunk last night. The initial trigger had been that he and Sarah had yet another stupid unnecessary row. Sarah had again claimed that he wasn't prepared to sort himself out, but what had really pissed him off was that she had alluded to Amy's recent problems being due to his out of control behaviour. The problem with Riordan and Skeggsy also hadn't helped his general mood and added to that stress he needed to talk to his chief handler, Detective Inspector Daryl Rice.

Rice had an operational overview of the strategic activity Jack was involved in, but Jack was not expected to report to him on a daily or even weekly basis. Should the operation go tits up or if Rice thought Jack had gone native then he would report this further up the chain of command to the Detective Superintendent who was in charge of the overall viability of the operation and its objectives against organised crime. If the operation had been compromised in any way the Superintendent's decision would be final and he could pull the plug on the whole undercover operation at any time.

Only Jack's weekly undercover handler and Rice were authorised to have direct contact with him as only they knew the case Jack was involved in. He knew the conversation with Rice would be difficult as they very rarely saw eye to eye.

Jack thought Rice was a sanctimonious twat who had risen through the ranks by kissing arse. Originally he had left Birmingham University and joined the Police Services on one of those accelerated management schemes for prize idiots and had always placed political correctness ahead of Jack doing his job.

Christ, when Jack went to his office, Rice never even offered him a seat. Some power game he had learnt in control training at Hendon. One day the bastard would trip up and all of his so called friends would probably hang him out to dry with the Independent Police Complaints Commission. He'd burnt too many people's fingers to get to where he was and never once had he been on the front line as a real copper in the true sense of the word.

Jack thought Rice didn't understand the stress of working undercover and the emotions that came with it. The need to bust Riordan was overwhelming for Jack, but to Rice it was just another statistic helping to push him up the egotistical ladder of success.

There were a lot of police services worldwide, such as Costa Rica and Colombia, that had Riordan on their radar and were very interested in his global criminal activities. These included wholesale drug trafficking, prostitution and even people trafficking, which was the latest criminal trend where vast amounts of money could be made out of defenceless victims. Riordan was heavily involved in all of these enterprises and yet he seemed out of reach of arrest and he was very careful to keep himself out of any involvement in the dirty work.

Jack was getting much more deeply involved investigating Riordan than his original remit from the NCA dictated. His life was on the line on a daily basis and one wrong move would place him in the shadow of death.

Throwing the remnants of the coffee which had failed miserably in waking him up in the sink, Jack turned the kettle on again, this time also putting some bread in the toaster. His hangover seemed to be coating his bones like a deadly virus and he rushed to the toilet to throw up the first cup of coffee of the day. Aside from a couple of slices of pizza last night, he hadn't eaten in days and his empty stomach heaved as he retched into the bowl. Recently Jack had recently been throwing up every morning in anticipation of the daily danger facing him.

CHAPTER 8

The Rihanna ringtone went off again and Jack looked at the mobile suspiciously. It was Skeggsy and he really didn't want to speak to him, he let the mobile ring for a while, but the Rihanna song kept on screeching at a high pitch fever. It was too much for his hangover so he pressed the green answer button. He silently swore that the next time he saw Amy he would make her change it to anything but Rihanna.

'Oi, where the fuck have you been? I've rung you twice this morning.' Skeggsy's voice roared out of the mobile.

Slipping into character Jack said, 'Fuck you, it's not even seven in the morning and I've been on a bender mate, know what I mean?'

'For some strange reason Mr Riordan wants you to do the Southall run instead of me, so you'll need the keys to Cavendish Road. Where do you want to meet?'

Jack swallowed another bit of the horrible acid puke that had come back up again, tearing into the insides of his throat. Coughing he said, 'Meet us at the greasy spoon on South Street.'

'No worries, bruv. See you there at about half-eight. Got to get rid of this bird first though and she might take a while if you get my meaning?' Skeggsy said, laughing at his own joke.

Jack despised Skeggsy and didn't laugh but at least Skeggsy might be a little bit more amiable than usual if he'd recently shot his load. Doubtful though as Skeggsy would happily shag a bird and then beat the hell out of anyone near him. Sometimes he even beat the hell out of the bird he had just shagged, claiming he was frustrated and no one liked him. He knew Skeggsy was paranoid from all the speed he took. The bloke was unpredictable and in Jack's line of work unpredictable was dangerous.

He looked out through the sash bay window on to the small street. The rain slid slowly down the pane, a river of droplets lit up by the imposing new floodlight in the car park opposite his flat. Jack thought it must be the worst start to spring on record. It was still early and nearly daylight, but the floodlight stubbornly strode into his living room like a menacing lighthouse lamp determined to blind him. He had complained to the local council but he knew they'd never do anything about it.

An hour later, Jack climbed into the black Audi A8 soft top that he had taken in part exchange for a payment that was owing from a drug gang up in Manchester. The bill was going to be paid eventually, but he took the car anyway to show the new gobshite gangbangers he didn't give a fuck. He had to show them who was running things. The bigger the name he made for himself on the street the closer he would get to Riordan.

He drove out of the flat's basement garage which sloped upwards onto the road. The electric garage door working for once, but still clanging loudly against the steel supports as it closed. He turned left onto the bypass and headed straight for the Dorking Cockerel roundabout. In the middle of the roundabout stood a bizarre ten-foot-high and five-toed cockerel. Every other week it had a road cone or else some form of clothing adorned on it by the local guerrilla knitters.

Driving through the rain towards the multi storey car park in Junction Road, Jack checked the Audi's electronic wing mirrors one final time to make sure that he hadn't been followed.

He parked the car on the third floor, satisfied that he hadn't been tailed and headed purposefully towards the café where he was to meet Skeggsy.

The café looked busy and he opened the door, which was covered with adverts for the return of a Beer festival the following Saturday at the Dorking Halls. Entering the room the heat from the kitchens made the burn scars in Jack's left leg tighten painfully for a moment. He tried to ignore the pain and the sudden flashbacks of the exploding RPG that came with it.

The café was brimming with its usual hungry builders and dope heads recovering from the night before. Jack took some comfort in the fact he looked no worse than anyone else in the room. The smell of greasy fry-up reminded him how hungry he was and he hoped his hangover had abated enough to allow him to eat.

Jack was nervous about the meeting with Skeggsy as he was so unpredictable. Skeggsy was Jack's boss as far as the gang pecking order went and yet Riordan had made it appear as though Jack was challenging for Skeggsy's position in the gang.

CHAPTER 9

Walking to the front of the café, Jack spotted Skeggsy sitting alone at a table for four on the left beside the counter. He was staring intently at the woman on page three of the *Sun*; it was almost as though he had never seen a naked women before in his life.

Skeggsy suddenly looked up. 'What took you so bleeding long? I'm skint after last night. Get yourself a tea and pay the cow will you. Oh, and don't leave her a tip she wouldn't give me her phone number, fucking lesbian,' Skeggsy whined.

'You didn't get us anything then?'

'Told you, I'm skint,' Skeggsy said, smiling as the yellow yoke of the runny fried egg dripped from his fork onto the breasts of Melanie, age twenty-three, from Birmingham.

The blackboard above the counter displayed numbered meals and also the specials for the day. As he looked up he felt his stomach reach inwards and then outwards. There was no way he was going to eat a lot, so he settled for fried eggs on toast. The young girl who had sensibly rejected Skeggsy's neanderthal attempt at chatting her up was serving at a table and there was now a spotty kid with Ray-Bans behind the counter waiting to take his order.

'Number three, mate,' he told him. 'On white. I'll have a mug of tea as well.'

The gangly kid moved out of sight briefly and shortly the sound of the kettle went on as he shouted through the back archway into the kitchen, 'Number three on white, Joe.'

The kid came back to the counter. 'Do you want the tea bag left in?'

'Might as well, cheers.'

After paying for both of them Jack grabbed a knife and fork and walked back to Skeggsy's table clutching his mug.

Tearing open a sachet of white sugar and pouring it into his tea, he looked at Skeggsy and said, 'So have you got the keys or what?'

'Don't get clever with me. They're under the newspaper, okay?'

Jack took a brief look behind him then leant over the table taking the hidden keys from under the newspaper. He slid them into his coat pocket.

A few minutes later, Mr Ray-Ban came over with his order and Jack covered his overcooked eggs with brown sauce and salt.

'So why is Riordan giving you the Southall run? I normally do it. Why the fuck are you his golden boy all of a sudden?' Skeggsy demanded, taking his eyes off Melanie and her tits for the first time. 'Is there something you're not telling me?'

Jack looked directly at Skeggsy and he could see the wild questioning look in his piercing blue eyes. The 'I've had no sleep' space saucer eyes of a paranoid speed freak stared back at him, making him more than a little nervous whilst he tried to concentrate on eating his breakfast.

'I dunno, he sounded well pissed off though.' Jack thought it was best to not further arouse Skeggsy's suspicions and continued, 'He said he had some other more important job coming up which he needed you for.'

Skeggsy sneered, 'Probably to do with the scousers up north ripping him off. I swear he thinks every twat is at it.'

'Yeah, he did mention something about that. Right, look, I'd better get going. Are you sure Riordan wants me to do the Southall run today?' Jack asked, letting Skeggsy feel that he was the one in charge.

'What do you think? You'll be the one in the shit for not doing the job, not fucking me!'

'Yeah, yeah.' Jack drank the last of his tea which had already gone cold. It had only been luke warm when Mr Ray-Ban had first given it to him. He decided to leave the half eaten eggs as he felt his stomach kicking again and wanted to get away from Skeggsy who was asking him far too many questions to which he didn't have any answers.

He suddenly stood up and said, 'I'll bell you later,' and walked quickly out of the café and back to his Audi in the car park.

At least Riordan now trusted Jack with the keys to the safe-house in Cavendish Road behind the railway station in Redhill. The house in Cavendish road was where most of the drugs they sold in the South East were stashed, weighed up, bagged and ready for distribution down the chain to the smaller dealers who didn't have the brains or bottle for wholesale dealing. It was one of the many safe-houses Riordan rented under fake names with fake references and fake driving licences as proof of identification to satisfy the curiosity of any of the nosey letting agents.

Jack would go to Southall later, but first he needed to make contact with Rice and explain things were moving quickly.

CHAPTER 10

Jack had a final nervous look around the car park and pushed the engine ignition button on the dashboard. He drove slowly down the exit ramps, spotting Skeggsy's black BMW 7 series on the second floor. He recognised it instantly by the personalised number plate: SKE77Y. Skeggsy called it his 'Black Man Wheels' and liked the attention the number plate drew. Jack's face creased into a wry smile. Any prat could have bought the number plate for about four hundred quid. Even so, he was a bit jealous of the top of the range 'E65' model with performance focused features. Whatever he thought of Skeggsy, the car was bloody dynamite and wasted on a tosser like that.

Outside, the weather had worsened. The rain came down heavily, violent shards of water attacking the windscreen. Flicking the windscreen wipers on, Jack joined the new two-way traffic system that was bound to have its first crash soon.

As he waited at traffic lights, he fished around in his jacket pocket and pulled out a crumpled packet of Marlborough Lights he'd bought the night before. Lighting a cigarette with his gold Zippo, he listened to the monotonous noise of the windscreen wipers.

Jack's thoughts turned to Sarah and especially Amy whom he hadn't seen for a month or so. He spoke to Sarah every day but he seemed to speak to Amy less and less. He was worried that Amy was becoming withdrawn again. He guessed that university could be a lonely place for someone as fragile as her. He missed them both a lot.

After a few miles, switching roads and making last-minute turns, he was sure that no one was following him. The rain continued to belt down and looked like it was settling in for the day. It was trying its utmost to piss off all of mankind. Jack drove a little further down the road and turned the Audi into the new Barratt Homes estate which was full of red brick two up and two down starter homes for spoilt rich kids with cash from Mummy and Daddy. Reversing into a space outside a red-brick house with a sky dish on the side and a large double-glazed conservatory that looked like it could do with a good clean, Jack killed the engine.

He took out his mobile, opened up the back of it and carefully took out the battery and removed the SIM card from its delicate holder, placing it on the top of the car dashboard in front of him. He reached into his pocket and took out a small cardboard packet that he had taken earlier from its hiding place underneath the spare wheel. He tore open the packet and removed a SIM card, placing it in the now empty SIM card holder in his mobile. He pushed the battery back into place with a loud click, then slid the back on to the phone.

He switched it on and punched in an eleven digit number that he had committed to memory three years ago. He let it ring four times and then cancelled the call. Waiting thirty seconds he again punched in the eleven digit number, the phone rang, rang and rang a third time. Then a very public school-educated voice answered.

'Is that you, X4, I hope this phone line is secure?'

'Yeah, long time no see, Mr Rice, have you missed me?' Jack asked laughing.

'Ha, bloody ha. I'm not your mother. Why are you calling me direct? Have there been some developments that you can't talk to your daily operational handler about?'

Jack started to answer, but Rice cut him off. 'Hang on, fuck it, give me a second. I'm at a presentation by the Chief Super reminding all of us about the importance of bloody police diversity and I can't hear a damn word you're saying.'

All Jack could hear was a lot of muffled voices and the noise of clashing cups. The sounds grew gradually fainter.

'Right, what have you got for me?' Rice asked sounding clearer but a little out of breath.

'Riordan rang me last night. He wants me to sort out some trouble he's been having. He thinks that he's being creamed off for quite a bit of coke somehow and it might be from the connection in Southall. I'm going up there later today and I'll have a snoop about if I get the chance. It seems I might've finally gained his trust.'

'Riordan rang you? Excellent work. That slimy piece of shit has finally shown his face at last. Right, be careful and remember we need to find a way to connect Riordan to the wholesale global trafficking of the drugs. Don't fuck this up or I'll have the police shrink declare you a fucking alcoholic psycho and you'll be eating shit out on the street with the rest of your skanky old army scum friends before you know it.'

'Thank you, sir, you're too kind,' Jack replied sarcastically, feeling his blood beginning to boil and not bothering to tell him his worries about his power struggle with Skeggsy. He absent mindedly started to rub the wound on his left leg. He did this out of habit whenever he was angry or nervous. Nothing else was said and immediately the line went dead.

A second later Jack's phone bleeped and he saw that it was a text message from Amy, *I'm really sorry Dad.* Reading the text message Jack's heart missed a beat. The message made no sense. He immediately rang Amy but her phone went to voicemail. He left a message asking her to call him as soon as possible. Becoming increasingly more anxious considering Amy's recent suicide attempt he rang Sarah and her phone went to voicemail as well.

Frustrated and worried Jack replaced the original SIM card in his phone. With his Zippo lighter, he burned the SIM card he'd used to call Rice between his fingers. Once it had disintegrated into a mess of curled plastic he threw the smouldering SIM card out of the window of the car. He started the car and headed off to Redhill. He tried to keep his mind on the job in hand but all he could think about was the strange message from Amy.

Chapter 11

Amy awoke slowly. Opening her eyes, she saw she was in a spartan but brightly lit room she had never seen before and was lying on a strange metal single bed. Her head was propped up with two starched white pillows.

She started to look around the small room, discovering painfully that she couldn't fully turn her neck as she had thin plastic tubing inserted up each nostril. The tubing was also hooked around her ears to hold it in place and pulled against the wall connection which had a large sign above it in red capital letters saying, *OXYGEN ONLY.*

After a few seconds she again tried to look around the room but the nasal oxygen tube defiantly restricted her movement. It hurt her nostrils as she turned, as did the IV drip catheter which had been inserted into the back of her right hand covered with a sterile gauze and tape to hold it in place. Amy noticed that her whole wrist was a yellow blackish colour, possibly from the tourniquet being too tight when her vein was accessed for the catheter and IV drip. She supposed she could probably have done a better job of it herself. She certainly had the experience with needles.

The catheter sticking obtrusively out the back of her hand was attached with long tubing to one of those steel tall walk about things on wheels with a bag full of 'liquid vitamins' hanging from one of the hooks on top of a portable stand. You saw patients in tacky television dramas pushing these stands aimlessly up and down long corridors, wheels squeaking quietly.

She stared up at the white square-tiled ceiling. The lights pierced deep into her over sensitive bloodshot eyes like car headlights stuck on full beam. Her body's physical reaction felt rather like the reverse of photosynthesis for plants. She was drained of energy.

As unconsciousness started to envelop her again, a female nurse, brunette hair styled into a short bob, walked briskly into the room banging the door loudly against the wall as she passed through it. Amy thought the look on her face resembled that of an owl who had eaten a raw onion. She was pretty but looked as though today had been one of those days and her face was not going to hide that fact. Stress lines streaked across her forehead as she spoke loudly to Amy.

'Amy, can you hear me, darling. Here, try to be sick in this bowl.'

Aware that Amy had only just regained consciousness, she repeatedly pressed the red emergency button to the top right of the bed whilst Amy stared at her through wildly dilated eyes. With one hand, the nurse quickly passed Amy a small grey cardboard bowl she had bought into the room with her, whilst with the other she tried to catch one of the pillows on the bed from slipping onto the floor.

Amy involuntarily sat bolt upright and all at once the lights in the room turned into a bright series of coloured flashes like lit fireworks as she started to vomit all over the bed she was lying in. Once her body had purged itself, she spat weakly into the bowl which the nurse had desperately thrust into her hands. Her stomach was empty, it hurt like hell and a sticky green acid stared up at her from the bowl in her hands.

Amy used all of her strength and tried to push herself further up in the bed, using her elbows. The door crashed open for a second time and a huge male nurse with tied back platted hair and another female nurse, a little younger than the first, ran in answering the emergency call. They grabbed Amy by the arms and legs and tried to hold her down as she struggled. She felt a fresh wave of nausea as she fought them off. Her catheter ripped out in one long zig zag agonizing movement, each bruised spike mark on her skin joining itself up in a dot-to-dot messy tear. Dark red blood sprayed all over the struggling nurses and splattered the clean white hospital walls and floor.

As the two junior nurses restrained Amy the pretty brunette nurse said, 'Amy, please relax, you're in hospital. I know everything seems a bit of a shock to you at the moment, but it won't do you any good to struggle. Please calm down, we're here to help you. We need to give you an injection. It'll help you stop vomiting.'

'Why the fuck should I? Why am I here? What's happened?' Amy screamed at the nurse as she struggled pathetically. Her weak, drug-ravaged body was no match against the strong nurses.

She noticed that the pretty brunette nurse had a small watch hanging from her breast pocket like one of those nurses in the old comedy films, but she knew that this was not a comedy film, nor was it one of her usual drug-induced fantasy dreams. It was some strange horrible form of reality. She couldn't remember when she had her last hit of smack, but she knew this was her body withdrawing.

The room started to spin again and she could hear the pretty nurse, who in an odd way reminded Amy of her mother, say warningly to the huge male nurse, 'Careful, Johnny, don't break the needle.'

Immediately she felt the warmth of the injected drug flow throughout her veins, dragging her slowly into unconsciousness. She could feel herself fall back against the bed and the room started to swirl into a greyish white mist with lots of faces looming over her. She could hear loud strange voices calling her name, fading off quietly into the distance. But she was unable to answer them as her head finally dropped heavily into the lumpy hospital pillow.

A while later, Amy woke up again. She didn't know how long she'd been asleep; there was no clock in the room. She felt groggy from the sedative and her stomach muscles and throat hurt from all of the earlier retching.

She tried to look around the small white hospital room and her eyes began to focus on the huge male nurse now quietly sitting in a high-backed wooden chair beside her bed reading a book.

Seeing she was awake, the nurse stood up, ready for any trouble she might give him. His name badge read 'Johnny Hutchings' and in a voice surprisingly gentle for a man of his size, he said, 'Alright, how are you feeling now? Amy, isn't it?' Johnny smiled at her.

He had a soft country voice, Norfolk or Suffolk, she couldn't quite place it, but she was no good at accents anyway, especially considering the crazy place her head was in right now.

'Like shit,' she replied. 'Have you got any water or juice? My mouth tastes like the inside of Gandhi's flip flop.'

Johnny walked over to the small four-door wooden cabinet beside Amy's bed and reached over for the jug of iced water on top of the cabinet. Grabbing a white plastic cup that was also on top of the cabinet, he poured the water out and handed it to her.

'You had us all worried there. You was a real goner for a while. Do you remember collapsing at home or coming here in the ambulance at all?'

'No, not a thing. Where am I?'

Amy sheepishly looked at him, her sunken blackened eyes peering over the top of the plastic cup of water as she sipped it. She flinched as the icy liquid hit her ravaged throat.

'You're at the Accident and Emergency Department Recovery Unit in Dublin's St Vincent's Hospital and have been here for three days. You stopped breathing twice. In essence you died twice from all of the shit you've been smoking and injecting into your body and we kindly bought you back to this planet from the one you were on. You owe a lot to the doctor's skills and your room-mate who called the ambulance, but you probably don't really feel very grateful at the moment? Am I right?' Johnny smiled pleasantly at Amy making her feel warm. Even though she knew she didn't look at all attractive at the moment, she could feel her deathly pale cheeks start to blush and began to feel a little embarrassed in front of this gentle giant.

'I don't remember much at all, but I'm sorry for the trouble I've caused.'

Suddenly Amy burst into tears and started to shake uncontrollably clutching the bed sheets close to her stick-thin body. She could feel the tremors of cold turkey 'clucking' through her body like a probing disease. Johnny left the room without Amy noticing. He left her crying under the stark bright lights, curled up in a foetal position on the cold metal hospital bed with the starched sheets clenched tightly in her fragile bony hands.

Twenty minutes later Johnny returned to check on Amy. The bed was empty and Amy's hospital gown was strewn across the bed, Johnny shouted for the ward nurse who quickly came running in.

'Do you know where the patient is?' Johnny frantically asked.

'No, she was here last time I checked but it looks like her clothes are gone.' The nurse pointed at the empty chair where Amy's clothes used to be.

'Oh shit, she's done a runner. She could die the state she's in. What the fuck do we do?'

CHAPTER 12

Turning the Audi left off the roundabout beside Redhill railway station, Jack drove under the bridge and noticed that the nightclub was still closed. It was an imposing grey listed building which had once upon a time been white, but was quite tatty looking now. There was a large neon sign above the boarded up windows saying *Liquid Envy*. This was the last of the many names that the club had been called over the years.

During the days when it was open, the club was always changing hands. The owners could never cope with the drunken violence and drugs which were rife, especially back in the 90s during the rave era. Before the licensing laws were radically amended in 2003, all of the pubs would shut at eleven thirty and people had nowhere to go to carry on drinking. So naturally they went to nightclubs which had extended licences. Of course, later drinking hours meant that most of the people in the clubs late at night were well pissed and the club in Redhill had been no different.

Most of the clubbers were too hammered to pick anyone up from the dance floor, so they would take more speed, pills or coke, fight or else end up vomiting in the toilets.

The bouncers ran all of the drugs allowed in the club and took their slice of the action - any dealer who thought he was hard enough to go it alone was dealt with swiftly and severely. The bouncers' other priority was to regularly deal with any brave idiot who thought he was hard enough to take them on.

These twats were usually dragged out of the emergency exit at the back by two or three bouncers and then had the living daylights beaten out of them.

It was fortunate that Redhill had a hospital only a mile and a half away as the Ambulance Service were regular visitors to the club, especially on Friday or Saturday nights. A&E would be full of clubbers suffering alcohol poisoning, broken bones or stab wounds.

A short distance further on, the Audi's new tyres screeched a little as Jack turned the car sharply into Cavendish Road. He overtook an old woman riding a Moped as he turned into a small disguised cul-de-sac.

Weaving the Audi around the potholes in the road the car slid on the loose gravel and finally came to a stop outside a bungalow set back from the road. Jack turned the engine off and watched the windscreen wipers jerk to a stop whilst the relentless rain continued to batter the car. Opening the car door he decided to make a dash for it and ran to the bungalow, stopping only when he reached the newly painted red front door where he sought refuge under the awning from the deluge. Turning round he pointed the key fob at the Audi to lock it, then used another key on the ring to open the front door before disappearing inside.

Dropping the keys on a small wooden cupboard which was hiding the electricity meter, Jack peeled off his rain-drenched leather jacket and hung it on one of the hooks above the radiator in the entrance hall as he pushed the front door shut. He wiped the rain off his closely shaven head and went into the living room. The flooring was made of expensive engineered hardwood planks that had the rustic oak feel of an alpine lodge and his boots made a squelching noise as he crossed the shiny floor to the solitary sofa. The room was bare apart from the sofa, a 32-inch widescreen television and a glass coffee table.

Jack tried to call Amy but annoyingly her phone still went to voicemail. He left a message saying, *Hi darling, I got your text. I just wanted to make sure everything is okay. Can you call me as soon as you get this, love you.* He decided that if Amy hadn't made contact with himself or Sarah in the next couple of hours then he would call the hospitals and the local Gardai in Dublin. He didn't want to panic unnecessarily and needed to get the drug delivery to Southall done first.

Jack was knackered from the night before and slumped exhausted into the sofa, which was still covered in its plastic delivery cover. He reached for a small box on the long glass topped table in front of him. Using a small glass spoon, he scooped up some of the contents of the box and slowly tapped it onto the table.

His hangover was still giving his brain cells a good kicking as were his problems with Amy. One small line he said to himself. It couldn't make the day any worse, surely? He looked with anticipation at the small mound of white powder that was staring up at him. Grabbing the misused loyalty points card out of the box, he wiped the remnants of white powder off the edge of the card using his mouth and could instantly feel his lips go numb at the edges. The coke was high grade Peruvian flake and could be 'washed up' and came back at nines. The process of 'washing up' was a way to test the grade of cocaine, turning it into home-made crack ready for smoking. Jack had learnt a lot since he'd gone undercover, probably too much if any of his police colleagues saw him right now.

You poured a couple of drops of ammonia onto a tablespoon already full with a gram of coke and then, using something like a safety pin that had been cooled in a freezer, the mixture was slowly stirred in a dragging motion, pulling the coke out of the ammonia to the edge of the spoon. The coke appeared from the ammonia like magic and stuck to the pin in a gooey compound. The secret was to then hold the tablespoon under running water to complete the chemical reaction and dilute the taste of the ammonia. The weight of pulled back coke reflected the quality grade of coke per gram once dried. In other words ninety percent of the gram coming back out of the ammonia meant it was pretty well ninety percent pure, hence the phrase 'coming back at nines'. Jack knew this stuff was high grade – it was his own personal stash of uncut coke.

Using the loyalty points card he dragged a line of the glistening powder across the table, then eagerly leant forward, snorting one line up his left nostril and then the other up the right. He leant back into the sofa holding a finger against each nostril one at a time and snorted loudly, forcing the coke as far up his nostrils as possible.

Jack wiped the back of his hand across his nostrils and sniffed quickly a few times.

He needed to get to Southall as quickly as possible and wriggled around like a fish in sand on the sofa with its plastic sheeting, eventually finding the phone in his trouser pocket. The effect of the coke was definitely kicking in as he scrolled down his phone contact list to the name 'Big V' and pressed call. The phone rang a few times and then a gruff Welsh voice answered.

An angry voice shouted at Jack. 'Skeggsy was meant to call me first thing this morning to arrange a drop, what the fuck happened? Do you think I'm having a laugh driving all over London with shit loads of paper work on me waiting for one of you two idiots to call?'

'Well, I'm arranging it now, not Skeggsy. We had some problems our end,' Jack lied. The coke was racing through his brain cells now and it felt good to make Big V sweat a bit. He was a pain in the arse and always wanted the gear cheaper than anyone else. He thought he ran all of the clubs, pubs and whores in and around London, but in reality he was a small dick in a big sea as far as Jack was concerned. Even so, Big V was still a very important link to Riordan and also to the wide distribution of all types of drugs. The London drug business was worth billions to the people at the top of the tree and it was Riordan who indirectly supplied at least seventy per cent of the drugs consumed in the city.

'Oh yeah, Riordan pushing you up the ranks is he? You'd better not be messing me about,' Big V growled.

'I'll meet you at the usual place in one hour. The Punjab – do you remember it, you fat bastard?'

'I'll have Davey meet you there,' Big V replied. 'And you call me a fat bastard again, I swear I'll eat your balls with my dinner. But in the meantime, it's been a pleasure doing business.'

'The pleasure is all mine. Did I mention your woman couldn't stop begging me for it last time I was in Southall? Your bitch was on heat so much you should keep her in a freezer. Laters.'

As Jack put the phone down on the table he could hear Big V laughing just before the line went dead. Jack thought most of the people he dealt with whilst undercover were scumbags but he occasionally enjoyed the banter.

Jack had been doing business with Big V since he'd first begun to infiltrate Riordan's network and he knew how dangerous the nutter was. But they had a strange sort of respect for each other built on the dangerous business they were in. Jack's business as the undercover cop posing as a wholesale drug dealer being the most dangerous of course, but his life depended on the fact that Big V didn't have a clue about that.

According to his undercover story, he'd lost his HGV licence after being nicked by the police, pissed at the wheel of his lorry. The DVLA had been happy to oblige with this story by banning him from driving and his licence was revoked with a three-year disqualification. He had the licence back now, but was not allowed to drive HGV's and was currently out of work and signing on benefits. This was helped by Covert Operations Support who had concocted his credentials – a fake employment history and fake passport so that he could travel abroad without arousing the suspicion of any other border agencies around the world.

Bringing him back to reality was the noise of the bloody Rihanna ring tone on his mobile again. He looked at the screen and it said the caller was Deano. He pressed the answer button. 'Yeah, alright, mate.'

Deano was one of the firm's trusted delivery guys having just got out from a five stretch in prison after being busted with two kilos of coke. He had dutifully swallowed the bust quietly. He did the time inside and told the police he had been forced into it by Albanian gangsters as he had owed them money from his drug habit. The story was total bollocks of course, but that was the criminal underworld code and you were a dead man if you broke it by grassing on someone. Jack knew that Riordan had looked after Deano whilst he was behind bars and had given Deano a tidy untraceable lump sum of cash for his silence.

'Yo, boss, what's happening?' Deano's high-pitched voice squeaked down the line. 'I waited in all day for your call yesterday.'

'Yeah, shit, sorry about that. I got caught up with something. Anyway, Riordan wants me to do the Southall drop instead of Skeggsy so I need your arse over here pronto. I'm at Cavendish Road.'

'Sure thing. See you in ten minutes. I'll be waiting outside. I'll drop call you when I'm there. By the way, don't forget your canoe – it's fucking pissing it down and we might need one in bandit country,' Deano joked.

Jack laughed and hit the end call button on the phone. Deano's jokes were dire and his squeaky west-country accent made them sound even worse.

Whilst he waited for Deano he tried calling Amy and Sarah again – still no answer.

CHAPTER 13

Sitting in the back room of the Tankard Pub in Kennington Road, Lambeth, which doubled as his office, Big V was sweating even more than usual and swore under his breath after ending his call from Jack. Beads of sweat streaked across his forehead and he continuously wiped them away with his hand.

Reaching past his huge stomach, Big V retrieved a lighter from the small square table in front of him. The huge conical-shaped spliff hanging from the corner of his mouth had temporarily gone out. He relit it and took a large drag of the exceptionally strong 'AK47' skunk. He had bought ten kilos – five on tick – of the weed off Jack last month but he thought Jack was a prick and couldn't quite put his finger on why he didn't trust or like him. Even though he didn't much like Jack, he always paid him the tick money he owed for the weed on time. Jack worked for Riordan, and if you didn't pay Riordan you ceased to breathe, it was as simple as that.

He had heard on the grapevine that Riordan had started to think of Jack like a long lost brother, giving him more responsibility in the firm. Big V reckoned Riordan needed a replacement since his elder brother Dougie had come to an untimely end and he suspected Riordan was going soft in his old age. Riordan couldn't continue to keep control of the gangs north or south of the quaint middle England divide known as the Watford Gap Services on the M1 motorway and therefore a lot of the drug business was for the taking.

And it wasn't just the drug trade that was profitable. There was prostitution and even people trafficking was getting more lucrative now. The police weren't so clued up on it either. Big V had heard from a few underworld sources that Skeggsy and Jack had now become a force to be reckoned with up and down the country, they were virtually running Riordan's firm. London was just as big and violent a city as any up in the north and people disappeared easily. A bit like Riordan's brother Dougie.

The thought of Dougie's brain splattering in small bits all over the pavement made Big V chuckle as he crushed the end of the finished spliff into the ash tray with his fat hand. His large gold signet ring encrusted with tiny diamonds glittered in the light from the strip light above him.

Big V's office was through the pub's kitchen and to get to it you had to get past Big V's lackey, Davey, who guarded his boss's every move and loved the sound and feel of a blade cutting against human skin. Davey was too much of a chicken shit junkie to use his fists and could only ever inflict harm with a weapon.

The back room of the Tankard was just about big enough to swing a small cat in. It was lit by one long strip light across the low ceiling and had a small bar in the corner which housed hand pumps for Kronenberg, Carlsberg, a traditional Welsh cask bitter called Brains and Guinness.

Big V was born and bred in Wales – hence the Welsh guest beer. Originally he came from Aberthaw in the Vale of Glamorgan, famous for its coal-fired power station and the local cement works. The power station and the cement works were the only jobs going in Aberthaw and Big V's talents were not suited to either type of employment on offer. As a young man he had risen through the criminal ranks of Barry town and eventually Cardiff city by selling shit loads of amphetamines. Speed was the Welshman's breakfast, lunch and dinner, along with tabs of acid. These were the favoured drugs of the unemployed and there were plenty of them available thanks to

Maggie Thatcher. Big V owed all of his current prosperity to Thatcher's crusade against the mineworkers and the unions, but always he had known there was bigger money to be made in London. If Howard Marks, the most famous drug dealer from Wales, could succeed as 'Mr Nice', then so could he.

Big V had moved his operations to London in the nineties when everyone had wanted vast quantities of any drug they could lay their hands on; speed, coke, ecstasy, mad mandy, acid, ketamine – you name it the punters wanted it. He had quickly built up a large drug network stretching from Bristol to London and he was currently trying to set up business in the north of England.

Joining forces with Riordan and using his global criminal network could help Big V expand his business, but it pissed him off that Riordan would have nothing to do with him personally and only let his foot soldiers deal with him. This was where Skeggsy and Jack came in. They only wanted his cash and he reckoned that they would have buried him under the Severn bridge for a laugh given half the chance, but the large amounts of money he generated, was too much for them to refuse. He also controlled large parts of south London and business was good for everyone at the moment. The last thing anyone wanted was a gang war, especially Riordan. And who was Big V to rock the boat?

'Davey, get your arse in here now!' Big V roared and suddenly the door leading into the small back room swung open and a skinny rakish looking man in his late twenties with big dark eyes like a weasel rushed in. He glanced nervously around the small darkened room, before his gaze settled on his boss's huge frame sat in his usual place at a table near the corner of the private back room bar.

'Yes, Mr V, you wanted something?' Davey stammered in his quiet South London accent. He had a bad stutter which had resulted in him being bullied terribly throughout his school years. The teachers had no control over the pupils and had almost actively encouraged the bullying. Davey had taken to only going to school when his dad had forced him to go. His education therefore was a bit like the Titanic – a complete disaster.

One particular kid, Shane O'Flaherty, an Irish traveller kid, had made it his personal aim in life to make Davey's life a complete hell. One day, Davey had decided he'd had enough of this kid. He had waited until the lunch break when everyone got changed into their football kit ready for Games in the afternoon and, in the changing rooms, he had walked up behind O'Flaherty and pulled out a knife from his school bag and stabbed him repeatedly in the arse as hard as he could. All of the other pupils just stared at him and the room went as quiet as a graveyard as O'Flaherty slowly crumpled to the floor slipping over in a pool of his own blood as it slowly spread across the changing room floor. Davey had never gone back to a normal school again. He was locked up with other maladjusted kids until he was old enough to finish his sentence in an adult prison from where he eventually emerged with an addiction to heroin and a tendency to extreme violence.

Big V glanced over in the direction of the door where Davey was now stood, lurking in the shadows.

'See the bag under the table. I want you to meet Jack Reynolds at the Punjab at two o'clock. Give him the bag and he'll give you a holdall to take to the lock up in Hounslow. When you get there make sure that there are ten bags of weed and two of coke in there. Weigh each bag and get back here afterwards pronto. Make sure you aren't followed. Got it?'

'Two o'clock, yeah, Mr V, no worries. I'll be careful. I always am.'

'Oh, one more thing, take Danny and Joe with you in case that cocksucker tries any shit,' Big V growled.

Danny and Joe were two black brothers who were semi-professional boxers. They were well known around London and both of the bastards were as hard as nails.

Davey disappeared out of the door leaving Big V to peel another large Rizla off the red packet of Kingsize papers on the table in front of him. Big V smiled and thought to himself that business was looking good and things were getting better every day. Now all he had to do was phone his sterile bitch of a wife and make an excuse for why he was going to be late home. He had a new fresh-faced sixteen-year-old boy lined up waiting for him in the flat above the pub. The spotty boy was homeless, a virgin. It was going to be his first time and that was the way Big V liked them….unspoilt.

'Life is great,' Big V said aloud to himself as he dragged hard on the spliff in his hand. He was innocently oblivious as to what was about to happen.

CHAPTER 14

Jack took a deep gulp of air, trying to compose himself and nervously started to punch Sarah's phone number into his mobile.

When they had last spoken it had ended in an argument about his drinking, but he was desperate to find out if she'd heard from Amy. The phone rang without going directly to the annoying voicemail message and Jack was just about to end the call when she finally picked up.

'Hello, Sarah Reynolds.'

'Sarah. It's Jack.'

'Oh Christ, Jack, what do you want now? I don't want another slanging match. Is it important? It's not a good time right now, what with work and everything.'

Jack could hear his dog H in the background barking loudly. It was almost as if H could hear Jack's voice and was trying to tell him something.

'I'm sorry about the other night. I wanted to apologise. It's just the job I'm on at the moment gets to me occasionally.'

'What? So you think it's okay to drink yourself under the bloody table and then take it out on me?'

'Okay, okay, I've said I'm sorry. I only wanted to see how you are and to see if I could come round soon and take H out for a walk before he forgets what I look like.'

'Cut the sarcasm, Jack, it never suited you. He's your bloody dog, you buy all the damn dog food yourself and you know you can come round anytime, just ring me beforehand, okay?' Sarah subconsciously let her anger subside. Jack could hear her relenting.

Jack was still in love with Sarah and desperately missed the way she flicked her brown curls when she was angry or frustrated, the way her nose wrinkled when she was really happy, the way her body felt entwined with his in their bed.

Damn there were so many things he missed about her and he hated the problems his job caused, his drinking and especially the drugs which had led to her deservedly kicking him into touch and out of their beautiful home.

Trying to get to the point of his phone call Jack said, 'Look, Sarah, there's something I need to tell you.'

'Wait, Jack, me first. I really need to talk to you about something.'

After all the years that he and Sarah had spent together, Jack could sense when there was something wrong in her voice and alarm bells started to ring in his head.

'What is it? What's happened?'

'It's Amy. I haven't heard from her for ages and she always calls at least once a week, usually on a Sunday when she needs money. I'm worried. Her phone is switched off, which is unusual.' Sarah's voice trailed off as she started to sob.

'Sarah, don't cry. She could have just lost her phone. There's loads of possibilities.' Jack decided against telling Sarah about Amy's strange text message, he didn't want to worry her any further before he'd spoken to Amy.

'Christ Jack, what if she's started taking drugs again?'

'Why don't you call her tutor, you know, the toffee-nosed one? At least it'll put your mind at rest,' Jack suggested. 'Text me as soon as you know something. I'm sure she's not back on drugs again but you know what teenagers are like and if you go barging into her personal life, she'll only run further away and become more distant. I'll call you later this afternoon, but I really have to go now. She'll be alright, I promise.'

Jack ended the call. He was starting to get very concerned about Amy.

The phone started ringing again. It was Deano.

'Boss? I've been trying to drop call you for ages. You had me worried. I'm outside.'

'Alright, Deano, I'll be out in a tick.'

Putting the phone down, Jack went into the tiny bare kitchen at the back of the hallway. He opened the door of the larder cupboard. Inside, neatly stacked, were at least one hundred sealed plastic bags full of the best grass money could buy. On the street it was known as 'AK47'.

He grabbed the large holdall sitting on top and started to count out ten bags of weed, placing them in the holdall as he counted them. The smell of the weed coming from the cupboard was nicely overpowering and he slammed it shut once he had recounted all of the bags in the holdall to make sure that he hadn't made a mistake. Opening the drawer beside the larder, he took out two brick sized packages of coke which were wrapped tightly with brown masking tape and threw them in the holdall as well.

The coke was a good money earner and he knew that Big V was partial to a bit of sniff himself when he was entertaining underage boys. The thought of what Big V got up to in that flat above the Tankard pub disgusted him and he slammed the drawer shut, trying to focus his mind on the job going down in the afternoon, knowing that hopefully it would help lead to a solid conviction and Big V serving a long stretch in prison. Also, the quicker the job was done the quicker he could start to track down Amy's whereabouts.

Zipping up the holdall, Jack ran back into the living room and grabbed his mobile, his only connection with Amy. He then grabbed his leather jacket and opened the front door to greet the driving spring rain.

CHAPTER 15

Ducking quickly through the rain, Jack could see Deano sitting in his recently hired black Kia, he was wearing his usual herringbone 'scally' flat cap. Jack banged loudly on the roof of the car with his fist as he opened the passenger door and jumped in.

'You tosser. Are you trying to scare me half to death banging on the roof like that? I'm right out of ciggies waiting for you. Got a spare one on you?' Deano said as Jack leant back between the front seats throwing the holdall into the back.

'Suppose so, here have one,' Jack sighed, getting a cigarette packet out of his jacket and passing the packet to Deano.

'Cheers, pissing down, ain't it?'

'Fuck me, there's no flies on you, are there, Deano?' Jack smirked, taking the packet of cigarettes back off Deano and lighting one off the lit match Deano was still holding in his fingernail-bitten hand.

'Right, listen carefully as I don't trust that fat Welsh twat. He may turn up with some extra muscle, first sign of anything iffy get the fuck out of there and don't let anyone in the car until I call you, got that? I'll be parked just behind you watching your fucking back.'

'Yes, boss, all coolio.' Deano slowly blew the cigarette smoke in small rings from his mouth up into the already misted up windscreen.

'Once I call you, you can let one of them and no more than one, into the motor and give him the holdall, but only after my phone call..... alright?'

'Yes, boss, only after you ring me. Told you it's all cool; I know the routine.'

'Right, stick to the speed limit will you and the meet is on the Punjab at two. Don't get fucking nicked on the way for perving at the lollipop ladies during the school kids lunch break either.'

Jack shoved open the car door and jumped out. It was a rented car of course. Automatic Number Plate Recognition meant the police could read any vehicle registration number plate and send the number back to a central database where in a number of seconds it could be checked against any vehicle of interest. Deano was a convicted drug courier so if he was driving a car in his own name the police would have a probable cause for a stop and search.

Jack's Audi may have been stolen from an active drug gang up north but the car was clean now as Jack had the forethought to have the car re-registered through a small time wholesale Turkish heroin dealer he knew who ran a Hertz car hire franchise in Hackney as a front for his illegal activities. He could have got the police to instruct the DVLA to clean the registration of the car but he didn't trust the authorities and couldn't afford any leaks. His life expectancy depended on secrecy. Having been in the Police for a number of years he knew how easy it was for criminals to have a copper on the payroll. A dirty copper led to dead coppers and he wasn't about to die anytime soon if he could help it.

Jack stood for a second watching Deano as he drove out onto the main road, wheel spinning the Kia in the wet, before getting into his Audi. He reached inside his leather jacket and took a cigarette out of the nearly empty packet of Marlborough Lights. He was still thinking about the phone call with Sarah. The last thing he needed at the moment was Amy doing a childish disappearing act or falling back into taking drugs, but the text message along with Amy not answering her phone had got him mad with worry. Recently, he'd thought Amy had turned a corner with her troubles and Sarah didn't normally get so upset without good reason. He finished off the cigarette, threw the stub out of the window and set off.

As Jack drove he listened to the song *Cold* by Stormzy using his mobile on bluetooth.

He joined the M25 motorway and headed for Heathrow Airport getting caught up in traffic that was nearly at a standstill. The traffic cleared and ignoring the idiot in a Highways Agency 4x4 Land Rover on the inside lane, Jack swerved into the fast lane and put his foot down on the accelerator.

Every time he drove into London he noticed how there were more and more homeless people of all ages crashed out in doorways, most of the day desperately trying to stay invisible from the feral gangs of youths that preyed on them mercilessly. He felt sorry for them today. It must be so depressing being wet through to the bone with nowhere to get warm or dry your clothes out. What pissed him off even more was that the homeless soup kitchens and food banks were full of people a lot less deserving. Some people who went there even had jobs but were too lazy to look after themselves properly or else had come into the country illegally and yet the Government were too weak to admit there was an increasing homeless problem staring them in the face. The sad thought reminded him of some of his ex-army buddies whom he knew had fallen on hard times and were sleeping rough on the streets. The forgotten heroes.

Driving along the Uxbridge Road, Jack overtook a black Kia which was parked half on the pavement beside a small row of shops and without thinking he suddenly braked hard. Tyres screeching, he nearly crashed into the stationary Golf in front of him waiting at the red traffic lights a hundred yards before a BP petrol station. He looked in the rear view mirror and could see Deano sitting as bold as brass in the Kia outside the row of shops talking to a policeman, he could tell it was him. He could see the stupid flat cap he insisted on wearing poking out of the wound down window of the hired car. Deano stupidly believed the cap made him look like landed gentry.

Jack thought the day was getting worse and worse and he could feel the terrible hangover he had earlier in the morning returning with renewed aggression. It began to creep all over his body like a bad ecstasy pill. The coke he had snorted earlier was wearing off and the side effect didn't help his mood. To top it all, he could also feel the greasy breakfast turning over violently in his stomach. Despite this, his eyes never strayed for a second from watching Deano in the rear view mirror of the car.

The traffic lights turned green and he drove off sticking two fingers up at the two chavs in the Golf in front of him who were shouting that he should go fuck his mother. He didn't want to attract any more unwanted attention so decided it was best to turn into the BP petrol station to see what was happening between Deano and the policeman. He was only too well aware that one bored policeman doing his duty could ruin years of his hard undercover work.

Jack parked the Audi near to the car wash and walked into the petrol station shop. As soon as he was in the shop he texted Deano: *Call me, right now or as soon as you can?*

Five seconds later Jack's phone rang. Answering Jack said, 'What the hell was all that about? I drove past you and you were chatting a copper up.'

'Mate, I pulled up at the shops to get some cigarettes and just as I was about to get out of the car, this copper appeared from nowhere. Stuck his head in through the window and said, "Do you realise you can't stop here as it's a double yellow line or are you blind." I nearly shat myself. My sphincter muscle was going like a bloody yoyo. I swear he was looking at the holdall in the back seat, but the stupid bastard kept on sneezing and moaning that the bloody weather was going to be the death of him. The funny thing was I don't think he could've smelt even my Grandad's old gardening socks as he had such a bad cold. Anyway, I said, "Of course, officer, my mistake, hope you feel better soon." And then got the fucking hell out of there and he was none the wiser, the prat. I'll be there as agreed in ten minutes but will have to double back a couple of times to make sure no one's following me.'

Jack sighed. Deano was good at what he did but he could be reckless if he'd smoked too much weed and he'd nearly ruined everything. The simplest mistakes could get you nicked.

Jack got back into the Audi and turned the car back onto the Uxbridge Road. After a few miles of passing one Indian restaurant after another, some falling apart with peeling paint and others with racist grafitti on the fronts, he started to get closer to the centre of Uxbridge. The restaurants and shops looked smarter and more upmarket. The local council had been spending millions of pounds of tax payer's money trying to improve the area and rid it of all the drunks and crack heads.

Turning into Herbert Road and then almost immediately into Punjab Lane, he pulled into the small car park behind Smallfields old peoples home. It was a quiet secluded car park surrounded by high fences and an entrance and exit where they were unlikely to be watched as the drug deal went down. He could see Deano sitting in the Kia and stopped the Audi in the space behind him and tooted the horn. He saw Deano's cap turn around and Deano gave him the thumbs up letting Jack know everything seemed okay and he hadn't been followed.

Almost immediately a black BMW swerved into the car park and came to an abrupt stop beside Deano. There were three men in the car; two of them were huge black men who were obviously the hired muscle and the driver was white. Jack instantly recognised him as Big V's right hand man, Davey.

The driver's door opened, Davey got out and walked over to the Audi carrying a brown holdall over his right shoulder. He got in. Jack could feel his stomach turning again as the pungent unclean smell emitting from Davey wafted through the car.

'Alright, Jack, how you doing, bruv? I want to get this done quickly, right, so don't fuck me about.'

'Careful, Davey, don't forget who you're talking to. What's the rush, are you still tickling the balls of that fat Welsh prick you call your boss?'

'Very clever, you're a funny man aren't you, Jack? Have you got the gear or what?'

'Pass me the bag and once I've checked it, call one of your goons and tell him to get the bag off my guy in the black Kia.'

Davey passed the holdall over and Jack unzipped it and counted the bundles of money wrapped up in elastic bands. He then rang Deano.

'Looks okay. You can tell your goon to collect the gear and then fuck off, you weasel.'

Davey pulled his mobile out of his pocket and scrolled through his contacts list and clicked on a phone number in it. One of the black guys got out of the BMW and got into the Kia. After a few seconds he got out and back into the BMW carrying the large holdall that Deano had given him. Immediately the switch had been completed, Davey got out of the Audi and Jack drove off, following Deano's car out of the car park as it blew blue wisps of smoke out of the overtired exhaust. The evidence against Riordan and now Big V was mounting up.

CHAPTER 16

So far the afternoon shift had been full of the usual mundane patients needing physio or bandages changed. Half of the patients at the hospital were time wasters who were only there to ensure that their benefit payments continued. Some of Sarah's colleagues despised these people, but Sarah felt sorry for them and the nature of the job meant that they had a duty of care to treat them.

The most regular patient Sarah had to treat was Mrs Stevens who was about fifty-five and had never done a stroke of work in her life. She had churned out children like a packing factory conveyor belt and now she had the brazen cheek to complain of a bad back. Unfortunately, she suffered from various mental issues and really only came to the hospital to have a cup of tea and a chat. These regular cups of tea took up a lot of Sarah's time but she didn't mind.

Since leaving the house and driving to Dorking Hospital where she had been working for the last five years, all Sarah could think about was Amy. Jack had said he would call her before her shift started but he hadn't; which was no surprise to her at all. She'd thrown him out of the house for being unreliable and drunk; so far he had proved no different. He was still drinking and she was sure he was still taking drugs.

Pushing open the large glass swing doors, Sarah walked past the X-Ray department, her padded shoes sticking to the freshly polished floor. She stopped and turned as she heard a voice behind her.

'Hello, Sarah. How was Mrs Stevens today?'

'She was fine thank you, Bob, but I think she may have used the last tea bag yet again.'

Bob was a Radiographer and a few years older than Sarah with an unsightly cleft lip. He was tall with thick glasses and his white hospital coat hung off his skinny frame as though it were dangling off a coat hanger. The main problem Sarah had with Bob was that he followed her around the hospital corridors pouncing on her when she least expected it. She thought he was creepy. He'd asked her out on a date a few times over the years, but seemed to have stepped up a gear since hearing she'd kicked Jack out. He was virtually stalking her around the hospital wards.

'Are you going to the canteen, Sarah? Perhaps we could have a coffee together?'

Bob's eyes strained hopefully through his milk bottle glasses as he looked Sarah up and down taking in every curve of her figure. It unnerved her. She felt as though he was undressing her with his eyes. Coughing into her hand, Sarah tried to hide her disgust and politely replied, 'Sorry, Bob, I can't at the moment. Perhaps another time when we aren't so busy on the ward.'

Turning quickly away she continued down the corridor towards the main entrance of the hospital feeling Bob's eyes following her intently from behind. She felt a cold shiver run down her shoulders at the thought of his beady little eyes watching her every move. The large automatic glass doors at the main entrance slid open quietly and Sarah rushed outside away from his prying eyes.

With a sense of desperation she had not felt recently, she lit a cigarette and dragged on it with as much strength as her lungs would allow in the unusually cold spring air. She exhaled the smoke, watching it disappear into the hazy mist. She walked over to a bench and sat down, rummaging around in the depths of her handbag for her mobile. She found it and clicked on the contact number for her parents. If Amy had contacted anyone it would be her grandparents. She knew how close Amy was to them as Jack and herself had been so wrapped up in their own problems lately that they hadn't had a lot of time for Amy.

'Hi, Mum. How are you and Dad?' she asked, not daring to jump blindly into the subject of Amy immediately.

'Hello, darling,' Amy's mother answered in a polished privately educated accent. 'We're both okay. Your father is on his last chemotherapy session and things are looking hopeful, fingers crossed. I've been busy helping out at the local church as you know. Gosh you would not believe how much of my time it takes up,' she said with a loud sigh. 'We're always tired. I suppose your father and I have to face the fact that we're not getting any younger.'

'I know, Mum. Will you tell Dad that I send my love. Look, there's a reason why I'm calling, but I don't want you to go into a mad panic.'

'Well, darling, just saying that starts me worrying. Goodness what is it? Nothing dreadful I hope. You're not getting back with Jack, are you, dear? I never trusted him. You're too good for him and he drinks too much. But I'm sure you know that anyway. You always were such a level-headed girl.'

'Mum, it's not Jack. And yes, he does drink too much and you know I still love him but we're not living together at the moment so you've no need to worry.'

'Heaven for small mercies then,' Sarah's mother sardonically retorted with a faintly sarcastic laugh.

'There's no need for alarm, but I was wondering if you'd heard from Amy recently. We've not heard from her for a week or so. It may well be she's just going through an adolescent phase at the moment and wants her own space. Well,

Jack thinks so anyway, but I was wondering....' Sarah trailed off, trying to keep any hint of worry or desperation out of her voice. They had deliberately chosen not to tell her parents about Amy's recent troubles.

'The last time we heard from Amy was just after Christmas when she rang thanking us for the winter duvet we bought her. I gather the Blackrock Halls of Residence are very badly heated. She seemed okay, but she did ask if we could send her a little money as she was too embarrassed to ask you or Jack when you were both arguing so much. So we sent her three hundred pounds to help her. Is that a problem, darling? We were only trying to help.'

'No, no problem, Mum. Thanks for being so thoughtful. Listen I've got to go now; my shift starts in a minute. If you hear from Amy can you ask her to call me straight away? But please don't worry; everything is fine. Love you and say hello to Dad for me. I promise I'll pop round soon. Things have been hectic with work; you know what it's like.'

'Okay, darling, big kiss from us both.'

'Bye, love you both too,' Sarah said tugging her free hand through her tangled brown hair in frustration. As soon as she ended the call, she started to cry, her shoulders jerking up and down involuntarily as she sobbed. Sitting on the bench, she held her head in her hands, ignoring the people coming and going around her.

Suddenly she heard a voice she knew only too well.

'Are you alright, Sarah? Is there anything I can do?'

'Bob, honestly, I just need a few moments to myself. I'm fine, nothing to worry about,' Sarah lied, praying to any religious being that maybe existed in this or any other universe that Bob would go away as soon as possible and stop prying into her personal business before she lost her temper and unprofessionally told him to just fuck off.

'Sorry, I didn't mean to upset you. I'd better get back and check on those X-rays,' Bob spluttered, quickly disappearing through the main entrance doors back into the hospital and Sarah watched him until he turned the corner to make sure that he'd gone. If he didn't act so weird all of the time she could maybe have felt sorry for him. But his weird behaviour was his undoing.

Reaching into her pocket for another cigarette, she took the last one out of the packet and, scrumpling up the empty packet, threw it into the bin at the end of the bench. It missed and fell on the floor amongst the other discarded cigarette ends.

Jack had suggested calling Amy's personal tutor. They'd met the tutor last summer when Amy had fallen behind with her course work. Trying to remember his name she scrolled through the contacts memory on her phone and finding the name, Mr Fitzpatrick, pressed the green dial button. Her hand shook and she wasn't sure if what she doing was the right thing. She could hear Jack's last words ringing in her ears: *If you go barging into her personal life she will only run further away*. She thought, sod you, Jack, somebody has to do something.

'Hello, University of Dublin, this is Mr Fitzpatrick, how can I help you?'

'Yes, hello, my name is Sarah Reynolds and my daughter Amy is studying law at your faculty. You were kindly helping her as she'd got a little behind on her course work.'

'Ah, yes... Amy Reynolds, of course. I remember meeting you and you're husband last summer. How are things with you, Mrs Reynolds?'

Sarah could picture the tutor in his study, sitting in his favourite old and slightly tattered armchair with the straight back, surrounded by books. He was more than likely holding a cut crystal glass half full of expensive brandy.

'I'm fine, thank you. I'll come straight to the point. My husband and I haven't heard from Amy for a while and recently we've not even been able to reach her by phone. We were wondering how her studies were going and whether you had recently seen her at lectures?' There, she'd said it now and she felt a little bit of relief mixed with lots of anxiety.

The tutor replied in a soft voice, 'Amy has been attending lectures sporadically, Mrs Reynolds, and recently we understand that she's been taken ill. But I'm sure there's nothing to worry about. However, on a personal level I am not too keen on the crowd that she's been hanging around with outside of the University and I feel that they have become a distraction to her studies and intend to talk to her about her attendance. She's heading for a fail on this part of the course unless she bucks her ideas up.'

Sarah could feel her heart rate increase. 'What exactly do you mean by the wrong crowd?'

'Well as you know I don't mix with the students socially, but I do have ears, you know, and I'm fully aware of what students get up to. You know what I mean, Mrs Reynolds, wild parties and the like. Just like when we were young, eh?'

'Wild parties?....What sex, drugs?' Sarah questioned.

'Mrs Reynolds, I'll be perfectly frank, I don't know if your daughter is messed up in anything, but I know that the group she's mixing with are heavily involved in the drug scene in and around Dublin. We try our best to keep the drugs off campus. There really isn't anything else I can tell you, but my advice would be to try not to worry and keep on trying to call your daughter. Perhaps try phoning some of her friends; they may be able to help put your mind at ease.'

Shaking, Sarah's voice started to break. 'I'd be grateful if you would ask Amy to call me immediately the next time you see her. Thank you for your help, goodbye.'

Sarah again delved into her handbag and took out a new packet of cigarettes. She tore the packet open and lit one, inhaling deeply. She tried to wipe away the tears streaming down her face as she wondered where Amy was and why she wasn't answering her phone. Where on earth was Jack when she really needed him? Sarah was now convinced that Amy had started using drugs again and her life could be in serious jeopardy.

CHAPTER 17

As soon as Jack had got back to Dorking from Southall he rang Amy at least a dozen times but her phone instantly went to voicemail. It was unusual that she wasn't answering but, aside from the drugs, he knew Amy was becoming her own woman and needed space to grow up and experience life. Since Amy's suicide attempt her mother was always molly coddling her and was afraid of letting go of the reins which Jack knew frustrated Amy and often left her embarrassed, especially in front of what few friends she had.

When Amy had first started to smoke she was only fifteen. She was underage and Sarah had gone up the wall. She'd raged and lectured and tried to ground her on more than one occasion. Jack had tried to play devil's advocate, explaining to Sarah that if she tried to stop Amy smoking, the likelihood was that Amy would only want to smoke more.

Jack remembered when he was a teenager – he must have been only about eleven or twelve – he'd been caught smoking his stepmother's Dunhill Kingsize cigarettes. As a punishment, his stepmother had sat him down on a chair in the kitchen and forced him to smoke a whole packet of twenty cigarettes one after the other, hoping that it would make him physically sick. Jack smiled to himself as he remembered telling his stepmother that it had made him feel like puking and he had promised that he would never smoke again. He'd only said it to shut her up and get her off his case. Secretly he'd enjoyed every single puff of each cigarette. He'd continued to smoke, but had stopped stealing cigarettes from his stepmother and learnt to be a bit more sneaky at covering the smell.

Skeggsy had rung him earlier and demanded to meet him in the Kings Arms as soon as he'd returned from Southall. Jack was already in the Kings Arms and was three quarters of the way down his first pint of Oranjeboom. He was the only customer and the only noise to break the silence was the anxious tapping of his pistol key ring on the wooden bar top and the occasional crashing sound of empty bottles being thrown into the bins out back. He wished Skeggsy would hurry up as he had much more important things to do.

Jim, in a navy suit, walked into the back part of the bar carrying a box of Shiraz and Jack caught his eye.

'Did you want another one?' Jim asked, hauling the box onto the bar.

'Just a quick one, Jim,' Jack said impatiently looking at his watch for the fourth time wondering where Skeggsy was and why he wanted to meet him so urgently.

Jim placed a pint of Oranjeboom on the bar. 'Three seventy.'

Jack had thought about giving Sarah a quick call, but seeing as he was on his second pint and still didn't have any news on Amy he thought better of it. Sarah had been pretty upset the last time they'd spoken and if she guessed that he was in the pub, she was likely to go ballistic at him.

One of the major reasons she had thrown him out of the marital home was his drinking and she didn't appreciate that a large part of his job involved blending in, mixing with the suspects of whatever case he was working on – and alcohol played an important part of that disguise. He knew in his heart of hearts though that his excessive drinking had spilled over into his private life and that recently there hadn't been many nights when he wasn't drunk. The main issue was he now liked being drunk and had got used to the hangovers. He had begun to enjoy living life close to the edge and sobriety no longer held much appeal.

As Jack got off the bar stool to go to the toilet a group of men came in – regulars, Jack noted, who usually put away two bottles of wine each in a session.

Going into the toilet he opened the single cubicle door and locked it behind him. He took a small wrap out of his pocket and unfolded it, using a twenty pound note he quickly snorted a line of coke. The rush hit him like a main line train to the brain.

Running the knuckles of his right hand under his nose to wipe away any tell-tale signs, Jack pushed the door of the toilet open and walked briskly back into the bar. Immediately he caught sight of a cropped head of ginger hair. Sitting in front of him, as bold as brass, was a grinning Skeggsy.

'Alright, you pisshead?' said Skeggsy. 'Blimey, you on the old marching powder again?' He laughed into his pint, sloshing it over the bar. Everything was a joke to Skeggsy and the drunker he got the more he laughed. Usually it was at nothing in particular and Jack was thankful that at least Skeggsy didn't seem too pissed.

'Everything go alright, did it?' Skeggsy continued loudly.

'Yeah, let's grab the table in the corner,' Jack said, taking his pint off the bar and walking over to the round table by the window so that they could talk without anyone overhearing. Sitting down Jack took a gulp of his pint and asked, 'Have you heard from Riordan at all?'

'Yeah, last night, but that's none of your business,' Skeggsy snarled, taking a seat across the table. 'Anyway, Southall?'

'Well I went there and that skinny creep Davey was at the drop. He was as jumpy as a pig in a pork factory. So was that pervert Big V when I spoke to him on the phone come to think of it. I don't trust any of that lot and Big V has always had it in for Riordan. He would snap up the chance in a second to take over his trade in London.'

Skeggsy picked up his pint and took a long pull on it. He drank nearly over half of it in one go before he said, 'I told Riordan you weren't to be trusted yet but he wants you to go to the flat in Wandsworth tomorrow morning and check up on a delivery that's arriving later tonight. There should be three hundred parcels of the best coke money can buy from our Peruvian friends. It needs cutting and pressing so that it's ready for distribution. That's if you can handle it? Deano will meet you there as he's shifting the gear. I asked him to start sorting things out. All you have to do is make sure they get a move on and the gear is ready to be shifted to the other distributors as quickly as possible. Just bell Deano when you get there and he'll let you in. He knows what to do.' Skeggsy paused. 'By the way, there'll be three Vietnamese girls there and they'll be in their underwear so they don't nick any of the gear. Just remember they're there to do a job, not to satisfy any of your personal sexual deviances. You can stick to the internet for any of that weird shit you're probably into. Fresh meat like that is my payday, not yours. Got it?'

Lighting a cigarette, Skeggsy sneered, his ginger eyebrows meeting in the middle of his forehead like tramlines.

Disgusted, Jack knew Skeggsy was thinking about the terrified trafficked women and what perverted things he could do to them.

'Hey, no smoking inside,' Jim shouted across the bar at Skeggsy.

'Fuck you. I'm going in a second so you can have your jollies off in the toilet in a minute, alright, you prick?'

Jack gave Jim a knowing nod to leave it and said, 'Yeah, Skeggsy, no worries. That's the flat in Armoury Way, isn't it? I think I've been there a couple of times.'

'Yeah right, that's me done,' Skeggsy said tilting his head back and finishing the last of his pint in one go. 'Make sure you call me when everything's pressed and packaged. Once it's all ready to go I'll take over on Mr Riordan's orders. But I'm trusting you with this, so don't let me down or else I'll cut your prick off, okay?'

'No worries. It'll all be sorted. I'll call you later.'

Jack watched Skeggsy duck down a little as he left the pub so that he didn't bang his head walking through the small doorway and then he stood up, taking his now empty pint glass to the bar. He'd been to the Armoury Way distribution flat, but had never actually been inside and this was a good opening for him to gather more intelligence on how Riordan's drug operation worked.

He didn't worry for one second about the implications of how deep undercover he was going and which side of the law he was starting to tread. Least of all he thought of the danger he was putting himself in. The question Jack asked himself was whether he had underestimated the danger he was in.

CHAPTER 18

Slowly waking up to the sound of Lorraine Kelly's voice flooding into his brain, Jack took a while to realise it was coming from the breakfast TV programme on the flat screen in the corner of the room. He'd never liked those desperate, almost pious, breakfast television presenters and resented them even more when they woke him up.

As he opened his eyes and looked around the room, it became clear that he wasn't in his bedroom. As usual he'd only made it as far as the leather sofa and he was still fully dressed – like a teenager after a heavy night out, Sarah would say. Stretching out his arms and legs, Jack knocked over the ash tray that had been balanced on his chest. He swore as the contents scattered over his carpet and the old wound in his left leg twinged with the unexpected movement.

Standing up, he clumsily stepped in the remains of a doner kebab which, hazarding a guess, he'd picked up the previous night.

Shuffling to the bathroom with kebab stuck to his feet, Jack undressed and threw his clothes on the floor. He studied himself in the bathroom mirror and could see that he still had a fit body, lean and muscular. His chest was well defined and still quite hairy but 'old age' rudely told him that he had a couple of white wisps of hair there and more would soon follow.

As he looked at his reflection, he barely recognised the hard-lined face staring back at him with large bloodshot eyes. He was shocked at how tired he looked and hated the crow's feet fanning out from his eyes and the three days' growth of stubble on his chin. His days of melting women's hearts were gone, he could live with that, but life without Sarah was destroying him minute by minute and day by day.

After showering and dressing, he switched the kettle on and switched the SIM cards in the mobile again. Immediately he could see that there were six missed calls from Sarah and a couple of text messages. He opened the last message sent and read it: *Where the bloody hell are you Jack? You promised to call me you bastard, I still can't get hold of Amy. I need you to call me immediately.*

The previous night Jack had tried calling some of Amy's friends, those he knew of, which weren't many. No one admitted to having seen Amy recently and he had the distinct impression they were hiding something. He'd intended to call Sarah but must've fallen asleep after drinking one too many cans of lager.

The tone of Sarah's text was explicit, he'd better bite the bullet, call her, and take whatever flack was going to fly his way.

Jack sat down on the sofa with a mug of strong coffee to prepare himself for a tirade of abuse from Sarah. He could feel the caffeine waking him up as he sipped, but the downside was it also intensified his hangover.

He decided against a morning 'livener' line of coke. She could always tell if he was on anything and for the first time in ages he didn't feel like snorting a line this early in the morning. He had an unsettling feeling that after speaking to Sarah his life was going to change dramatically.

Jack scrolled down to Sarah's number in his mobile and hesitated before hitting the green dial button. He sat back against the soft leather of the sofa and listened to the rhythmical dialing tone buzzing in his ears. Jack could feel each pulsating ring of the phone bursting through his blood vessels and then at last he heard Sarah's voice.

'Jack, is that you? Thank God, I've been so worried.' Her voice was high-pitched, filled with anxiety and exhaustion.

Jack was flooded with guilt for not calling sooner. He could be such an insensitive idiot sometimes.

'Yeah, it's me. Have you heard anything from Amy?'

He knew that his subconscious radar was spot on most of the time where trouble was concerned and his bad leg started to ache almost immediately just to prove that his radar was working fine.

'Just listen will you! I spoke to my parents and they said that they haven't heard from her for a few weeks and I also spoke to Mr Fitzpatrick, her personal tutor, and he's hardly seen her since Christmas. Amy's basically not been attending her lectures regularly at all and he hinted that she's involved in drugs. When I say that, I mean more than just a bit of weed on campus; she's involved with fucking scumbags and I'm terrified of history repeating itself,' Sarah's voice broke. A sob echoing down the line. 'It's happening again Jack. You've got to find my daughter and bring her back.'

'Our daughter, Sarah.'

'Yes, fucking whatever. Jack, this is our daughter we're talking about and I'm really scared. Christ, if you'd set a better example to Amy none of this would be happening. But no, you were too interested in getting off your head and wrecking our marriage.'

Jack took a deep breath and said, 'I'll ignore that mega-barbed comment. I admit it's worrying and I'm terrified that she might've gone back to drugs. Last night I rang some of her friends and left messages asking her to call either of us immediately. If we don't hear something soon I'll fly over to Dublin and speak to this Fitzpatrick guy myself. Worrying yourself senseless won't help.' Immediately he regretted telling her not to worry, he only wanted to protect Sarah.

'Don't you dare tell me not to worry, Jack! This is Amy we're talking about. Our daughter.' Sarah shouted at Jack more in frustration than anything else.

Neither of them knew where Amy was and even worse was the inconsolable horror that she might be in some real trouble and that there was nothing either of them could do.

'Sarah, shouting at me won't help the situation. Are you absolutely sure that the tutor said Amy was on drugs?' Jack still didn't want to tell Sarah about the strange text message from Amy.

'He didn't exactly say it outright, but you could tell he thought so. He said she was hanging around with the druggie crowd and missing lectures. It all adds up now. I feel so stupid for not seeing this earlier.' Sarah was crying uncontrollably now.

Jack leaned forwards on the sofa and said, 'Sarah, before I fly out there I'll ring some mates in Ireland from my army days and perhaps they can find Amy. I know some who work for the local Gardai. If she calls you, you call me straight away. If you can't get through then send me a text, but I'll try to keep the phone on when I can. Alright?'

'Okay, Jack, but I'm petrified. I'm so worried about my little girl. I mean drugs, not again surely?'

'Don't worry, I'll get to the bottom of it.' Jack put the phone down and as he did he could still hear Sarah crying.

CHAPTER 19

The NCA main offices were based at Spring Gardens in Vauxhall, London. Spring Gardens used to house a facility used by the now disbanded SOCA and was a large, unimpressive set of red brick buildings surrounded by high wrought iron fencing. The site originally only consisted of just two units of offices, but over the years the necessity to fight organised crime had increased and it was now composed of various strategic units dedicated to fighting all types of crime in the UK and abroad.

The NCA had been forging a name for themselves with some high-profile arrests recently. One of their biggest seizures to date was five hundred million pounds worth of coke discovered on the Ukrainian tug boat Hamal, just off the Scottish coast of Aberdeen. The NCA had also been working hard to manage a better working relationship with their colleagues at MI5 and MI6, who mainly dealt in trying to stop all aspects of terrorism. These acts of terrorism were blatantly funded from the misery of the vast wealth generated by the wholesale international drug market, prostitution and recently from the spoils of people trafficking, which was becoming increasingly popular to the crime lords of the underworld.

DI Daryl Rice showed his NCA identity card to the security guard at the gate as he drove his silver Mercedes SLK into the secure underground car park.

Once parked, Daryl sat in the car for a few minutes listening to the end of a documentary about obesity in Britain on

Radio 4's 'The Today' programme. He enjoyed Radio 4 as it had some hard-hitting factual current affairs programmes on it, mixed with a splattering of middle of the road music which suited him completely. He was no musical expert or geek but it played none of that gangster rap crap that people listened to nowadays, which he hated with a passion.

He leaned forward stretching up close to the rear view mirror and straightened his tie and checked that his top button was covered by the tie. As an afterthought he checked to make sure the flies on his trousers were done up.

He was making a more concerted effort this morning than usual. Yesterday he'd received an email from Detective Chief Inspector Peter Smith summoning him to a meeting at 8 a.m. The DCI had asked for an operational overview of how the strategy they were deploying with Jack as an undercover was working. Daryl knew that the DCI had a reputation as a ruthless bastard and being Cambridge educated he was only concerned in statistics. He had to ensure that all costs were operationally effective and tied neatly into the NCA objectives. If they did not, he'd been known to pull the plug on an investigation without any warning. The way things were in this current period of austerity meant that the senior ranks quite often didn't have the funding to let an operation run its full course anymore.

What made Daryl particularly nervous today was that the senior ranks very rarely got involved unless they had a whiff of things turning sour and Daryl knew that he had kept regular updates with all of his field operatives except for Jack who was a bit of a lone wolf. Maybe word had reached the DCI about Jack. He couldn't believe that was true for an instant as he'd fed regular reports to the DCI on the investigation into Riordan's criminal activities and the undercover operation involving Jack was so secret that there could not have been a leak within the NCA to necessitate this meeting.

He dreaded the possibility of extracting Jack from the field. It would mean three years of hard work going down the drain for all involved, which was not an order he was easily prepared to accept. It would also mean his career on the line. His career and the Mercedes he was sitting in were the most important things in Daryl's life and he wasn't going to let an out of control undercover prick like Jack or a snotty-nosed wanker like the DCI fuck things up for him.

The programme on Radio 4 had just finished. The resounding decision from the discussions held was that Britain was full of lots of young fat bastards who were not intent on working at all and as a result the tax payer would have to fork out for specialised modified ambulances that could carry patients weighing up to one hundred and forty-four kilos and the cost to the tax payer would be around £90,000 for each ambulance. The presenter on the radio announced that the discussion tomorrow morning was about parents hitting their children.

Sighing at the state of Britain, Daryl turned the radio off and locked the Mercedes. He quickly strode towards the entrance and punched the code into the security system to let himself into the building. He loved the bustle of the NCA offices and walked towards the lift which would take him to the third floor where the DCI's office was and where he presumed the meeting was going to be held.

His heart suddenly missed a beat. He stopped walking and leant against the wall beside the main desk, attempting to blend into the stained magnolia-coloured wall. He had just noticed a pretty female uniformed constable walking directly towards him.

He felt his balls tighten, but it was in horror and not sexual excitement. It was the same pretty blonde constable he had met at the area Christmas party last year. If his hazy memory served him correctly her name was Julie and she was married to the desk sergeant at Wandsworth nick. He had a reputation as a hard bastard who hated the higher ranks. He knew the sergeant despised what Daryl stood for as Daryl had only risen through the ranks due to the police accelerated programme for 'posh boys' with a paid-for educational background to fit the senior jobs. This was so that the media and the do-gooder fraternity were kept happy, but the 'bobbies' on the pavement felt that this was taking the piss.

He wasn't too sure of the sergeant's name, but was damn sure Julie had probably told him about the incident at the Christmas party. Daryl had followed her into the ladies toilet after buying her a gin and tonic, along with at least his fifteenth pint, and he had grabbed her pretty little bum cheeks and tried to kiss her neck from behind as she fixed her makeup in the mirror. Julie was tougher than she looked as she had turned around slowly and seductively smiled at him. Her small breasts straining through her tight white blouse had been tempting him to lean in for a kiss on her lips, but she had put her arms on his shoulders and surprisingly quickly pulled him towards her and kneed him in the balls as hard as she could. She had then slowly walked out of the ladies toilets leaving him writhing on the floor in agony clutching his balls.

Daryl didn't directly work alongside the constable and this was the first time he had seen her since the incident. She hadn't reported him and he could only put it down to the fact that making such an accusation against a senior officer could possibly ruin any future chance of promotion. There hadn't been any witnesses and as sexism was rife amongst the male officers her making a complaint wouldn't have gone down well with any of her male colleagues.

The pretty blonde constable walked past Daryl without noticing him, or so he guessed as she had ignored his presence completely. Perhaps she had decided to ignore him on purpose, probably a good thing but he was never going to find out either way. Once she had walked past him the pain in his balls subsided as quickly as it had started and he took his handkerchief from his pocket and wiped the nervous sweat from his forehead. There was no way he was going to risk going to another Christmas party, especially if it got out he had sexually assaulted a young female constable at last year's party, then his fast track career would definitely be over in a flash. The PC brigade that existed in the police would make sure of his suspension or sacking.

The yellow arrow lit up on the control pad beside the lift confirming that the lift was on its way down and Daryl let out a quiet sigh of relief on its arrival. The doors slid open and he thankfully stepped into the empty lift. Pressing the button for the third floor, Daryl rubbed his aching balls through his freshly pressed trousers with his left hand and could feel a faint stirring as he thought back to the close call a minute ago where Julie might have recognised him, but more vividly he thought back to the memory of his having held her small but tight bum cheeks in his hands for those few furtive dangerous seconds.

Stepping out of the lift, Daryl carefully smoothed down any creases that were left in his uniform with his hands and walked towards the double doors at the end of the empty corridor. A gold nameplate read *DCI Peter Smith*.

With a deep breath, Daryl gave his tie a final, nervous check, then clasping his peaked cap tightly under his arm he knocked firmly on the door with his knuckles.

With his career on the line, Daryl heard a deep but educated voice bark loudly, 'Come in.'

CHAPTER 20

At last the sun had finally come out and shown its face. The view from Jack's flat of Boxhill had been spectacular when he had woken up earlier in the morning and looked out of the window. He could see all the way up to the viewpoint at the top of the hill. It was emblazoned in the early morning sunshine and already had pockets of tourists milling around like small foraging soldier ants.

After his phone call to Sarah he had racked his brains thinking of which ex-army buddy he could call in Ireland that might be able to help him locate Amy or at least look into the worrying drug allegations made by Amy's tutor. As he was right in the middle of an undercover operation it might blow his cover if he suddenly disappeared and flew to Ireland, but if Amy definitely was in danger he wouldn't have a choice. He hoped the tutor had been mistaken.

One man he had thought of was someone from way back when he had been serving in Bosnia – Corporal Stan Wacameyer, a crazy American dude who had liked his drugs and was usually high on something during a firefight. Nearly every soldier was on some sort of drug back in those days. It had been the only way to alleviate the mental anguish caused by all of the atrocities that they had encountered during the savage war. After seeing your close friends blown to pieces in front of your eyes, any normal human being would have felt the need to have something to calm their nerves and take the edge off the daily terror they had to endure.

He had heard on the grapevine that on leaving the army Stan had gone to work in Northern Ireland. He thought he'd heard that Stan was either working for the Security Services or else working in an advisory capacity combatting terrorism. Since the loyalist paramilitary ceasefire, following the Good Friday agreement on the 10 April 1988, there was still a lot of security work to be done in Ireland as various terrorist organisations had since split into vigilante groups and were now trying to stir up the troubles again. Jack thought that if Stan was still working over in Ireland, he might agree to help him for old time's sake. It wasn't going to be an easy or quick task to track Stan down and he was already late meeting Deano in Wandsworth. He decided to try and track him down after he had returned from seeing Deano at Armoury Way.

After clearing up last night's kebab, which was not a pleasant experience, he decided to quickly report in. From memory he tapped in the number for his daily Cover Officer, Gary or Gazza as he liked to call him. He'd only met him once at Spring Gardens when the undercover operation had first got the go ahead from the top brass, but he liked him enough and trusted him.

'Hey, Gazza, it's your long lost—' An irate Brummie voice stopped Jack in his tracks.

'Don't take the piss. I haven't heard from you for days and you know I have to make a report weekly to the DI. I've covered for you recently but I'm not putting my fucking job on the line for you, got it?'

'Okay, okay, keep your hair on. I promise to be a good boy and call in every day as instructed,' Jack replied sarcastically. He hated all of the mundane rules governing undercover work which got in the way of concentrating on the real job in hand.

'Well you might be interested to know that Rice has been called into a meeting with the DCI.'

'Oh fuck. We're not up for review yet. What's all that about?' Jack asked, feeling a cold shudder go through him.

'Don't know, but I wouldn't be surprised if the DCI pulls you out after the way you've been acting lately, unless you can get some results pretty damned quick.'

'Well I'm going to Wandsworth in a minute and they've asked me to oversee the cutting and pressing of the latest shipment of coke that's come in. I think I'm finally making some headway and Riordan seems to trust me now.'

'Alright, I'm just warning you, so don't be too surprised if we suddenly sweep you up off the street if the shit hits the fan.'

'Thanks for the warning, Gazza. I'll call you soon. I promise.'

Switching the SIM cards over he flushed the card he had just used down the toilet. He knew that his security was a bit over the top but it was what made him feel comfortable that mattered. So what if he was a bit OCD about things – being paranoid had kept him alive so far.

With alarm bells still ringing in his head from the conversation he had just had with Gazza, Jack left the flat and climbed into the Audi. Jack had a lot of music stored on his phone, from contemporary musicians like Ed Sheeran to bands of his own era. He turned on the bluetooth and chose to listen to Oasis's sixth studio album, *Don't Believe the Truth*.

Driving out onto the bypass, he lit a Marlborough Light and inhaled deeply. A loud aggressive tooting of a car horn behind him abruptly bought him to his senses and he swerved the Audi back into the correct lane as some young chav in a baseball cap quickly put his foot down and overtook him on the outside lane in a souped-up silver Astra whilst giving him the one-fingered salute.

The playlist changed to one of Jack's favourite Oasis songs, *'Mucky Fingers'*, so he turned the volume up a bit just before he turned onto the A3 dual carriageway which went all the way up to Wandsworth. He drove listening to the song, chuckling to himself at the obvious connotations of the title of the song.

Jack had been to Armoury Way a couple of times but had never been trusted to go into the flat by Skeggsy or Riordan. He had only ever met Skeggsy or Deano outside the flat and then given them a lift somewhere. Jack suspected that being ordered to go to the flat was just another test set by Riordan who, after Jack's years of careful undercover work, was perhaps beginning to trust him and welcome him into the fold by giving him more responsibility.

This was to be the second major safe-house that Jack had been in where the gang kept large consignments of drugs and Jack knew that he could blow the gang's whole distribution network apart in an instant by busting them right now. There was no way the top brass would be happy with closing down just a small part of the network in the UK. Busting them now was not an option and if he did it would mean that the NCA would be unlikely to get the budget for such a major operation again.

Jack reached Armoury Way, turning the engine off but leaving the music playing. He lit another cigarette, noticing that he only had two left. The last thing he wanted to do was wander down Wandsworth high street looking for fags. He hated Wandsworth as he thought it was a shithole, pretty much like the rest of London.

Leaning back into the Audi's exceptionally comfy driving seat he took a nervous drag on his cigarette and looked up and down the street. The only attraction of London was how cosmopolitan it had become; there were Asian women, Afro Caribbean women, there were also plenty of Eastern Bloc women living in London now which was a big 'thank you' to the last Labour Government and their immigration policies. Jack didn't discriminate when it came to admiring the fairer sex and now the sun was out so were the women and most of them were confidently wearing clothes that left little to the imagination.

Suddenly the sound of his phone ringing broke his train of thought and he looked at the number calling him and could see that it was Skeggsy. What the fuck did he want?

'Alright, Skeggsy, how's it hanging?'

'Better than you ever will be, you twat. Are you there yet?' Skeggsy growled.

'I've just pulled up, okay. Give us a chance will ya? If you get off the phone I'll be able to call Deano and get on with it.' Jack started to sweat a little as Skeggsy was unpredictable and that made him nervous, he also sounded as high as a kite.

'Mr Riordan asked me to keep an eye on you. He also rang me this morning to remind you that he expects you to have an answer very soon to that small problem he discussed with you about the product being short. Mr Riordan is not a man who takes kindly to being kept waiting and I wouldn't want to be in your shoes if he has to ask again.'

Jack could hear loud voices in the background and guessed that Skeggsy was either already in the pub or else he was in the bookies, both venues being his regular pastime. Skeggsy regularly lost most of his ill-gotten gains in the bookies or else he blew the cash on booze and drugs. Whatever he did, he never saved much money as far as Jack could tell. He was always skint.

'I hear you, loud and clear, but these things take time, you know?' Jack said, knowing that Riordan suspected it might even be Skeggsy ripping him off.

'No good telling me, mate, say that to Mr Riordan. Bell me later once you've sorted the job out with Deano.'

The phone went dead and Jack wasn't quite sure whether the call had been a veiled threat or just Skeggsy being his usual menacing self. Either way he knew he needed to find out something quickly about who was ripping Riordan off as his safety relied on him keeping Riordan pacified. He knew Riordan was playing him against Skeggsy but if Riordan didn't trust him then the operation was finished and Jack knew he would become a dead man walking.

It was time to call Deano.

CHAPTER 21

'Yeah, alright, boss?' Deano's distinctive squeaky voice echoed out of the mobile, as though he was in an area with bad reception.

'I'm good, so are all the birds walking around here, the fucking sun don't half bring them out if you know what I mean. Nothing like you get back in Dorking. Probably why they used to have a butchers in Dorking – to get rid of the rough meat!' Jack said laughing at his own joke. This undercover work was getting to him – he was even starting to sound like the scumbags he was trying to bust.

'The Vietnamese birds up here doing the business with the gear ain't bad either. Skeggsy might be a complete psycho who'd more than likely have an argument with a lamp post if it answered back, but he's got good taste in birds. They're fucking gorgeous.'

'Take some bromide Deano and remember hands off. So what's the flat number then?'

'I'll come down. I haven't left the flat since late last night and could do with a breath of fresh air anyway, if that's alright with you, boss?'

'See you in a sec then. I'm just outside parked across the road.'

Lighting another cigarette, Jack waited for Deano to appear. His immediate thought was why was Deano being cagey? Perhaps it was a set up and his cover had been compromised. Or on second thoughts it was probably the paranoia of the job kicking in. He felt slightly dizzy from the adrenalin mixed with all of the coke racing through his veins and yet again the burn scars on his left leg started to pulsate slowly.

The danger of what Armoury Way could have in store for him made him anxious and adrenalin continued to surge through his veins like an out of control canoe racing down rapids towards dangerous rocks. He looked at his hands and saw that they were shaking. He had also accidentally bitten his bottom lip drawing blood and guessed it was either the coke or the adrenalin, or perhaps a mixture of the two.

Jack thought back to the Armoury Way he had known when he was growing up as an out of control youngster. He remembered how the flats had been busted in a very much publicised show of intent by the police back in the late eighties. It was the evening news report on television which had stuck in his memory. It had shown footage of police officers dressed from head to foot in black with balaclavas and 'romper stomper' boots. They had abseiled down off the roof of the flats and burst through the windows of each individual flat simultaneously like a precision timed military attack by the SAS. Nearly all of the flats at the time were being used by drug dealers and the drug gangs had even made pipes in the flooring leading down through the floor of the flats and eventually to the sewage system. The dealers were ready to throw the drugs down the pipes if they were ever raided. The police though were one step ahead of the dealers who were the Jamaican 'Yardies'. At that time the Yardies were taking over London by using levels of extreme violence that had never before been seen in mainland Britain. The police had cleverly blocked all of the drains and entrances to the sewage system under the flats by using wire mesh which trapped all of the drugs that the dealers hurriedly disposed of down the pipes whilst the bust went down.

Since the large scale 'clean up' by the police, the area around Armoury Way had been transformed by the local council and the Yardies and their druggie hangers-on had either been locked up in prison or kicked out. Jack cynically thought to himself, but also with some admiration, that perhaps Riordan was actually quite clever in thinking Armoury Way would now be a good place to stash his drugs for a short time and that they would fall under the police radar.

Tap, tap, tap.

Jack turned his head, praying on his mother's grave it wasn't a traffic warden knocking on the window and peering through the darkened Audi window he was greeted with the outline of Deano's ugly face and piercing rat-like eyes. Deano was still wearing his manky scally cap. Opening the car door Jack shouted at him, 'Fuck's sake, don't creep up on me like that.'

'Sorry, boss, you said it was ok to come down, I didn't think there was a problem,' Deano replied.

'Yeah, true. Right let's get up there then, you'd better not have left those girls up there by themselves?' Jack questioned Deano giving him a hard stare.

'No way, I left Sean up there looking after things. He helped us last night on the collection of the gear. I'm not sure if you've met him before but he's a good lad, I shared a cell with him in Ford nick when I was finishing my last stretch inside. He's as good as gold and well tasty with his fists. He got me out of a few scrapes with people trying to tax me on money owed for gear whilst I was on the inside. We've done a few jobs on the outside together and if Skeggsy has no work for me, Sean sometimes gets me a bit of legit work on the scaffold.'

They crossed the road and on reaching the entrance to the flats Deano punched in a series of numbers on the entrance keypad and the metal door made a beeping noise. Deano pushed the door quite hard and the screeching noise of the scraping metal against the floor set Jack's teeth on edge. However, he wasn't prepared for the foul stench of urine that hit him full in the face as the door opened.

Deano nodded at him with a look of resignation saying, 'I know, the kids think it is funny to piss against the door, the lift is even worse.'

'Right, let's take the stairs then,' Jack said, quickly becoming convinced that maybe this area around Wandsworth hadn't quite gone as upmarket as he had at first thought. The entrance hall to the flats was pretty bleak apart from the artistic gang grafitti colourfully covering all of the walls which had at one time presumably been painted an off white, sort of magnolia colour. Following Deano up the concrete flight of stairs, Jack's eyes zoomed in on the tacky tiled mural of a scene from what looked like *The Jungle Book*. The mural spiralled up the wall alongside the staircase. He thought the artwork was actually quite good but any artistic thoughts he had were rapidly drowned out by the noise of rap music echoing from each of the surrounding flats that they walked past.

Reaching the fifth floor, Deano clearly unfit and a little out of breath said, 'This place is becoming far too rough and on top so Mr Riordan wants us out of here within twenty four hours. We just need to package the product and then this place is closed down, finito.'

The news that the drug safe-house was going to be closed wasn't music to Jack's ears but he hoped that maybe he could at least salvage some sort of useful information that he could then pass on to DI Rice.

Deano delved into his trouser pocket and whipped out some latex gloves. He also passed a pair to Jack saying, 'You can't be too careful, one careless finger print and the whole gig comes down like a pack of cards, know what I mean? Put them on will you, Mr Riordan insists.'

Jack hurriedly pulled the gloves on, which was not an easy task, and looked at Deano standing there in his scally cap and the latex gloves. The gloves were too big for his hands and he had empty bits of latex flopping over his fingertips like rabbits ears, which made Jack burst out laughing. He felt as though he was in some sort of surreal film written by Oliver Stone. He loved *Scarface*, but he had no intention of dying any day soon unlike almost all of the characters in the film.

'Shit, sorry, Deano, but this is kind of weird. My missus doesn't even ask me to dress like this,' Jack laughed, waving his latex gloved hands at Deano's bemused face.

'Yeah, yeah, I know, but it's better than getting busted. It's a little bit more weird inside though.'

Deano made a quick phone call, mumbling quietly into his mobile and instantly Jack could hear what he thought was the sound of the sliding of a series of bolts unlocking the door and then Deano took a gold Yale key out of his pocket and turned it in the lock.

When they walked into the flat Jack could see that it had been reinforced with steel together with four long sliding bolts and there was also a gate protecting it as well. 'Bloody hell, it's a bit like Fort Knox, isn't it?' Jack joked as they walked in.

'It has to be with all of the crack heads and nutters about, never mind the Old Bill.'

'There's no way Old Bill would get through that door with their bloody great big red key.' Jack laughed, thinking a copper would probably be bashing against the reinforced door for a good few minutes with a battering ram and the door probably wouldn't even move half an inch. By that time any drugs in the flat would have been flushed down the toilet and long gone.

Peering over Deano's shoulder as they walked in, Jack wasn't really prepared for what he saw in the flat. There was a three seater beige cloth sofa in the corner covered in plastic sheeting and Deano walked over and sat down on it making a strange squelching noise. He started to roll what looked to Jack like a joint judging by the size of the large Rizla that he held in his hand.

The whole flat was covered in thick plastic sheeting. It was spread all over the floor of the flat and even nailed up the walls and over the dirty windows.

In another corner of the room stood a large hydraulic press. Standing over it was a strikingly beautiful Vietnamese girl wearing just a skimpy pair of knickers and the same style of latex gloves that Jack and Deano were wearing on their hands. The girl was swinging her hips in time to the music blasting out of a radio on the floor beside her. Jack smiled and said to Deano, 'It's that bloody Rihanna song, I've got the same song as a ringtone on my mobile and don't know how to change it.'

'I quite like the song and she's a cracking fit bird anyway,' Deano said, blowing a thick stream of cloudy smoke from the spliff between his lips as he spoke.

Sensing someone's presence behind him, Jack quickly turned around and found himself looking directly at a large youngish man with short-cropped blonde hair and sleeve tattoos on both of his massive forearms. He was closing the sliding bolts on the door and then using his weight he forced the gate behind the door closed.

As the gate finally clunked shut Jack said, 'You must be Sean then?' For a horrible second he thought he recognised Sean, or even worse Sean had recognised him. His instinct warned him not to trust Sean and his left leg started to throb in agreement. The wound was years old but as time went on the hassle it gave him was beginning to piss him off the older he got. It hurt a lot more nowadays than when he was a testosterone filled youngster, but then so did the two-day hangovers as well.

'Yeah, alright, mate?' the big man replied in a strong Liverpool accent. Jack noticed that Sean was also wearing a pair of latex gloves, which in itself was a feat of engineering considering his hands were the size of large boulders. Seeing the size of Sean had unsettled Jack and for a fleeting moment he was unsure whether he had been bought to the flat for a different reason.

Deano was a professional crook in his book. He knew the ropes and had kept his mouth shut and done his time whilst he was in prison, but he hadn't expected him to be stupid enough to leave someone else unwatched in the flat with the Vietnamese girls.

Even if Deano had given Sean the okay he was still taking unnecessary chances. Skeggsy had made it very clear that in the flat there was only meant to be the girls cutting and pressing the coke in their skimpies and no one else.

'Give us a toke on that spliff then, Deano?' Jack asked, in an attempt to defuse any tension that may have arisen on his reaction to meeting Sean.

'Yeah, sure, boss,' Deano stretched across the sofa so that Jack could take the spliff from him.

There was a trestle table beside the blacked out window of the room with slabs of coke piled on top each other like house bricks. A tiny little Vietnamese girl was crushing each slab of coke in a large bowl with a huge pestle half the size of her and mixing it with what Jack could only think was the cutting agent Benzocaine.

Suddenly there was the noise of a toilet flushing and another girl with latex gloves on walked into the room listening to headphones in just her knickers with her small perfectly formed breasts jutting out in front of her. Jack struggled to take his eyes off the third girl and could fully understand what Deano had meant when he had said the women sorting out the gear were gorgeous.

'Fucking hell, Deano, there's only one place these girls are going to hide anything, isn't there?' Jack joked, with a dirty smirk on his face even though he felt sick to the pit of his stomach at having to hide his true feelings towards the situation the girls were in.

CHAPTER 22

Daryl Rice took a deep breath and then strode with false confidence into the DCI's office, praying that his fear about his career possibly coming to an abrupt end in the next few minutes was not etched all over his face.

The carpeted office was spacious and, seated behind a large polished wooden surround desk, was DCI Peter Smith. Behind the DCI was a large window and the sunlight streaming through it lit up the DCI's balding globe-shaped head. The DCI had tried to hide his baldness by side combing his greying hair across his head. The gel that he had used to complete the image glistenened on the thin wispy strands of his hair in the bright morning sunshine. On his desk propped up beside a large jug of presumably fresh water were stood the obligatory small framed family photos of his rather plump wife, who was looking a little past her sell-by date, and their two young children.

Looking around the room, Daryl could see that adorning the walls on each side of the large desk were larger framed photos of the DCI in various stages throughout his career. In some of the photos he was posing on a small stage shaking hands with a senior police officer whilst accepting a commendation. Daryl noticed one particularly old photo that must have been of the DCI relaxing after his passing out parade at Hendon Police Training College. He had a full head of hair in the photo and he barely looked old enough to be served alcohol in a pub.

'Take a chair please, Daryl,' DCI Smith said. There was an empty chair in front of the DCI's desk placed between two men who were smartly dressed in similar tailored dark suits. 'I'm not sure if any of you gentlemen have met before in a professional capacity, but let me introduce you anyway. To DI Rice's left is DI David Scally attached to MI5 and to his right is DI Peter Steele seconded to 6.'

'Thank you, sir,' Daryl said, taking the empty seat as he shook both men's hands and said to the MI5 man on his left, 'Hello, Dave, it's been quite a while. Are you still trying to get that golf handicap of yours down?'

'Still trying, thanks, Daryl. I got it below a ten handicap a few years ago but I can't seem to find the time to get out on the course much nowadays. The job doesn't really allow for it. What about you?'

'I'm the same, too busy, but I was never in the same league as you on the golf course anyway,' Daryl laughed. He hadn't seen Dave Scally for a number of years since they had both done a short stint working at Reigate nick when they were fresh-faced bobbies on the beat. Dave had been a good laugh to work with and had also been a very good golfer compared to Daryl. When their shifts allowed it they had played golf together on their days off work at Dorking Golf Club or sometimes at Effingham Golf Club, but Effingham Golf Club was a bit snooty and a junior rank's wages didn't really stretch to paying the exorbitant green fees.

Back in those days he would never have guessed that Dave would have been the type of man who would end up working in MI5. He had always seen Dave as a live life fast type of guy like himself. The NCA or high-ranking Met maybe but never the Intelligence Services, it goes to show that you can never tell with some people.

'Right, that's the meet and greet done. Obviously you two already know each other but can we now get down to business please?' DCI Smith interrupted, nervously brushing his right hand over the front of his gelled hair. The three men immediately straightened their chairs to face the DCI and nodded in unison.

'Thank you, gentlemen. I have invited all of you here to discuss the cover operation the NCA have had running for a while with the target being Mick Riordan and the prime objective of bringing down his criminal empire. Now this has been a long-term deployment and I thought it was about time that Daryl was made aware that 5 and 6 also have a concerned interest in our Mr Riordan. This is to be a joint operation across international borders going forward and we must work together to ensure that anything material or any person that we have on the ground isn't compromised in any shape or form. Does everyone understand?'

All three men understood that whatever individual agenda they might have had when they had initially walked into the DCI's office was just about to rapidly change and there was a strained silence before anyone spoke.

DI Steele took the initiative and shifted in his chair to look at DCI Smith but also kept the other two men in his line of sight.

'Sir, MI6 have had an interest for quite a while in Riordan and his gang and as you know amongst other things the 6 remit is keeping terrorism off our shores. Our recent intelligence confirms that Riordan's drug activities are funding various aspects of terrorism abroad and possibly more worryingly they are funding terrorism at home on a growing scale. 6 and also 5, which is where Dave comes in, have been running a joint operation for a number of months and we're concerned that the NCA don't trip over our own agents working undercover and vice versa. You guys deal with stopping the drugs arriving on our shores but we have to deal with global terrorism.

Your man is currently funding this with his involvement in the wholesale drug trade.'

Steele continued, 'We know he's recently been importing a large amount of coke from Central and South America, we also know that he's joined forces with a criminal narco-terrorist organisation called, "The Shining Path". These guys are a Peruvian Maoist rebel group and as quickly as one leader is killed or locked up another replaces him. They're a real force to be dealt with and are using the money from the export of the cocaine paste to fund their cause. We have now discovered that Riordan has been in discussions with rebel guerrilla factions in Iran and Iraq. This guy's balls have grown so big that we now suspect he's thinking of climbing in to bed with Al-Quaeda. Basically, we believe your man is attempting to branch out into the heroin trade as well.'

'The NCA have a man deployed on the ground who is working very closely with the higher echelon of Riordan's gang and we don't want 5 or 6 to regard our interest in this as just a peripheral matter,' Smith barked back curtly, his face starting to glow an angry red colour as there was no way he was going to let either service bully their way in on his operation without a fight.

'I understand that and I think that I can speak for all of us when I say none of us want to compromise anyone. MI6 don't want to get involved in any evidential chain and DI Scally can confirm that 5 have the same intentions. That's down to you guys. We just want this bastard Riordan and his gang off the streets as his dealings with known terrorists are making the people traffickers rich, his drug cash is also arming various rebel armies around the globe wanting to blow up anyone that doesn't follow their particular cause or religion. In fact gentlemen, he is quickly becoming the Pablo Escobar of the Western world and needs to be stopped unilaterally.'

'I can only agree with DI Steele that Riordan's activities are having a global effect in many extremist criminal areas and 5 and 6, along with GCHQ, have been following his activities for a while,' Dave Scally interjected.

'My primary concern is for the safety of my man on the ground,' Daryl piped up feeling a little bit left out of the conversation.

DCI Smith replied, 'I'm just coming to that point, thank you, Daryl.' Then looking at all three men he continued, 'The NCA have a duty of care and we all do irrespective of whether it is 5 or 6 or any other bloody agency. But we might have a serious problem. Intelligence indicates that there may be a leak somewhere as we can't understand how Riordan seems to keep one step ahead of all of us and still appear to be squeaky clean. But this information stays in this room and goes no further, everyone understand? I'm not prepared to explain today where this information comes from, but I want you all to be aware of it,' DCI Smith said, reaching for the jug of water beside the photos of his children and pouring himself a glass without offering anyone else in the room a drink.

'So we're letting the operation run and we're not sweeping our guy off the streets? Considering this new information isn't that a bit risky?' Daryl queried.

'It might be but the NCA are not the only undercover involved as this is also an overseas operation now. The top brass have given the go ahead but you just need to be aware of the potential for this turning nasty.' The DCI looked at each of the men in the room for confirmation of what he had just said. 'Right, thank you for your time, gentleman. I'm sure you all know, as I said earlier, that nothing goes outside of this room. Please remember that any reports that are written up for assessment must be kept sanitised and the existence of any covert source must be kept as tight as possible between those around this table. Daryl, can I ask you to stay behind for a minute please?'

Steele and Scally got up and left the room after shaking hands with Daryl and the DCI. Daryl thought that this was the moment when the DCI was going to remove him from being the main cover officer on the operation and looked straight at him, trying not to stare at his dreadful comb over of hair which had started to flop down over his forehead in the heat.

'Daryl, I am aware that your covert source has not been reporting in daily as he should and you haven't been handling him weekly as your remit instructs. If this continues I will remove you from the operation, do you understand? Go on, get out of my bloody office,' DCI Smith ordered in a raised voice.

'Yes, sir,' Daryl mumbled nearly tripping over the chair he had been sitting in as he left the DCI's office as quickly as he could.

A few seconds later he was standing at the end of the corridor waiting for the lift to arrive. He let out a huge strained sigh of relief. The meeting with the DCI had been a close call. Jack Reynolds was a bastard and he was really beginning to piss him off now.

The yellow arrow signalled the arrival of the lift and as the doors slid open Daryl walked quickly inside without looking. As the doors slid shut Daryl's nostrils recognised the sweet smell of perfume which had enveloped the lift and looking to his left he was horrified to see the young constable from the Christmas party staring straight back at him.

Julie was standing with her arms folded underneath her firm breasts and the tight WPC's skirt that she wore accentuated her slender hips.

'Hello, sir,' Julie said in voice heavily weighted with sarcasm and Daryl could tell that she had more to say to him. 'How are your wandering hands? Have you groped any young WPC's lately?'

'Look...... Julie, isn't it?'

'Save your breath, you slimy pervert, you're lucky you're not up in front of the IPCC on a disciplinary charge.'

'I'm really sorry, I'd drunk far too much, it wasn't very professional of me and I can only apologise for my behaviour.

However, may I remind you that I am still your senior officer,' Daryl mumbled in a futile attempt to regain some sort of control before the situation got out of hand.

'Bollocks to you, sir.'

The lift had reached the reception floor and Julie angrily pushed past Daryl and stormed off down the corridor. Daryl waited until Julie had disappeared around the corner before he cautiously stepped out of the lift. What with the DCI having a go at him and now Julie, he wondered what was going to happen to him next. And as they say, bad things always come in threes and today was definitely turning out to be one of those days.

CHAPTER 23

Jack had been in the flat for about five hours now and was gasping for a Marlborough Light.

On the floor beside the trestle table were some freshly pressed kilo blocks of high purity cocaine. Each block was in a vacuum-sealed see-through plastic bag and they were piled high on top of each other with some of the blocks also piled up in stacks on the trestle table. Jack guessed that there must have been about fifty kilos of coke and they had already cut it and pressed it using the hydraulic press. It would still get cut time and time again by each dealer whose hands it went through before it reached the street level of the pubs and clubs.

A kilo of high purity coke would cost in the region of about four to five hundred pounds when it initially left Colombia where it has been processed from the coca paste imported from Peru. However, by the time the coke had reached the shores of England the cost of a kilo would have rocketed to anywhere from thirty to forty-five thousand pounds depending upon the stability of the market at the time.

Deano went into another room and came back carrying four large duffle bags which he threw on the floor beside the piles of coke. Throwing their confiscated clothes at them, he told the three Vietnamese girls to go and get dressed and said to Sean, 'Give me a hand putting the coke in the bags, will you?'

'Yeah, sure,' Sean said, tearing his eyes away from the three tight bottoms in skimpy knickers hurrying past him into the other room to get dressed.

As they finished packing the coke away, the three Vietnamese girls came back in the room looking very different now that they had their clothes on. They had a sort of innocent 'butter wouldn't melt in their mouths' look about them. Deano told them to sit down on the sofa and took out his wallet. He pulled out a wad of notes and carefully counted them before giving each girl in turn some of the cash. The girls each smiled and nodded in appreciation whilst saying what Jack presumed was 'thank you' in Vietnamese.

Turning to Jack, Deano said, 'Come on let's go. We can leave the place as it is. I'll send some of the lads back up here later to move the press and clear the flat up. Sean, you take two of the bags down to the car and I'll carry the rest.'

'Okay, just let me get my gear.' Sean went into the other room and quickly came back wearing a faded blue denim jacket with a small six litre hiking rucksack strapped to his back. He picked up the two large duffle bags using just one of his huge hands and with his other hand he opened the gate and slid the bolts across to open the door. Deano roughly pushed the Vietnamese girls out of the door and they all trooped off together down the stairs.

Deano's black Kia was parked a couple of spaces behind Jack's Audi. Opening the boot he threw the heavy duffle bags in and said to Sean, 'Where are you parked? I'll drop the girls off and bell you later to sort your wages out, alright?'

'No worries, the motor's only over there.' Sean threw the other two duffle bags into the boot of Deano's car whilst with his other hand he pointed at a rusty blue Toyota Hilux parked on the opposite side of the road. 'Cheers, Deano. See you later, you too Jack.'

'Cheers Sean,' Jack muttered watching Sean cross the road. Jack turned and said to Deano, 'Good job. You know the addresses to drop the gear off to, don't you? I've already rung them so they should be expecting you. Hide the rest of the gear at Cavendish Road and drive carefully. I'll let Skeggsy know the job's done but I can't follow you back as I've got some other business to do whilst I'm up here.'

'Okay, boss.' Deano jumped in his car and Jack watched him as he slowly drove off in his little Kia car weighted down with a shit load of drugs.

Sitting in his Audi, Jack waited for Sean to drive off but he could see Sean was talking to someone on his mobile. He was nodding and frantically gesticulating with his huge arms, almost as though he was having an argument with somebody. There was something niggling Jack about Sean and his instinct told him something was not right. He had felt the same nervous feeling earlier in the flat as well. Sean had finished his phone call now. Jack could see the Hilux was indicating to pull out so he made a snap decision and decided to follow at a discreet distance. Checking his rear view mirror he indicated to pull out into the traffic a few cars behind.

Jack started to follow the Hilux at a discreet distance, trying not to alert Sean to the fact that he was there, but it wasn't easy as Sean was turning out to be quite an erratic driver who rarely indicated whenever he decided to turn off the main road and drive down a smaller side road. It was close to four o'clock now and the traffic was building up into rush hour. This would mean London would soon come to a virtual standstill and Jack still hadn't had the chance to buy some cigarettes.

He tried to keep an eye on where they were driving to without losing sight of Sean in the battered Hilux. Jack had caught glimpses of road signs giving directions to Brixton and Camberwell and his imagination started to go into overdrive the closer they got to Lambeth as it was an area he shouldn't be seen in without permission. Not being one of Big V's boys, any gang member of his might take a chance and have a pop at him. Jack knew the layout of London but he was no expert on driving around the city.

He hit the brakes hard when the Hilux suddenly turned without indicating into Brixton's Ferndale Road. The Hilux almost immediately pulled up without indicating yet again. It had stopped outside a quaint old-fashioned red-brick pub called the Duke of Edinburgh, which had wicker hanging baskets above the entrance. The baskets had been recently over watered and were dripping everywhere. There were a few trestle tables in front of the pub with people desperate for a sun tan sitting in the warm sun having a few drinks in what had turned out to be quite a nice day, not that Jack had seen much of the sun after being cooped up in the flat in Armoury Way for the last few hours.

Jack drove a short way past the pub before pulling into the first available parking space that he could find. He ignored the fact that he was parking on a double yellow line as he needed a good vantage point from where he could closely watch the big fucker Sean in his rear view mirror. Sean opened the driver's door of the Hilux and climbed out. Even if you were as big as Sean was you still had to climb down out of a Hilux as they're raised so high off the ground. He then stubbed out a rollup on the ground with his right foot and reached into the car and took out the rucksack he was wearing earlier. Holding his rucksack in his left hand he looked carefully in both directions before he ran across the road in a gap in the traffic and disappeared inside the pub.

Sitting in the Audi, Jack slammed his fist into the steering wheel in sheer frustration at how stupid he had been. Of course it was the damn rucksack!

Thinking back to when they had all been in the flat in Armoury Way, the Vietnamese girls had worn almost nothing and the girls had all been searched thoroughly by Deano, but it had never even occurred to either of them to search Sean when they left the flat.

Jack thought back to when they had been talking earlier as they had stood in the street outside the flat in Wandsworth and

Deano had said that Sean had watched his back whilst he was on the inside. However, on meeting Sean, his police instinct had kicked in and there had been something about the man he hadn't liked the look of, but he hoped for Deano's sake that for once his instinct was off the mark.

Jack got out of the Audi and darted across the road between the oncoming traffic and for a moment he stood outside the entrance to the pub. He was unsure about what he would discover the other side of the door, but eventually with a nervous sigh he decided it was now or never and pushing the door to the pub open he walked in.

CHAPTER 24

Standing in the doorway of the pub, Jack looked around and could see that it must have been renovated only a few years ago as it had a modern look to it, but in a nice quirky way, it also looked as though it had expensive trendy feature lighting throughout. The pub initially appeared to be spacious and Jack could see that it had various function rooms, not just one large room with a bar like a lot of pubs, which possibly explained why he couldn't see Sean anywhere.

As he walked towards the main bar he passed a room with a pool table which was a dying breed in any pub in England. In the pool room there was a group of young lads wearing hoodies and baseball hats who were playing and it looked like two of the lads were thrashing their mates as they were on the black ball and the others still had five red balls left on the table.

He walked past another room which was filled with comfy chairs and sofas. Some of them were made of that hard tanned brown leather like the sofa your grandfather used to have in the sitting room. Some of the other sofas were made from cloth in various bright and garish colours. There was still no sight of Sean anywhere.

Jack headed towards the large polished wooden bar which had a generous selection of recently polished brass pumps selling a wide range of ale and cask beers. Leaning on the end of the bar he waited until he caught the eye of the barman, a tall man in his early twenties with studs in his nose and stretched ear piercings in both earlobes. Jack thought the ear piercings looked stupid and couldn't understand their popularity.

The barman with the large holes in his earlobes walked towards Jack and said, 'Yes, mate, can I help you?'

'Yeah, where are the gents toilets, please?'

'Over there, turn right and you should see the sign straight opposite you.'

'Thanks, mate. Can I have a pint of Stella as well?' Jack asked, giving him a five pound note. Mr Holey Ears walked off and soon came back dripping a pint of Stella over the top of the bar and gave him back his forty pence change. Jack stared at the two twenty pence coins in the palm of his hand and grumbled, 'Bloody hell, how much is a Stella in here?'

'Four pounds sixty, mate.... Problem?'

'Nope, I suppose it's London prices. I come from way out in the sticks where it's a bit cheaper.'

Mr. Holey Ears walked off down the other end of the bar making it abundantly clear to Jack that he wasn't going to have the experience of any more friendly chat from him today.

Jack nervously downed his pint in a couple of gulps and headed off to find the toilet. It wasn't a sensible option to leave his pint on the bar as it would either get nicked by some tosser or even worse drugged by some freak who thought putting a pill in a stranger's drink was funny.

As he walked towards the gents his eyes carefully swept every corner of the pub looking for Sean but he was nowhere to be seen. He guessed that he was either in the toilets or else he had gone outside into the pub garden. If he bumped into Sean in the toilets he wasn't sure how he would explain his presence there, but he was positive that his adrenalin would kick in and he could come up with some sort of bullshit to explain things. If he couldn't he was going to be in a whole shitload of trouble.

He pushed open the door into the gents and could see that the room was almost empty, there was one lonely bloke standing slashing in the middle urinal which was a real no go area in

Jack's book. You were a bit of a weirdo if you used the middle urinal.

London was definitely becoming too eclectic for Jack as he noticed that the toilet walls were covered in childish comic-like wall paper. At least if you went to any one of the gastro pubs in Dorking you'd find interesting historic pictures hanging from the walls to look at whilst you went for a piss. That was much more to his taste.

He had a quick piss thinking the only option was that Sean had gone outside or else he had somehow given him the slip. He disregarded Sean giving him the slip as he had been very careful in making sure that he had tailed him from a distance and would have been surprised if he'd been spotted. Anyway, he still hoped that his suspicions about Sean could turn out to be completely wrong.

The pub was beginning to get quite rowdy as it was slowly filling up with the after-work drinkers. He could see some builders camped in the far corner surrounded by their concrete footprints on the wooden floor. The smartly dressed office workers were easy to spot and of course there were the usual benefit scroungers who had been there for most of the day. Jack sneaked a look through one of the windows into the huge pub garden which seemed to stretch on forever. At the end of the garden was a brick wall covered with a gigantic mural of a rhinoceros. He had never seen anything like it in a pub garden before and sitting at a table just in front of the rhino mural were Sean and the weasel eyed scroat Davey. They appeared to be chatting just like best mates would do over an ice cold lager on a hot summer's day.

Shocked, but also pleasantly pleased that his instinct hadn't failed him, he realised all of his suspicions about Sean had been right but he also realised the implications of what Davey meeting up with Sean meant. Worryingly, it meant Big V was involved in ripping off Riordan and that spelt serious trouble on the street and even more so to Jack's investigation.

Suddenly his phone started to vibrate and seeing Skeggsy's name staring up at him, he pressed his thumb down on the 'reject' button.

Jack knew that discovering Sean's disloyalty and proving that Big V was behind it gave him a real chance of getting in deeper with Riordan's gang. Based on this information Riordan would have no choice but to trust him now. Riordan had asked him to find out who was ripping him off and the culprits were sitting twenty yards away from him without a care in the world and he was just about to burst their happy little bubble.

Looking down the garden, Jack set his mobile to the camera app and smiling to himself he quickly took a photo of Davey and the traitor Sean, he could use the photo as evidence for Riordan and it could also be used as evidence by the NCA in any future prosecution of the gang. He then casually walked down the garden past the innocent laughing drinkers sitting happily in the sunshine who were oblivious as to what was about to happen.

This was Jack's chance to prove to Riordan that he was his new number one enforcer and Skeggsy was history. It was going to kick off and he had to get in first and go in hard. It was extremely unlikely that Davey and Sean were going to offer to buy him a pint and ask if he wanted to join them.

Jack could feel his left leg starting to hurt a little as every sinew in his body went taught with the anticipation of the exploding violence that was about to occur. Sean was a huge muscular man who towered over the pathetic excuse of a frame that represented Davey's body, so he was going to have to take Sean out first.

Trying to keep the sun out of his eyes he approached the table Davey was the first to see him. He looked up at Jack and his eyes did a double take as they suddenly bulged out of his eye sockets in recognition and total horror at seeing Jack. He froze just like a rabbit does when it's caught in the headlights of a car.

Davey shouted, 'What the fuck are you doing here?'

'Uh?' Sean said, not realising that Davey wasn't talking to him.

At the exact same moment Sean turned around Jack hit him with as hard a punch as he could catching him on the left side of his head directly on his temple. Jack could not have tried to deliver a better punch as the pint glasses went crashing across the table and Sean slowly slumped to the ground in a large unconscious heap. Looking around the ground beside the now upturned table for Sean's small rucksack meant that he had taken his eyes off Davey for a second too long; he should have known better as his eyes caught the twinkling in the sunlight of cold steel flashing towards him.

Instinctively, he put his forearm up in front of his face to protect himself as Davey lunged at him making quick stabbing motions with a long blade which would have been better suited to a late night horror film. The blade was at least eight inches long and double edged, ending in a sharp point. In his haste to stay out of the reach of Davey who was wildly slashing at him with the knife he stepped back and fell onto one of the pub garden tables and then screamed in agony when he felt the long point of Davey's knife puncture deep into the flesh of his scarred left leg. The pain was excruciating as the knife tore through the burn scars and he could feel the tissue and muscle tearing with each twist of the knife. He fell to the ground writhing in agony whilst clutching his left leg with both hands.

As he rolled around on the ground, he could feel the warm flow of blood seeping freely between his fingers as he clutched his leg. He tried to fight the waves of nausea from flooding over him and fought the dizziness which was trying to envelop him.

'I always said you were a fucking prick, Jack,' Davey hissed at him as he grabbed the small rucksack off the ground and as a final insult he leant close over Jack's body and spat at him full in the face before turning and running through the crowd of people that had started to gather to see what all of the commotion was about. Nobody made any foolish attempt to be a hero by trying to stop Davey as he ran past them manically slashing the air with the knife whilst shouting loudly, 'Get out my fucking way.'

'Are you alright, mate? Someone call an ambulance now.' Jack heard somebody shout out as he fought against drifting into unconsciousness. He could hear a woman crying as the large crowd began quickly gathering around him. He guessed that there were some sickos taking photos and knew he had to get the hell out of there.

With a loud groan he forced himself to stand up and started to push his way through the crowd of onlookers. He saw a gate at the side of the garden and ignoring people's pleas for him to stay and wait for the ambulance which was on its way, he hobbled towards the gate dragging his left leg along the ground behind him. Fortunately the gate was unlocked and on opening it Jack fell crashing onto the pavement out on the street, using what little strength he had left he got to his feet and hobbled around the corner to where the Audi was parked. As he turned the corner he saw Sean's Hilux swerving into the traffic with smoke bellowing from the tyres as it sped off down the road. Sean was the least of his worries as he quickly hobbled to the Audi with blood spilling in thick dark red drops onto the pavement and on reaching the car he almost collapsed into the driver's seat. He started the engine and drove off muttering a massive thank you to Audi for designing the A8 with automatic transmission. Jack struggled to drive the car in a straight line as he tried to stay conscious; he looked down at the amount of blood pouring from his leg and wondered if he was going to die.

CHAPTER 25

During Jack's army and police careers he had been given plenty of medical training and swore at himself as he remembered that his army issue medical trauma kit was in the kitchen cupboard back in his flat. So, improvising he frantically tore his belt from his trousers and using it as a makeshift tourniquet tied it tightly around his wounded thigh to stem the bleeding.

Experience told him that the stab wound was serious but at least the knife had not hit an artery. If it had been an artery, the blood would be spurting in powerful jets all over the roof of the Audi and he would be dead within ten minutes.

Jack weaved the Audi through the nearly gridlocked rush hour traffic whilst continually flashing the car's headlights and pressing the horn at everyone and anyone who wouldn't move out of his way. He drove as quickly as he could towards the closest accident and emergency hospital he knew which was King's College Hospital in Camberwell. It was roughly ten minutes drive away from Brixton but felt more like ten hours to Jack before he finally pulled up into the hospital car park. His leg was completely covered in blood which had also soaked into the upholstery of the car. The front of the Audi looked like someone had thrown a five litre tin of red paint over it and Jack promised himself that he was going to break every bone in that weasel Davey's body once he had recovered.

Opening the car door Jack used all of what little strength he had left to pull himself out of the car. Taking a few steps he stumbled out of the car park onto the road falling painfully to the ground just as a passing ambulance screeched to a halt.

The driver and a paramedic jumped out of the ambulance and ran towards Jack. The paramedic took one look at him lying on the ground and shouted to her colleague in a strong Scottish accent, 'Quickly, go and get some help from inside the hospital. He's lost a lot of blood so tell them we'll need a trauma team on standby.'

The ambulance driver ran off in the direction of the hospital entrance and then everything started to go hazy as Jack rested his head in the paramedic's arms until finally he let unconsciousness get the better of him.

He felt as though he was on a slide as the ceiling flashed past above him with a strobe effect of bright strip lighting. The lights were blinding him and all he could hear were voices shouting at him as he tried to say something, but there were no words coming out of his dry mouth.

After investigation, the trauma team had taken the decision to rush him on a trolley into the operating theatre and were now busy getting gloved and masked up as the surgeon on call had arrived.

'Okay, listen up everyone,' the masked surgeon shouted to the team. 'The entry wound is a nasty deep puncture possibly from a long sharp knife and we'll need to stem the internal blood flow, otherwise, in the next few minutes the patient is likely to haemorrhage.' He leant over Jack. 'You have a nasty wound and we're going to have to operate immediately. You'll feel a small prick in your wrist and then the gentle flow of anaesthetic as you drift off into sleep. Try to count aloud to ten but I can guarantee you won't reach number six let alone ten.' Jack tried to say something but the oxygen mask on his face was too constricting and all he could do was nod his head whilst listening to the voice slowly counting. 'One, two, three …………'

'Hello, are you back in the land of the living now? Do you know we nearly lost you there?'

'What the hell happened? Where am I?' Jack growled in pain at the tiny middle-aged Jamaican woman standing over his bed. Her name badge read *Blossom.*

The pain in his leg was increasing as the anaesthetic from the operation wore off and he tried to gather his thoughts, but he was still finding it hard to wake up properly after all of the morphine the doctors had pumped into him.

'We found you collapsed in the car park near the hospital entrance with a stab wound in your left leg, which by the way looks as though it has already been through enough trauma already.' Blossom scribbled a note on the chart in her hands. 'Your previously burnt scar tissue has been badly ripped by the knife blade and it is going to take some time for your leg to recover fully, if it ever does. I'm sorry to say but if you didn't limp before from your earlier burns injury you most definitely will now. The police are outside waiting to speak to you. I've told them you need to rest but I can't keep them away from you forever.' Blossom's tone was matter of fact. She leant over him and pulled him towards her chest so that she could puff up his pillows and then gently leant him back down again.

'Thanks, I appreciate it. I'm sure you've heard all sorts of rubbish before, but it really isn't what it looks like.' Using his elbows for leverage, Jack pushed himself into a more upright position in the bed and tried to manage his best smile possible. 'Can I make a phone call please, Blossom?'

'I can't allow it. Not until the police have spoken to you. Then you can. Sorry it's hospital policy when a suspected crime may have been committed.'

'Okay no problem. Can you send the rozzers in then, but if I press the buzzer can you please get rid of them straight away as I'm very tired and don't feel like I can put up with too many questions, obviously.'

Blossom left and returned in a moment ushering two men in identical suits into the room. Jack laughed to himself thinking that if these two coppers in their cheap supermarket suits thought they were fooling anyone about not being in 'The Job', then his mother was the Queen of England.

The taller of the two policemen standing beside Jack's bed introduced himself and explained to Jack he was not under arrest but they needed to question him as they believed a crime may have been committed. After listening to Jack's explanation, the taller policeman, who seemed to be the only one doing the talking, said with a distinctive tone of sarcasm in his voice, 'So, sir, let me get this right for the record. Your explanation is that you were strolling through Brockwell Park, enjoying the sunshine where you saw a cat which you presumed was stuck up a tree. You'll stop me if I get anything in your statement wrong, won't you, sir?'

'Of course I will, thank you officer.'

'As I was saying, you saw the cat in the tree and decided to rescue it instead of calling the emergency services, such as the Fire Brigade and as you were climbing the tree you slipped and fell. Unfortunately when you fell you landed on some sort of spike in the ground and it punctured your left thigh. You could see that the wound was quite deep and decided to heroically drive all the way to this lovely hospital where you were found collapsed in the car park from loss of blood.'

'Yes, that's exactly what happened.'

'I haven't quite finished yet. You have also confirmed to us that you have not been in Ferndale Road recently, particularly a pub called the Duke of Edinburgh from where we received a report of a stabbing earlier on today.'

'As I said, that's exactly what happened. Now if you don't mind, I need to get some rest please.'

'Sorry, sir, of course you need to rest. We'll be checking out your story and seeing what CCTV shows up, but you have no need to worry if you really were nowhere near the Duke of Edinburgh today, do you? Feel better soon, sir.'

'Thank you.' Jack watched the two policemen leave the room and as they left they spoke to the uniformed officer stationed outside his room who got up and then followed them down the corridor. As soon as they were out of sight Jack pressed the buzzer and waited for Blossom to appear.

Blossom stuck her head around the door and said, 'I saw the policemen leave. Did you want to make that phone call now?'

'Yes please, Blossom.' Jack had left his mobile in the Audi and needed to urgently call his undercover handler, because as soon as the police looked at the CCTV playback they would see his ugly mug plastered all over it covered in blood outside the Duke of Edinburgh and then his cover would be completely blown. Blossom returned pushing a payphone on a trolley. Jack took his trousers from the locker beside his bed and found some loose change to use in the payphone. Waiting until Blossom had left the room, he dialled his handler Gazza's number as he couldn't face talking to DI Rice and listening to his sanctimonious crap.

'Gazza, it's X4.'

'What's this? Two calls in one day, I am privileged.'

'Shut up and listen as I'm on a payphone. I'm in the King's College Hospital in Camberwell, I've been stabbed.'

'Oh fuck,' Gazza shouted down the phone.

'I'll live. I've had an operation but the local Old Bill have been asking me all sorts of questions and it won't take them long to link me to a stabbing in the Duke of Edinburgh pub in Brixton. I've stalled them by feeding them a load of bullshit but I need you to speak to the senior detective for the area and brief him as to what's happened. He needs to square the incident away and ensure that the report on it is discreetly filed away under the heading of victim unwilling to help the police. He needs to do this pronto.'

'Right, I'll get on it straight away but you know that I have to report this to DI Rice, don't you?'

'Yes I know. I hope it makes the prick's day.' Jack put the phone down.

There was no physical way he was getting out of hospital that afternoon but he was going to discharge himself as soon as he could. He was thankful he was still alive but it wasn't long before his thoughts soon turned to the possibility that Amy might not be.

CHAPTER 26

Opening the locker by his bed, Jack took out his clothes and started to try to get dressed, grunting with the effort it took to pull on his ruined trousers. He eventually managed it, despite the shooting pain in his leg. Sitting on the bed in his bloody clothes he put the pain killers he'd been prescribed in his pocket and rested for a moment before holding the crutch and hobbling as best as he could out of the room and down the brightly lit corridor.

It was only six o'clock in the morning and the day staff were starting their shift but Jack wasn't staying there a minute longer. After a huge row with the duty nurse on the ward desk, Jack managed to discharge himself, despite all of her advice and loud protestations. On reaching the main reception at the front entrance to the hospital, he sat down in a chair for a few minutes to get his breath back as it was hard going using the crutch.

Wiping the sweat from his forehead, he got up from the chair and went through the sliding doors at the front entrance, he started off on the long hobble to the car park whilst trying to remember where he had parked the Audi before he had collapsed.

It didn't take long to find the car and an over-keen traffic warden had left a parking ticket on the windscreen. The driver's seat was covered in dried blood which had soaked into the interior. Jack made a mental note it was going to need a thorough valet throughout to clean it. Whether it would ever look as good as new again was a good question and one Jack would be reminding himself of that the exact moment he beat Davey to a pulp in revenge for the stabbing. The bastard was definitely going to get a good kicking.

After a slow and painful drive, Jack eventually reached Dorking and cursed the local council for not mending the potholes in the High Street. He tried to swerve the car around the potholes in the road but still accidentally drove over some of them and each time he did, the bumping up and down of the car made his leg feel as though someone was hammering a blunt skewer slowly into his leg. Arriving at his flat he parked the blood stained Audi and limped into the flat.

He'd found his mobile in the car and had also taken one of the SIM cards from the hiding place in the boot of the Audi. As soon as he had switched the cards over the phone bleeped in rapid succession and he could see that Sarah had left at least twelve messages for him. He quickly read them and could see that she was very pretty fucked off at him for not calling her.

He steeled himself ready for the forthcoming abuse and rang Sarah's number.

'Jack, is that you?' Sarah's voice was barely audible over the sound of barking in the background.

'Yeah, it's me. I can barely hear you. What's up with H? Aren't you feeding him?' Jack asked, trying to stall the torrent of abuse which he knew was coming.

'Of course I bloody well am. I'm in the middle of feeding your damn dog right now – hence the barking. What's it got to do with you anyway? You're never here to feed or walk him anyway. Christ, you sound like you care more about the dog than you do about me. More importantly do you even give a toss about your own daughter, or have you forgotten about her as well?' Hardly stopping to take a breath Sarah continued, 'Have you managed to find out anything about Amy since we last spoke or have you just spent the last twenty four hours getting drunk and stoned, or whatever you do nowadays?' Sarah spat her words at him down the phone with more venom than a rattlesnake in a death strike.

'I've been busting my balls trying to find out how she is and will explain in a second. There's something I need to tell you first. It's not as bad as it sounds, but I've been stabbed in my leg and worst of all it was my wounded leg. I had to have an emergency operation and lost shed loads of blood. They gave me a blood transfusion but at least I haven't lost my fucking leg. I'm really sorry I didn't call about Amy but all hell broke loose, I was on a job and—'

'Oh, Jack, you should've said. I'm so sorry for kicking off at you. It's just all this stuff with Amy. Is there anything I can do?'

'No, don't worry about me, I'll be fine. I've left messages about Amy's disappearance with people I know in Ireland and I'm also waiting for the local Gardai to get back to me. As I promised you before, if we don't get any news soon I'll fly out there.'

'Okay.... But call me or a hospital if your leg starts to get any worse. And make sure your friends find Amy as soon as possible. I'm going out of my mind with worry.' Sarah's voice was quickly starting to lose its earlier compassionate tone.

'I promise, honey,' Jack whispered as he ended the call and immediately groaned in pain as he tried to stretch out his injured leg. Jack noticed that Sarah had actually shown what appeared to be genuine concern for him and she had also let him call her 'honey' twice in one week. It wasn't the right time to think about it but maybe in a perverse way Amy's disappearance could bring them closer together.

Having tried to put Sarah's mind at rest Jack knew it was imperative that he didn't lose sight of his undercover work. He needed to find out whether Skeggsy or Riordan had found out about the stabbing. He would be royally fucked if Skeggsy knew about it and became suspicious as to why he hadn't been nicked. He decided there was no way round it, he couldn't avoid the situation any longer and he would have to call him. So yet again he switched SIM cards and scrolled down the list of contacts in his phone. Finding Skeggsy's name in the list he hesitated for a few seconds before he eventually pressed the green dial button.

'Where the fuck have you been?' Skeggsy roared down the phone. 'All of the deliveries have been made and yet you go on the missing list. Your mobile has been going to answer-phone and Mr Riordan has been busting my bollocks to get some answers about Armoury Way and why the delivery was short yet again. Believe me, it's only my soft and caring nature that has stopped you from being hunted down and tossed into the Thames to drown with a breeze block tied to your fucking bollocks. Never do a Harold Houdini on me again, you got it you fucking prick?' Skeggsy was working himself up into a frenzy but at least Jack knew that Skeggsy didn't have a clue about him being stabbed.

'If you call me a prick one more time it will be you eating plankton in the Thames, alright, Skeggsy? Whilst you were out balling some old ginger minger, I found out who's been robbing Mr Riordan and also got fucking stabbed for the effort I've been putting in to protect Mr Riordan's interests. I don't want to talk about this on the phone, so meet me in the greasy spoon on South Street in twenty minutes. You know the café I mean, the place from the other morning with that idiot waiter in Ray-Bans. Oh, and incidentally, you might need to wear Ray-Bans if you call me a prick again. By the way are you going to give me a number I can contact Mr Riordan on to tell him I've sorted out his problem?' Jack asked, knowing he already had Riordan's number but fishing for any further developments since he'd been stabbed.

'Well, how do I know the problem has been sorted until I see you?' Skeggsy replied sarcastically. Jack guessed that he had probably already had a quick sniff of marching powder or else he had been using his arm as a pin cushion again. 'I'll speak to Mr Riordan, just you remember who's in charge here and who's the fucking errand boy. If anything needs explaining it will be on my say so.'

Jack was left listening to the dial tone after Skeggsy had put the phone down on him. He slammed the mobile down onto the table whilst breathing a sigh of relief at how the conversation with Skeggsy had gone. The bloke was a moron and had a way of riling him. He knew that Skeggsy was trying to play the 'big man' to prove a point about the pecking order. But reading between the lines Jack knew he was getting closer to Riordan and Skeggsy was getting worried about his position in the gang. Skeggsy took pride in being Riordan's right hand man and wasn't going to roll over easily.

Jack knew he should report in to either Gazza or DI Rice but the morphine was starting to wear off and was making him feel a little hazy. He decided that if he was meant to hand in a comprehensive report about the events of the last few days it could wait until later.

Smiling to himself he wished he could have seen DI Rice's face when Gazza had briefed him on yesterday's stabbing. The sanctimonious twat must have looked like he was trying to shit a hedgehog out of his arse as he wondered how he was going to explain the news to the top brass that his undercover man had been stabbed.

The last call he had to make was to Major Hewlan Morgan whom he thought might be able to put him in contact with Stan Wacameyer. He had served alongside Hewlan back in the hell which was Bosnia when they were both the rank of lieutenant.

He remembered Hewlan well and was glad that he had stuck with the army and had risen to the rank of major. If there was any man he would have wished to serve with, he would have chosen Hewlan over any other. Hewlan was the sort of soldier who led from the front and he wore the army virtues on his sleeve.

After ringing Hewlan and briefly chatting about 'the old days', he discovered that Stan was godfather to Hewlan's youngest daughter but he hadn't seen him in a while as Stan was no longer a serving soldier which was as Jack had suspected. Hewlan had said Stan had a few problems and he skirted around the subject until Jack explained the reason why he urgently needed to contact him. It quickly became clear Stan had fallen a little deeper into the murky world of drugs than since his army days when he had only used recreationally.

Hewlan had said that regrettably the battles Stan had fought in all over the world had taken their toll on him mentally as well as physically and he was probably suffering from PTSD because the drugs seemed to have taken over his life. He made a point of saying that until Stan straightened himself out, Hewlan would not let him near his family.

Jack didn't like to press Hewlan for details but it was imperative he located Amy's whereabouts quickly and if Stan was the only person who could help then so be it.

It turned out that Stan had been working in Belfast for MI5 but had been sacked for testing positive for heroin. He had then worked as a security guard on an industrial estate but had also got sacked from that job after being found in a drunken coma on the night shift. The one positive thing to come out of the conversation with Hewlan was that he knew Stan had moved to Dublin and had a phone number of some junkie girl called Lisa that Stan was known to hang around with. He only had the number because Stan would use it to constantly phone him up at any time of day or night completely out of his mind on whatever gear he could lay his hands on and asking for money whilst saying that all army buddies should stick together. Hewlan had felt sorry for Stan and had given him a small amount of money knowing it would probably be blown on drugs but he had also tried to put Stan in contact with a veterans charity called 'Combat Stress' to see if they could help him.

Hewlan hadn't heard from Stan for a while and presumed he was either still on the drugs or even worse dead. He hoped in the back of his mind that the charity had been able to help him, but he couldn't see it really happening. Stan was just another ex-soldier out on the streets who was slowly killing himself with drink, drugs and self-harming.

Jack rang the phone number Hewlan had given him but it went to voicemail so he had no alternative but to leave a message and asked Stan to call him urgently or email him and left his details. He didn't put too much hope in Stan being any help after what Hewlan had told him, but as he was desperate it was worth a try… Anything was.

CHAPTER 27

Amy Reynolds knew that today was going to be yet another one of those really bad days. It seemed that lately every day was a really bad day for Amy and at the moment the days tended to blend into one another.

Struggling to stop her body shaking, she propped her head up in her hands using her elbows and looked around the filthy squat she was staying in. She swung her legs awkwardly around to the side of the bed so that she was perched on the edge of the urine soaked mattress and reached for the packet of rolling tobacco that was on the floor. Searching amongst the debris from the night before, she at last found some scrumpled Rizla papers and burning a little bit of the hash that she had left from last night into the paper she rolled a single skinner between her shaking fingers.

She was surprised that no one else in the squat had stolen the hash or the baccy whilst she had been asleep. The drug-induced sleep she'd just woken from was more like a coma than a refreshing sleep and there was no way anything, apart from the clucking feeling of needing another hit of smack, was going to wake her up.

She was getting desperate for a quick early morning hit and rubbed the bruising from the fresh needle marks on her left forearm. Recently she had started to use her left arm as her right arm had blistered and the veins had imploded so badly that they were unusable.

Trying to think back to the previous night, she only had a vague recollection of what she had done. The last thing she remembered was cooking up some smack that she and her so-called housemates had scored from the Sillogue district in Ballymun.

Amy's eyes started to focus more clearly and she looked at the unconscious young girl with dirty dreadlocked hair tied in a bun on the top of her head who was spreadeagled uncomfortably on the torn leather sofa. The girl was hugging an old grey blanket tightly around her shoulders which she had obviously used to try to keep the cold Dublin night at bay. Trying to stay warm was futile in the unheated squat, however the girl had probably not even felt the cold once the warm Afghani heroin had begun to flow deep into her veins.

Amy knew this feeling only too well as she and Luke had gone halves with the girl the previous night on the fifty euro bag of brown they had bought from some dickhead on the Ballymun estate. The scumbag had initially wanted thirty euro and a blowjob, but she had refused and paid fifty instead. There was absolutely no way on earth she was going to suck his cock but the girl on the sofa might have without them knowing and had probably pocketed the twenty euro. She didn't even know the girl's name.

This was the third squat that Amy had stayed in since she had been kicked out of the Blackrock Halls. The governors had found out that she'd overdosed and been rushed by ambulance to St Vincent's hospital. The governors' reputation was far more important than her welfare so she was out on the street.

Since the overdose she had attached herself to Luke, another squatter and she supposed she could call him her boyfriend even though she hadn't known him long. They'd met in the last squat she'd stayed in when he had stopped a crackhead trying to rape her and they had been together ever since.

She only knew him as Luke. He had told her his parents had named him after the 1967 Paul Newman film *Cool Hand Luke*. She had no idea at all of what his surname was, but he made her feel protected and when you lived in squats you learnt not to question people too much. Everyone had a past; they were either trying to hide from someone or else wanted to bury themselves in a world of drugs and alcohol to compensate for the sexual abuse they had suffered in their childhood.

Luke was a lot older than Amy and together they shared the same incorrigible love of drugs. The problem was that one minute he was with her telling her how much he loved her and then the next minute he would disappear into thin air, only to turn up a couple of weeks later with a big nose bag of coke or smack.

He was always promising her a way out of squatting and the mess she was in and he was constantly telling her that from now on she was the only girl for him. She wasn't frightened of him and guessed that she loved him, but there were odd moments when she realised she didn't really know him at all and maybe it was just the drugs that kept them together.

She looked at her phone. During the night her mum had left at least a dozen text messages and so had her dad, both of them leaving voicemail messages as well. She'd deleted the hundreds of other messages they'd left over the last few days. All of the messages had been asking her to call them urgently. Most of the messages left by her mum were virtually unintelligible because of her crying.

When she had been a little girl she had craved love and attention and her father had always been there for her. As she grew up she had seen less and less of him. He was always working away on one damned job or another. If it wasn't the army it was the police and she was sick of it. She had never really had a close relationship with her mother and she felt quite isolated from them both.

Now that she was back on the drugs she felt ashamed and was too frightened to ask her parents for help. She thought they were too wrapped up in their own problems to care. She didn't know what to say to her parents so she took the easy option and put off answering their messages. Anyway, she had Luke to look after her now.

Luke had been there last night but there was no sign of him in the squat this morning. It wasn't the first time over the last few weeks that Amy had wondered where the hell her boyfriend had gone to.

Taking one last deep drag of the joint before it burnt her fingers she put the finished roach end in an empty can of Guinness on the floor. She felt as though she was keeping her self-respect by trying to be tidy even though the floor was covered in cigarette butts, empty beer cans, pizza boxes and used syringes. There were even supermarket plastic bags stacked in the corner of the room full of human excrement.

She kidded herself that she had only got wrecked out of her head last night because she was worried about what was going to happen today when she met her personal tutor to explain her lack of attendance at lectures. She was resigned to being kicked out of uni but still a single tear leaked out of her right eye and slowly ran down her freckled pale face. At one o'clock her fate with the uni was going to be sealed and all of her dreams that she'd had since she was a little girl of having a successful career in law would be over in an instant. Then she was going to have to explain to her parents why she was no longer studying law.

Well, she wasn't going to tell them the whole truth, she thought to herself. So far she had kept all of her problems away from them and there was no reason for them to know anything different until she was at least off the gear. As far as she was concerned, her parents had enough problems of their own trying to keep their joke of a marriage intact. She hated the fact that her parents were living apart and just wanted them to be back together living as one happy family, just like when she had been a little girl.

The need for a quick hit was making her feel ill and she needed to do something about it quickly.

There was little point sitting in the squat surrounded by the stench of human urine and shit whilst waiting for Luke to return. It could be days before he returned, so Amy pulled on a jumper and picked up her fur-lined khaki parka coat from off the floor and decided to head into the city to score some methadone. If she scored some smack on the way then all the better, she thought to herself. Surely one small hit before she met the tutor wouldn't hurt?

Sheltering from the rain on the bus, Amy thought to herself how miserable and cold Dublin was. In the grimy bus window, someone had written *Dan Stevens is a cock*. How mature, she thought. She tried to peer through the rain at the houses as the bus passed them. Most were happy homes with loving families. She could see couples sitting on their sofas in their living rooms cuddling each other or playing with their laughing children. Amy wiped away a tear as she wished that she was a child again. All of that innocence and none of the pressures of an adult life to contend with. Life was so easy back then. If you were unhappy you cried and then your mother would sweep you up in her arms and make all of the unhappiness disappear in a second with her kisses and cuddles.

Noticing that it was almost her stop, she pressed the bell and the bus came to a halt at O'Connell Street. Amy squeezed past a young mum who was ignorantly blocking the aisle with her bags of shopping and a twin buggy full of screaming children. Quickly stepping off the bus, Amy landed in a large puddle which immediately soaked through the holes in her trainers.

Holding the parka fur hood down as far as she could over her forehead, Amy tried to decide in which direction to walk. Whichever direction she chose didn't really matter as all of the car drivers thought that it was funny to drive too close to the pavement and splash her with water as their cars ploughed through the flooded road. It was alright for them in their flash cars and with their perfect lives. Bastards.

Amy stopped beside the Charles Stewart Parnell monument and tried to use it to shelter out of the rain as she attempted to light the cigarette she had rolled earlier on the bus. Unfortunately, the fifty-seven foot high obelisk with Parnell's large out-stretched arm wasn't giving her much shelter from the driving Dublin rain, nor was it giving much shelter to the small group of strangers that had huddled together under the monument with the same intention as Amy.

The spring weather had begun to take a turn for the worse, if that was possible, and her rollup was sodden right through before she'd even managed to light it. Giving up, Amy was taken aback when an old woman in her seventies roughly barged past her running her shopping trolley over Amy's toes.

'Hey! Careful, you nearly had my toes off,' Amy said.

The old woman glared and shouted at Amy, 'Foc il leat, you English bitch.' Amy had lived in Ireland long enough to know the Gaelic for 'Fuck off' and was incensed at the old woman's anger towards her. The old woman shouted something else but Amy didn't understand it and her attention was now caught by the sight of the old woman's purse which was dangling half-out of the trolley.

In a fit of anger and still strung out from the previous night Amy reached into the old woman's trolley and grabbed the purse. She tried to jump over the trolley to make her escape but in her weakened drugless state she only managed to trip over the trolley and fell into the group of strangers huddled around the monument.

'Soith, gadaí. Stop her. The bitch has nicked my purse,' the old woman shrieked.

As Amy leapt up off the ground she found the group of strangers had surrounded her and her arms were pinned behind her. She struggled to get free and in desperation she wriggled out of her parka coat to escape from her captors. Ducking low she ran through the small crowd bumping straight into a policeman from the local Gardai who had run over on hearing the commotion He grabbed her by the arm and shouted that she was under arrest.

'Go fuck yourself,' Amy screamed as she struggled with him and using all of her remaining strength she kneed him between his legs as hard as she could. The overweight Garda dropped his handcuffs which he had been trying to put on Amy's wrists and almost fell to the ground. Before she knew what was happening, the Garda had wrenched a pepper spray from its holder strapped to his waist and stretching his arm out he pepper sprayed Amy in the face.

The instant pain that Amy felt in her eyes from the pepper spray was excruciating. Her eyes shut tight involuntarily but she was fortunate that the full force of the pepper spray had blown away in the wind and rain before most of it had reached her face. She ran off as fast as she could whilst wiping the spray from her eyes with the back of her hands and ignoring the shouts of hostility from behind her.

Amy ran as though she was attempting to break Usain Bolt's Olympic record. She darted between the wet shoppers walking towards her and ran down a couple of small side streets until her legs could not run any further. She slumped down beside a skip that was being used to clear out yet another shop that had gone to the wall in the recession. If the Garda was still following her she was too tired from running to resist any attempt he might make to arrest her again. Her eyes stung like hell so she cupped her hands and scooped up some water from the rain puddles to wash the pepper spray out of her stinging eyes. The dirt from the rain water couldn't hurt her eyes more than the pepper spray.

Once her eyes had settled down from the effect of the pepper spray she crawled behind the skip to get her breath back before she called a dealer she knew living around the corner to get a small ten euro bag of smack.

Today was definitely turning out to be the nightmare that she had thought it would be. She had the Gardai looking for her, Luke had disappeared again and the tutor probably never wanted to see her again after one o'clock today. Her life was in a real mess and she didn't know what to do.

CHAPTER 28

Jack had set his phone's alarm to ring twenty minutes after he had last spoken to Skeggsy. It still gave him a shock when it suddenly went off, it was that fucking Rihanna song again – also set by Amy. Jack promised himself that once he'd made sure that Amy was safe and sound he would kill her himself.

He was meant to meet Skeggsy at the café but he wasn't going to make their meeting – even if he rang for a taxi now – and he knew Skeggsy would be pissed off. Skeggsy was like a time bomb waiting to go off and he was obviously worried about maintaining his position in the gang. So why didn't Jack use him as a catalyst to get to Riordan?

He picked up his mobile and checked it had the right SIM card in it and then rang Skeggsy.

'Is that you, Jack?'

'Yeah.'

'Where the fuck are you? I'm sitting in this sodding café all by myself,' Skeggsy shouted, his voice echoing down the phone from the noise in the café.

'Yeah, sorry about that. I can't make it, my leg is killing me. Can you give me Riordan's phone number as I think he'll want to hear what I have to say.'

'Not until you tell me what happened first,' Skeggsy shouted above the din of the café.

'Listen, Skeggsy, Riordan told you to give me his number when I had some news and I have big fucking news for him.' Jack started to raise his voice.

'Don't fuck with me, Jack, or you'll regret it. Who stabbed you? What's going on?'

'I told you I want to speak to Riordan. There is a real danger of a turf war kicking off and you don't want to be responsible for any trouble that gets in the way of Riordan's business, do you? You fucking ginger ape.'

Jack put the phone down and left Skeggsy to think about his threat. It would take a while for his small brain to work it out, but he knew that Skeggsy would tell Riordan that Jack was winding him up. He'd set the cat amongst the pigeons by getting Skeggsy angry and his plan could go one of two ways. If it worked, he had made the right decision. If it didn't, then he could well be a dead man.

Jack washed as best he could without getting his leg wet. Afterwards, he rang the valet company and they said it would be two days before the Audi was ready and would call him to arrange delivery. He also rang for a taxi and gave them Sarah's address as the destination. He needed to see Sarah and he knew that Sarah wouldn't be at work today. She was panicking about Amy going missing and he'd promised to visit her anyway. He missed her and was looking forward to seeing her, despite the circumstances.

Waiting for the taxi he had one more thing to do. He texted the number Riordan had given him: C*an you call me? Jack*.

When the taxi arrived, Jack gave the driver directions to Sarah's house. The journey took a while as the taxi driver – a man Jack thought was from either Iran or Syria – he didn't know his left from his right and kept taking wrong turns.

Finally they arrived at Sarah's house and Jack paid the driver without giving him a tip. The man made a disapproving hissing noise before speeding off. Jack was pretty certain he caught the words 'Fucking tight bastard' before the door had slammed shut.

Standing outside the front door of Sarah's house he was trying to decide whether to use his key or to ring the doorbell when the door suddenly swung open and Sarah was standing there looking beautiful with just a towel wrapped around her. She was bent forward holding tightly onto H's collar. H was frantically jumping up at the open door, barking loudly in excitement. Jack tried to bend down to pat him on the head when his left leg suddenly gave way and all he managed to do was fall into the hallway in a crumpled heap. H immediately started to jump all over him trying to lick his face like a cheap hooker with a punter.

He felt like a complete prick as this was not the entrance to Sarah's that he had planned at all. Sarah hauled H into the kitchen as, with spectacularly bad timing, Jack's phone went off. He mouthed *sorry* to Sarah as he answered it. Sarah mouthed back, *Fuck you*, before heading upstairs without saying another word or looking back at him.

'Jack?' It was Riordan's gruff northern voice at the other end of the line. 'I hear that you've had a little bit of trouble but you may have some important information for me?'

'Yeah, hello Mr Riordan.' Jack dusted himself off and painfully stood to his feet.

'What have you got for me? And what's this crap about you not having a number to get me on?'

'Sorry, I was just winding Skeggsy up.'

'Well fucking don't. I know he's like a pit bull dog guarding its territory, but he can be gentle if you know when to tickle him. Get it wrong and he's like a dog who's had his bone taken away. He can be extremely dangerous, which is of course why I employ him. At the moment I want you two to stop squabbling like runts of the litter, or I'm going to have you put down. Are you listening to me?' The menacing undertones of what

Riordan was saying were not lost on Jack at all and he now knew that his plan to rile Skeggsy was working, but he didn't want to push the advantage too far.

'Yeah, sorry about that but he can be a real prick sometimes. If he laid off the gear…'

'I employ him for results and he gets them. What he does in his own life, be it drugs or fucking your sister, your wife or even your fucking daughter, is not my problem.' Riordan's voice was raised now. Tell me, what happened with my product and who stabbed you?'

'I ain't being funny, Mr Riordan, but I need to tell you face to face and not on the phone. After being stabbed, I'm not sure who I can trust. Let's just say I don't think Lambeth is a safe area to be working in at the moment.'

'Okay, I think I get the gist of what you're saying, but I want you on the next available flight to Manchester. You might have a bad leg but if I don't see your sorry arse up here pronto with an explanation of what the hell's been going on down there with my business you won't need to worry about your gammy leg. I'll slowly and painfully devour you like a pufferfish kills its prey with its tetrodotoxin, you southern tosser. Look it up in the *National Geographic*. Oh and by the way, I want this meeting strictly between you and me, not Skeggsy, I can't trust you two twats together. Text me when you arrive at Gorton Railway Station and I'll send one of my lads to collect you. One more thing, bring your passport and if you aren't there in a few hours you'll be breathing less than my brother Dougie and he's buried six foot under, God rest his soul.'

The phone went dead.

'H leave it alone.' Jack shouted at the dog who was now humping his hospital crutch. If only Sarah acted the same way Jack thought, instead of running back up the stairs in a fit of temper after he'd fallen in a messy, hungover heap in the hallway.

'Sarah….can we talk please. I can't get up the stairs with my leg the way it is. Can you please come down, honey?' Jack shouted up the empty stairs.

Sarah's voice echoed down the stairs, 'I'm not your bloody honey and you stink of booze.'

Jack looked at H who was wagging his tail and looking straight back at him with his pink tongue lolling from the side of his mouth. H recognised Sarah's serious tone of voice and promptly curled up in his basket beside the sofa. Jack decided that H was in a better position to know Sarah's moods than he was lately and followed him into the living room. He sat on the sofa and H quickly jumped up out of his basket and curled up beside him where they both promptly fell into a deep sleep.

CHAPTER 29

Sarah wrapped her legs around Jack and he could feel her smooth heels digging into the small of his back as he thrust himself deep inside her with ever increasing force. With each pumping motion he watched her skin ripple in waves across her nearly flat stomach and marvelled at how pert her breasts were even when she was lying down. He could hear her shouting his name louder and louder, 'Jack, Jack……..Wake up….. Jack.'

Sarah was leaning over him shaking his shoulder trying to wake him up. He groaned, 'What the… Oh God.' He wiped a hand over his face. 'I was having one hell of a dream there. How long have I been asleep?'

'A couple of hours. You looked like you needed it so I put a blanket over you and left you snoring with H curled up beside you,' Sarah answered.

Jack noticed that Sarah had been crying.

'It's serious Jack, I woke you up because Amy's tutor rang. He said that Amy's been kicked off her course as she hasn't been attending any lectures recently and he also said that she'd been kicked out of her halls after a drugs overdose. He hasn't got a clue where she's living now. He was meant to have a meeting with her yesterday but she didn't turn up so he had no choice but to exclude her from the rest of the course.'

'What the hell…. and nobody knows where she is? Well that explains the strange text message.' Jack could feel the anger growing inside him and it seemed to awaken the nerves in his leg as it started to pulsate with rhythmic pain, rapidly bringing him back to reality and the dream that he had been enjoying quickly became a distant memory.

'What text message?' Sarah screamed at him.

'I received a strange text message from her a few days ago.'

'And you never thought to tell me?' Sarah slumped onto the sofa breaking down into tears.

'I didn't want to worry you.'

'Well, it's a little late for that,' Sarah spat at him, 'Jack, what are we going to do? Our baby girl is out there somewhere and she could be in trouble. I'm going to call the police.'

'I already have and they are out looking for her as we speak,' Jack said, putting his arms around her and drawing her closer to him so that she wiped her tears dry against his cheek. 'I also have a mate in Ireland looking for her right now, we'll find her.'

Jack was torn between his family and his undercover work. Remembering Riordan's menacing phone call, if he didn't go to Manchester immediately he risked jeopardising the best chance he'd had in years of getting close to Riordan.

'Listen Sarah, I have to go to Manchester for work but shouldn't be there longer than a few hours. I'll book a connecting flight to Dublin and find out what the fuck is going on.'

'Oh God, thank you, Jack' Sarah said drying her tears.

'Can I use your internet to book the flights and check up on my mate in Ireland and see if there's any news? Oh, and where's my coffee?' Jack joked, smiling at Sarah, trying to reassure her and alleviate the tension.

Whilst Sarah made him a coffee he checked his emails and booked a lunchtime flight to Manchester on one of those cheap 'last minute' websites. There was an email from Stan Wacameyer saying that he had traced Amy to a squat, but she hadn't been seen there for a week and the other squatters thought that she'd moved on. Jack emailed his thanks back to Stan for his help and told him that he would be coming out to Ireland himself hopefully later today and he'd call him as soon as he arrived. Considering Stan's prompt response maybe rehab had worked.

He breathed a sigh of relief, at least the trail had not gone completely cold and he was sure that he would be able to find Amy once he had arrived in Ireland.

Sarah drove him to Gatwick and the conversation in the car had been a little frosty, to say the least. Sarah was furious that Jack was going to Manchester and wasn't going straight out to Ireland. He'd tried to explain that he had no choice because of the job he was working on and it wouldn't take long but his words fell on deaf ears. He thought better of reminding her that she couldn't fly out to Ireland herself as she didn't have a passport.

As Jack got out of the car he tried to give Sarah a kiss on the cheek but she pushed him away saying, 'Go to hell, Jack. Get our little girl back soon or I'll never forgive you. Just do whatever it takes to bring her home.' Jack felt that it was always one step forward and two steps back in his relationship with Sarah and he had absolutely no chance of ever understanding the way a woman thinks.

The flight to Manchester had left half an hour late, which meant Jack had just about enough time to down a couple of much needed pints at a bar in the airport before the last call for his plane came over the intercom. Whilst he had been in the bar he had looked around at all of the other travellers who were laughing and enjoying themselves, he was envious of them flying off to sunnier climates without a care in the world.

Each set of travellers was oblivious as to where the people seated at the next table were flying and none of them were interested in where Jack was going. He would have given someone the shirt off his back to swap his life with them rather than flying off to the unknown dangers that lay ahead for him in cold and wet Manchester. He didn't intend to stay in Manchester one second longer than necessary.

It was a short flight and Jack had been relieved when the plane had finally landed. It meant he could get away from the grossly overweight man called Trev who had been sat next to him. His body mass had spilled out over and under the arm rest leaving him little or no room to move in his seat. Trev smelt like he hadn't washed in a week and he'd continually tried to talk to him during the flight, boring him with tales about visiting his unemployed children called Gavin and Porsche. He told Jack that his wife had run off with a double glazing salesman. The worst thing about the man, besides his mind numbing and incessant chatter, was his horrendous breath, which would have knocked Tyson Fury out cold at ten paces.

It was one of Jack's pet hates that people always stood up in planes and got their luggage out of the overhead compartments before the airline staff advised that it was safe for them to do so, but such was his desperation to get away from Trev that he found himself grabbing his rucksack and doing exactly that. As Jack took the small rucksack that Sarah had lent him out of the overhead compartment, Trev was trying to explain to him for the fourth time that he still loved his wife. Jack struggled down the plane towards the exit and could hear Trev's high-pitched voice starting to whine at another innocent victim about the unfair hand life had dealt him.

Once Jack had passed through security control he could feel his leg starting to hurt. Sitting on the plane in the cramped seat beside Trev and his undulating flesh had certainly not helped his path to recovery from his recent surgery.

Leaning painfully on the crutch under his arm he limped out of the airport towards the taxi rank which was nowhere near the exit. Jack was fully aware that he could be walking into a trap and from the intelligence he had gained whilst tracking

Riordan it was more than likely that his every movement was being watched by someone on Riordan's payroll. Therefore, not wishing to attract any unwanted attention, he decided that at the moment it wasn't safe for him to report into Gazza or DI Rice. He was going to have to get on with the job in hand and hope that the passport he had used for identification at check in was flagged up and at least that way the NCA might know where he was…. and more importantly that he was still alive. For now anyway.

Jack swallowed another painkiller with the help of a can of lager whilst he was waiting in the queue at the taxi rank and regretted not having booked one of the Private Hire taxis before he had arrived at the airport. After about ten minutes of waiting he had finished his can of lager and was eventually at the front of the queue and said to the taxi driver, 'Gorton Railway Station please, mate?'

'Why don't you take the train pal? It's cheaper,' the driver replied in a broad Mancunian accent.

'Because I want to take a taxi, is that alright with you, pal?' Jack growled back at the young taxi driver who was wearing a tracksuit with white stripes down the arms and legs, a half smoked cigarette dangling from his mouth.

'Yeah, okay. Just trying to help you. It'll be forty quid.'

'Listen, I might be a southerner but don't treat me like some sort of a prick. I'll give you twenty-five quid or else you can put it on the meter and don't try and be clever by putting it on time and a half,' Jack grunted, slinging his rucksack on the back seat and plonking himself down in the passenger seat beside the young driver.

'Bloody hell, are they all as moody as you down south? Don't worry, pal, twenty-five quid'll do.'

'Okay, let's go then and cut the small talk. I'm not in the mood.'

The young lad put the car in gear and on purpose pulled away sharply giving Jack such a jolt it pushed him back into the seat and a bolt of pain immediately shot through his leg.

'Hey, take it easy with the driving will you and I'll take it easy with my mouth,' Jack said, trying to make amends for his foul mood.

After a minute or two, Jack offered the taxi driver a cigarette as a peace offering. The driver gratefully took it and they drove on towards Gorton in silence apart from the noise of the radio which was pumping out rap music, which Jack hated with a passion but didn't comment on as he reckoned he'd pissed the driver off enough.

Remembering Riordan had said he would arrange for him to be picked up he sent him a text message: *I've just left the airport and should be there in twenty minutes as long as the taxi driver doesn't take me round the houses or get lost.* Leaning back into the passenger seat he thought he could only cross his fingers and hope that the day couldn't get any worse.

As they neared Manchester the area they drove through started to get more and more built up and it had also started to rain. *Welcome to the fucking north*, Jack thought to himself as they drove past row upon row of weather beaten old red brick terraced houses with dirty net curtains hanging in the windows to keep out any prying eyes. Jack was surprised to see a sign giving directions to a Franciscan Monastery in Gorton which dated back as far as 1863. It seemed a little out of place considering his knowledge about the crime riddled area and, as they drove over the brow of the hill, Jack could see the train station a couple of hundred yards ahead of them. He could also see parked on double yellow lines outside the entrance to the train station a large, obviously very expensive silver Bentley, with two huge smartly dressed men casually leaning on the bonnet of the car smoking cigarettes.

'Do me a favour, mate. Drive slowly past the station and drop me off just round the corner? I'll give you an extra tenner okay?' Jack said, taking a bundle of notes out of his pocket.

'Sure, your cash speaks my language.' The young taxi driver drove slowly past the Bentley giving Jack a chance to get a good look at the two men smoking beside the car and the taxi pulled up on the side of the road once they were out of view of the station.

Jack retrieved his rucksack off the back seat and as he got out of the taxi the driver said, 'I don't know what kind of shit you're in, but this isn't the sort of place to go looking for trouble, especially as you don't come from around here, so watch your back. Cheers for the cash and look after yourself.'

The taxi sped off leaving Jack standing on the side of the road holding his rucksack under one arm and the crutch under his other.

There could only be one reason the Bentley was waiting outside the station, so Jack walked up behind it and said, 'Are you two fellas waiting for me, by any chance?'

The two smartly dressed steroid-pumped bodyguards spun round, but before they could do anything the rear passenger door swung open and a voice in a thick Mancunian accent shouted, 'Get in the fucking car, Jack.'

Jack climbed into the Bentley and his trousers made a squeaking noise as he slid across the smooth leather interior. He looked at the man sitting next to him who had a hard leathered looking face and a bald bullet-shaped head and said, 'Hello, Mr Riordan. You should take those goons you employ to Specsavers and get their eyes checked. They're no good as lookouts.' He held his hand out offering to shake hands with Riordan who ignored his hand completely.

'Very funny. So you're a comedian as well as a secretive cunt, are you? I hope you had a pleasant flight as you'll be going on another one shortly. I have a job for you, but first I want you to tell me everything you know about who's fucking with my operations down south and who the hell stabbed you whilst you were working for me.'

Riordan stared at Jack and Jack felt a slight shiver run down his spine as Riordan's ice cold blue eyes drilled into him.

CHAPTER 30

The early morning mist had started to lift and it was beginning to look like it was going to be yet another wet and dreary day in London. Skeggsy fiddled with the top of the range digital tuner on the car radio but couldn't find anything he wanted to listen to, so in frustration he turned it off.

He hadn't had a wink of sleep the previous night after he'd taken the phone call from Riordan. His mind had gone onto overdrive when his boss had told him that Jack was with him in Manchester. He'd also told him that it was Deano's mate Sean who had been stealing the coke from each delivery and Big V's sidekick Davey had stabbed Jack because he'd caught Davey picking up the stolen coke from Sean.

Skeggsy was really pissed off that Riordan had invited Jack to Manchester without him and he'd been left in London to look after things. He wished Davey had done the job properly when he'd stabbed Jack, but it just meant that one day soon he would have to do the job himself. He didn't like or trust Jack at all. Skeggsy thought that there was something that didn't smell right about him and he prided himself on being able to spot a 'wrong'un' when he saw one. He also didn't like the way that Jack seemed to be muscling his way into the top spot in Riordan's business. Skeggsy was becoming increasingly worried that Riordan might not want him as his right-hand man much longer, especially if Jack had anything to do with it.

Skeggsy licked the wrap of speed in his hand clean and tossed it out of the car window. He knew that his dealings with Jack would have to wait as Riordan had ordered him to deal with Sean immediately. So after he'd finished speaking to Riordan he had made a few phone calls and it hadn't taken long to find out where Sean was hiding out.

Sean's brother had a caravan down by the old disused Wapping Tobacco Docks. His brother was in prison doing a five year stretch for aggravated burglary and Skeggsy had learnt that Sean often used the caravan as a bolt hole. The yuppie money and the riverside apartments had gone and all that was left of the thriving docks was an empty shell. The caravan was parked in a secluded spot beside the canal behind the docks and for the last hour Skeggsy had been sat in the car, mulling over exactly what method of extreme violence he was going to use against Sean in revenge for his treachery.

Skeggsy turned around and leaning between the two car seats he looked at Deano who was sitting there with a face as white as sheet wedged between two very large muscular skinheads. His nose was bleeding from one nostril and his right eye was swollen shut. Skeggsy said to him, 'Right you little prick, I want you to knock on the caravan door and tell your pal Sean you're outside and that he's to let you in. If you fuck this up and give him any hint that it's a trap I'll tear your fucking kneecaps off with a claw hammer.'

Creeping up to the caravan Deano banged on the door while Skeggsy and the skinheads stood to the side of the door out of sight. They listened to every word as Deano said, 'Sean, I'm outside. It's me, Deano. I need to talk to you. Open up the door, will you?'

After what seemed like an eternity the noise of a bolt being drawn back and a key turning in a lock broke the silence and then the door opened slightly and a voice could be heard saying, 'Fucking hell, Deano, what the hell happened to—'

Skeggsy kicked the door with all of his strength and Sean's nose exploded in a bloody mess of shattered bone as it took the full force of the door smashing into his face and he went flying backwards into the opposite wall of the caravan.

Skeggsy ran in immediately kicking Sean in the bollocks as he lay stunned on the floor holding his nose not fully understanding what was happening. Skeggsy hit him with a hammer on the side of the face and there was a resounding crunching of shattering bone as Sean's cheekbone caved in under the weight of the hammer. Skeggsy shouted at the two skinheads to pick up the now unconscious Sean and tie him to a chair in what was supposed to be the caravan's kitchen area.

The skinheads picked up Seans's limp body and dumped him on the chair. Skeggsy roughly dragged Deano into the caravan as he'd been standing outside pretending to himself the shit he was in wasn't happening.

Skeggsy poked Deano hard in the stomach saying, 'You want to choose your mates more carefully.' Meanwhile the taller of the two skinheads tied a rope around Sean's limp body and the smaller pug-faced skinhead fastened cable ties around his wrists and ankles. The tying up took a few minutes so Skeggsy sat down on the only other chair in the dilapidated caravan. Smiling at Deano whimpering in the corner he took another wrap of speed from his pocket and taking a large dab using his middle finger greedily licked it.

The floor of the caravan was now stained with a long tram line blood stain from where the skinheads had dragged the unconscious Sean across the floor to the chair on which he was now securely tied.

'One of you two go and get a bucket of water or something so that we can wake this prick up and then the party can begin,' Skeggsy ordered. His eyeballs were almost bursting out of their sockets and the veins in his neck pulsated from the amount of speed he had taken.

The pug faced skinhead ran off and filled the bucket used to clean the toilet with water from a standing tap outside. He then came back into the caravan and threw the water in Sean's face to bring him back to consciousness.

Sean coughed and spat blood from his mouth onto the floor. Spluttering as his teeth had been broken, he stared Skeggsy straight in his eyes and mumbled, 'What the fuck do you want?'

'Well now, you've been a naughty boy, Sean, and I'm here to make sure that you pay for it. If or when I decide to end your pathetic existence on this earth it will send a message to Big V warning him that Mr Riordan runs London and nobody steals from him,' Skeggsy snarled.

'I haven't done anything and don't know any Big V,' Sean whimpered.

'Save it for your maker. At least have the decency to admit it, you thieving shit. If you carry on lying I'll just make the pain that you're going to suffer last even longer,' Skeggsy said, reaching down to a bag he had put on the floor. He slowly unzipped the bag and pulled out a mini petrol chainsaw, a knuckle duster, a packet of long galvanised nails and some lighter fuel and carefully laid them out on the floor in front of him.

Sean started to cry and pleaded, 'I'm sorry, please don't hurt me. I'll give you Big V. I'll do whatever you want.'

'Shut up, it's too late. You made your choice and now you have to pay.'

A trickle of urine started to flow across the floor as Sean wet himself.

The two skinheads started to laugh and Skeggsy shot them an angry look which stopped them in their tracks. Skeggsy shouted at them, 'Hold his legs down.' He then walked over towards Sean and knelt down at his feet and started to hammer a nail through his left foot into the floor. Once he had finished he proceeded to drive another nail through his right foot. Sean screamed in pain as the nails splintered the bones in his feet and stuck into the flooring, but nobody could hear his bloodcurdling screams as unfortunately for Sean his brother's caravan was in the middle of nowhere. Not even the homeless stayed down by the docks as the cold wind off the canal drove them away.

Skeggsy lit another cigarette and took a knuckle duster out of his pocket as Sean looked at him with wide eyes pleading for Skeggsy to leave him alone. Skeggsy grinned and ignoring his pleas for mercy started to pound his face with the knuckle duster. After a few minutes Sean's face was a bloody pulp and even the skinheads felt a little bit sickened at Skeggsy's ferocity. The sweat from the effort of half beating Sean to death had started to run down Skeggsy's face and was dripping from his smiling lips onto the floor.

Skeggsy sat back down on the chair and looked up at Deano who was standing there scared witless wondering if he was going to get out of the flat alive. 'Make yourself useful. Go and get me a coffee or something. White with two sugars.' Deano stepped over Sean's nailed feet and switched the kettle on. Two minutes later after searching through the caravan's cupboards he passed a mug of coffee to Skeggsy.

After taking a few sips of the coffee, Skeggsy took his mobile from his pocket and rang a number in the phone's contact list. He waited a few seconds until his call was answered and he said, 'Hello, you fucking Welsh paedophile. I have a message for you from Mr Riordan.'

Skeggsy proceeded to tell Big V that Riordan knew all about his little deal with Sean and that Riordan was going to make sure Big V never operated in London again.

Skeggsy then held out the phone to Sean, who was slumped and bloody on the chair.

'Talk to the prick, you bastard.'

'Please help me.' Sean could barely get the words out. 'Oh God . . . he's going to kill me . . . please……'

Skeggsy brought the phone back to his ear, but Big V had gone.

'Oh dear, Sean, your friend hung up on me. Now that's not very nice, is it?" Skeggsy said.

Sean let out a deep groan from the pain and wet himself again, this time draining his bladder completely.

Skeggsy shouted, 'Right, that's enough. You two hold his head tight and open his mouth.' He walked over towards Sean holding the tin of lighter fluid in his hand. Sean started to struggle frantically in a desperate attempt to escape, but realised that his struggling was completely futile and that nobody was likely to hear to hear his screaming either.

'I've had enough of your screaming Sean and I have the perfect remedy to make you shut the fuck up.' Skeggsy held the tin of lighter fuel over Sean's face and squirted a long thick jet of the lighter fluid into Sean's mouth as he struggled with the two skinheads who held his mouth open in a vice like grip. Skeggsy calmly winked at Sean and took a lighter out of his pocket, this was the part of his plan that he had been really looking forward to. He then put the flame from the lighter inside Sean's mouth and as the petrol took alight he stood back to admire his handiwork. Light blue flames curled out of Sean's mouth and he made a weird gargling noise as his vocal cords started to burn. The skin around his mouth started to melt and then his lower lip peeled away from his mouth and fell smouldering to the floor, leaving a small burn mark in the flooring as it lay there. It had not been an easy task to roll Sean's muscular body up in the old carpet they had bought with them. The two skinheads had carried his heavy body to the car and had stuffed it in the boot. Skeggsy had found some music on the radio that he liked and was singing to the song *BLEM* by Drake as he drove. The two skinheads and Deano sat in the back of the car in shocked silence at Skeggsy's transition from a violent maniac to then calmly singing as he drove after having just murdered someone.

The car stopped in Kennington Road outside the Tankard pub and Skeggsy said, 'You know what to do.' He leant forward and pressed a button and the boot of the car flipped open as the three men got out of the back of the car. The two skinheads reached into the boot and took out the now blood soaked carpet containing Sean's body and walked over to the door of the pub. Deano held open the door of the pub as the two skinheads threw the carpet with Sean's mutilated body into the middle of the pub and they ran back to the car.

The car wasn't Skeggsy's BMW. He wasn't that stupid. He'd stolen it earlier that morning. Skeggsy said, 'We'll torch the motor and then you lot can get off. Well done.' He threw an envelope at each of the skinheads saying, 'Don't spend it all at once, boys. Oh, and you, Deano, don't get paid anything. Just thank your lucky stars that you're still breathing.'

Skeggsy turned the music up and said out loud to himself, 'Job satisfaction, what a feeling. You can't beat it.'

Inside the pub Big V stared at the mutilated body splayed out on the unrolled carpet and roared loudly, 'Skeggsy is a fucking dead man.'

CHAPTER 31

Jack woke up to the smell of a softly scented feather pillow and for a fleeting moment forgot where he was. He remembered that he'd tried his best to persuade Riordan he couldn't stay the night but Riordan wouldn't have any of it. With a menacing undertone Riordan had made it very plain that he wanted Jack to stay overnight at his house in Gorton. He was virtually a prisoner.

He looked around the large bedroom which was expensively furnished and got out of the canopy four-poster bed as he desperately needed to use the toilet in the en suite bathroom. The bathroom was bigger than the living room in Jack's flat and in the middle of the shiny marble floor stood a huge white porcelain bath tub with gold taps.

The day before, after being picked up in the Bentley by Riordan and his two goons, they had driven up to a large gated mock Georgian mansion on the outskirts of Gorton where Riordan lived. Looking at the size of the impressive house, Jack could tell that the proceeds of crime paid very well. He couldn't help but look at the sprawling mansion through slightly jealous eyes and felt slightly envious of the wealth Riordan had accumulated through violence and drugs.

They'd driven up the long and winding gravel driveway which was aligned by ugly stone gargoyles sat on plinths which were evenly spaced along each side of the driveway. Riordan had seemed especially proud of the gargoyles and had told

Jack that he had given each one of them a special name, just like someone would give a name to a pet. Jack would never forget Riordan's cold eyes when he had casually told him that each gargoyle represented a man he had ordered to be killed because they'd crossed him.

After the Bentley had stopped in front of the house Jack had followed Riordan up the steps of the large porch which was supported by four large pillars and they had entered the house. Jack had only ever seen a house like it in Hollywood blockbuster films and he had been in complete awe of the size of the entrance hall. It had a huge two-tier crystal chandelier hanging from the ceiling and at the far end of the hall was a large double stairway leading upstairs to the rest of the house.

Jack hadn't known what to expect that day but Riordan had acted the perfect host and had taken him into a large living room and offered him a drink before excusing himself for five minutes as he had some urgent calls to make before they went out for dinner. Whilst Jack waited patiently a butler had come into the room and had said that Mr Riordan was unfortunately going to be longer than he had at first thought so he had been asked to show him to his room where he could freshen up.

Later, they had driven in the Bentley to the city's Chinatown where they had dined at Riordan's favourite restaurant called Red Chilli. The waiters at the restaurant had treated Riordan like royalty and he was clearly a well-known and notorious man from the nervous looks they had gotten from the other customers as they had taken their seats in the restaurant.

The waiters had hurriedly asked a family who were already eating to move from their table to make room for them in the packed restaurant. The family had quickly moved from their seats without the slightest hint of an argument once they had realised with whom they were being asked to change table. Jack suspected that the respect their party was being shown was only due to the fearsome grip that Riordan held on the inhabitants of Manchester and especially the locals in the area.

During the meal, Riordan had chatted about everything from politics to religion and he had spoken passionately about his love for horse racing explaining to Jack that he owned five race horses. Jack had genuinely found himself beginning to like the articulate and strangely charismatic man sitting in front of him and was impressed at the depth of his knowledge in all aspects of life. Jack had suspected that Riordan was taking his time and enjoying sounding him out. The bottles of champagne, which kept appearing on their table without asking, were to soften him up and to loosen his tongue.

Admittedly, he had probably drunk too much last night and the banging headache that he was suffering from this morning confirmed how drunk he must have been.

Jack's memory of the end of the evening was a little hazy and he had a vague recollection of going into a lap-dancing club called Secrets where Riordan had paid for countless private dances for them both of them in the VIP area of the club. The sexiest girls he had ever had the luck to lay his eyes on had danced erotically for both of them in private booths. Jack had tried to refuse as he didn't like the way the girls were being exploited but Riordan had insisted and he didn't want to arouse any suspicions. The booths were paid for by Riordan.

They had taken line after line of coke which they had poured onto the pert breasts of the girls before snorting, and he remembered with embarrassment that they had even snorted some lines of coke off the thongs stuck between the girls' tight bum cheeks. It had been one hell of a night ending with Riordan paying for a girl of Jack's choice to suck him off. Jack had gone into a private booth, feeling sorry for the girl he'd turned down her offer and had given her fifty quid to pretend to Riordan that she'd sucked him off.

The two goons had driven them in the Bentley back to Gorton at the end of the night and he remembered quickly sobering up as Riordan, without any explanation, had handed him a first class flight ticket with his name on it to Lima in Peru, with an onward flight to Cusco in the Andes. This was the worst news ever for Jack; he needed to go to Ireland, not Peru. Riordan had explained that the flight was early in the morning so Jack should to be ready to leave by six o'clock and he would explain exactly why he wanted him to fly to Peru in the morning.

Jack had initially thought that Riordan might be playing games with him by making him wait until the morning before he explained why he wanted him to go to Peru, but he had noticed that the ticket was for a return flight which gave him some sort of comfort in that he was possibly going to stay alive.

Jack was disturbed in his recollections of the previous night by a knock on the door. The same butler that he had met the previous day was standing there dressed in a dark suit with tails and a waistcoat.

'Mr Riordan is expecting you downstairs now, sir. The car is waiting outside to take you to the airport.'

About fifteen hours later, as his connection from Lima had been slightly delayed due to fog, Jack stepped down the retractable stairs from the twin propeller aircraft and walked across the runway tarmac at Cusco Airport having had plenty of time to digest what Riordan had said to him during the drive to the airport before he had left England.

Riordan had passed him an envelope and had said he would be met at Cusco by an ex-mercenary called Malkie McNeishe who was looking after his business interests in Peru and it was through Malkie's army connections that he was able to fly the cocaine paste out of Peru without any intervention from the authorities once they had been paid off. He had explained that in Peru every official had their price and if you didn't pay them off it would be impossible to run a successful drug business.

He had said that the envelope contained the last three numbers of a bank account that held the money he owed the Peruvian Maoist rebel group, the Shining Path, for the next shipment of coke and he was to give the envelope to Malkie. Riordan had been getting a bad feeling about Malkie recently and wanted a fresh set of eyes he could trust to keep an eye on him. He wasn't sure if Malkie had got into bed with the Shining Path and that he might be getting a bit too greedy. Riordan suspected that Malkie might be ripping him off and he wanted Jack to watch him like a hawk and see if his suspicions were true.

There didn't appear to be too many people Riordan trusted – Skeggsy and now this guy Malkie.

As Jack strolled across the tarmac in the hot midday sun the high altitude sucked the air from his lungs and he started to feel dizzy. He began to develop a pounding headache; he had read in a magazine on the plane that Cusco was 11,152 feet above sea level and even Olympic athletes could become dangerously ill if they weren't careful. The article had gone on to explain that a lot of people assume the ancient historical Inca site of Machu Picchu is higher than Cusco and that you have to acclimatize before going to Machu Picchu, whereas Machu Picchu is actually at an altitude where you are unlikely to have any problems at all as it is only 8,000 feet above sea level.

Jack couldn't help but laugh when he had read that the Andean people consider chewing coca leaves sacred and that it helps to overcome altitude sickness. There was no way using 'sacred' as mitigating circumstances for a coke charge would stand up in court back in London.

Jack was getting more and more irritated with having to use the crutch as he hobbled across the arrivals hall and was thinking about how he would break every bone in Davey's body when he glanced over and saw a tanned man wearing aviator sunglasses. The man had a wide grin on his podgy face which was almost hidden under the dense foliage of a large brown handlebar moustache. He was holding a large card in front of his bulging chest with *Mr Reynolds* written on it in a childlike scrawl.

Jack hobbled up to him and asked, 'Malkie?'

'Aye, that's me, laddie.' The man replied in a thick Scottish accent which Jack tried to place whilst he watched the man's huge moustache move up and down as he spoke.

'Let's get this straight from the start. My name is Jack, not laddie. Okay?'

'Aye, makes no difference to me, laddie. Come on, let's get out of this shithole'

Jack couldn't help but warm to the brash Scottish man with the wild fanny duster on his top lip who gestured for him to follow him out of the airport. He asked himself if anyone wore aviator sunglasses anymore, apart from Jim in the Kings Arms who was a confused Tom Cruise fan. He decided that the answer to his question was a big 'No' and followed the large Scotsman out through the exit doors where Malkie immediately climbed into a black Range Rover SVR which was parked right outside.

Jack nervously took a quick look around before he climbed up into the back seat of the brand new Range Rover. On opening the door he found himself staring at a scrawny young Peruvian man who said his name was Carlos. He was wearing a Foo Fighters t-shirt and scruffy jeans and smiled at him with a big toothless grin, flashing what was left of a couple of ground down yellow stumps in his mouth which looked like they were going to fall out of his gums at any moment. Malkie sat in the front of the car and said something to the driver in a language which Jack didn't understand. The driver started laughing and turned the stereo volume up a couple of notches as the car pulled away and he eased the Range Rover into the flow of the busy lunchtime Peruvian traffic.

After about two hours of careful driving up steep winding mountainous roads, they eventually turned off the main road and drove for what seemed like hours down a small bumpy mud track which took them deep into the Amazon forest but the drive was probably no more than ten miles due to the roughness of the terrain and density of the lush green forest. During the journey Carlos had continually smoked some foul cheap smelling tobacco and constantly chewed coca leaves which he periodically spat in large lumps out of the window. Jack was relieved when they finally arrived at a small grassy clearing and the Range Rover suddenly screeched to a stop as it meant he would have a break from looking at Carlos' grinning face staring silently at him and also it meant a break from the stench of Carlos' rotten breath.

Malkie shouted something and Carlos leant over Jack and opened the door whilst suddenly pushing him out of the Range Rover in one simultaneous movement.

As Jack tumbled out, falling painfully onto the hard ground, he shouted, 'What the fuck?'

'Carlos, search him for weapons but don't hurt him,' Malkie shouted.

'Malkie, what the hell is going on? Get this scrawny little monkey off me before I flatten the prick.'

Ignoring Jack's shouting Carlos started to run his hands up and down Jack's body, he grabbed him by the balls with his right hand and gave a hard squeeze to let him know that he understood English a little bit.

Malkie shouted back, 'Don't worry, laddie, it's just a precaution, you could be DEA, NCA or even Tactical Anti-Drug Operations. You could be any sort of prick and I need to watch my back as it's very fucking dangerous out here.'

Malkie then said something in Peruvian to Carlos who immediately forced Jack to the ground by kicking him in the back of his bad leg which made Jack scream in pain and he fell writhing in agony to the floor. Carlos roughly dragged him back up into a kneeling position by his shirt and pulled out a Ruger Blackhawk .357 Magnum handgun from inside of the waistband of his dirty jeans.

Jack screamed every expletive he could think of at Carlos as waves of pain from his leg shot through him like bolts of lightning and just a split second before Carlos hit him in the side of the head, knocking him unconscious with the butt of the pistol. His eyes caught the sight of Malkie's podgy face grinning and laughing as his head fell into the mud-soaked ground.

CHAPTER 32

Daryl Rice stood shivering on the Albert Embankment beside the banks of the River Thames, he was thinking about Jack. He blamed Jack for putting his career on the line and, to top it all, Jack had vanished into thin air and hadn't reported in for four days now. His handler, Gazza, hadn't heard anything either and the last contact the NCA could trace was when an interest marker was triggered on the Border Agency database at the airport because Jack had used his passport. Daryl thought to himself, *The lunatic has just discharged himself from hospital, he still has some explaining to do over that fiasco, and yet he's now jetting off abroad on an unsanctioned trip.*

Daryl could feel his hernia kicking up and took a deep drag on a cigarette. He'd given up smoking for six months but the stress Jack was putting him under with his wild antics had made him take up the dirty habit again.

Earlier that morning, at about half past eight, Daryl had been sitting at his desk in the NCA building pondering on what he would do with himself if he lost his career, when the ringing of his mobile had interrupted his train of thought. He hadn't recognised the number but answered it immediately, hoping it might be Jack calling so that he could give him a piece of his mind.

Unfortunately, the call hadn't been from Jack, but it had resulted in him now being stood beside the banks of the Thames waiting for the Clipper ferry to arrive and he had a horrible sinking feeling in his gut that he may live to regret having answered his phone.

Two blasts of the ferry horn signified its arrival and Daryl waited for it to dock beside the jetty's gangplank which was swaying wildly from side to side in the blustery wind. In the distance next to Vauxhall Bridge, Daryl could see the Secret Intelligence Service MI6 building referred to locally as 'Babylon-on-Thames' due to its resemblance to an ancient Babylonian ziggurat.

The phone call he had received earlier had probably been made from inside that very building.

Through the rain he saw the figure of the caller, DI Peter Steele, standing on the starboard side of the Clipper looking directly at him. Steele was sheltering from the wind dressed in a black knee-length raincoat with a cigarette cupped in one hand whilst he tried to hold his flat cap on his head with the other.

Steele had rung Daryl and asked to meet him here at ten o'clock but had stressed that he couldn't discuss the subject on the phone for security reasons. Daryl had tried to ascertain what the meeting was about, but Steele had refused to reveal anything and had also demanded that Daryl didn't mention his phone call to anyone and to keep their meeting a secret.

Daryl was unsure why Steele wanted to meet him off the record without DI Scally present and, more importantly, it seemed a little odd that he wanted to keep the DCI out of the picture as well. All in all, there was something that didn't seem quite right about this secret meeting on the Thames and it was starting to make Daryl sweat nervously even in the freezing cold.

He hoped the meeting would provide the necessary intelligence he required from MI6 to salvage his undercover operation, because as far as he could tell the whole operation surrounding Jack was going down the proverbial pan quicker than a dodgy curry on a Friday night.

The perversity of 'walking down the gangplank' wasn't lost on Daryl as he climbed onto the ferry, jostling amongst the foreign tourists who immediately got out their selfie sticks and started taking ridiculous photos of themselves posing in silly postures against the impressive outline of the City.

Daryl had been careful in making sure that he wasn't followed but didn't want to risk any security leak by being photographed on the Clipper so, pulling his raincoat over his head to hide his face, he pushed his way past the selfie sticks forcing the tourists out of his way and walked over to the stern and sat down.

The ferry wasn't very spacious and the journey across the Thames would only take about fifteen to twenty minutes depending on the roughness of the river swells, so Daryl stayed sitting on the wet bench and anxiously waited for Steele to make contact. He used the time to check to see that he couldn't spot any other agents on the ferry or anything that looked like it was a possible trap. His mind was playing games on him and his nerves were making his stomach growl. However, he found himself laughing at how secretive and melodramatic some of the MI6 agents who didn't work out in the field acted, they were the 'plastic coppers' of the Secret Service.

After five long minutes, Steele finally came over and sat down beside Daryl who was becoming more impatient by the second.

'So what's all the cloak and dagger crap about then, Steele?' Daryl asked.

'Call me Peter.'

'Okay, Peter. What the fuck is all this about? I'm a busy man and could do without playing at sailors on boats in crap weather like this. It's freezing out here, if you hadn't noticed.' To emphasise the fact, Daryl rubbed his hands together and blew on them, the warm moisture from his breath misting in the cold air.

The Clipper cut through the rough waters of the Thames as it made its way to the opposite bank of the river and bounced the two men about on the hard wooden bench. As Steele steadied himself for the next surge of the Clipper as it crashed through the water, he reached inside his raincoat and took out a large envelope and passed it to Daryl.

'I think you should look at the contents of the envelope and then we can discuss a proposition that I have.' Steele had to shout into Daryl's ear so that he could be heard above the wind and the noise from the twin-engines of the ferry.

Daryl didn't like the tone in Steele's voice. He took the envelope in his hand and waited a few seconds before cautiously tearing it open. He then slid out from the envelope what appeared to be colour photos. Some were close-ups and some appeared to have been taken with the help of a telephoto lens from a long distance. What was very apparent to Daryl was that it was his face staring out at him from every single one of the photos he was holding in his hands.

As Daryl stared intently at each of the photos he felt a tightening in his stomach as a wave of nausea swept over him which he knew wasn't from suddenly developing sea sickness.

'This is just a small selection of photographs that my employer has and obviously these are not the originals. You can keep these and stick them in your photo album.'

Daryl ignored what Steele was saying to him as he struggled to digest what he was looking at and how anyone had managed to take the extremely incriminating photographs. There were images of Daryl in various sexual poses, some were sadomasochistic and he was either tied up naked playing a bondage whipping game with a whore or else having sex with young vulnerable children. In some of the photos there were young girls looking as though they were screaming in pain and begging him to stop hurting them. There were even photos of him sodomising young boys. In every photo the children involved looked no older than twelve years old and Daryl felt himself go as white as a sheet.

He had always known that it was risky to visit prostitutes and he'd tried to stop, but it had become more than fantasy; it was an addiction. He'd become obsessed with sex ever since his daughter, Alice, had been killed in a multiple car crash on the M25 motorway three years ago and he had been forced to take six months off work with depression. Since returning to work, his obsession had taken a more sinister twist and he'd gotten involved with the child prostitution scene in and around London. It had been easy for him to find like-minded people when he had access to criminal files on the NCA computer and he had quickly sunk further into depths of depravity which he had never previously envisaged.

'You're very photogenic, Daryl. We even have you on video, but I don't think that you're likely to win any BAFTA's.'

Spluttering, Daryl whispered, 'What.....where......how the fuck did you get these? Oh Christ, I think I'm going to be sick.'

Steele patted Daryl on the back and said, 'I need you to listen very carefully or else you will be going to prison for a very long time. I hate men like you. You disgust me and if I had my way I'd cut your balls off and leave you to bleed slowly to death. But luckily for you it's not my decision.'

'What.... are you going to do? I didn't mean to hurt anyone.'

'Stop whining, you pathetic piece of shit!' Steele shouted at Daryl. 'My employer is concerned that an operation you are running may have an adverse effect on certain activities that he is concerned with. You have an undercover operative known as X4 and my employer wants him taken off the case immediately. I'm instructed to give you forty-eight hours or else these photos will land on DCI Smith's desk.'

'How the hell am I meant to do that? You know very well that the case involves MI5 and 6 and stretches across different continents.'

The ferry horn blasted twice to announce its arrival at the jetty and drowned out DI Steele's reply.

Steele then turned away, walking quickly towards the gang-plank leaving Daryl sitting with his head in his hands, crying like one of the little children in the photos whose lives he had destroyed.

CHAPTER 33

The deafening noise sounded like a van's diesel engine and the continual jolting as it was being driven over bumpy terrain had woken Jack up. The noise didn't help as he had the headache from hell from when Carlos had cracked him on the side of the head with the pistol butt and the noise of the van was amplified inside the confined space he now found himself in. When he'd opened his eyes, the first thing he saw as his blurred vision had begun to clear was the outline of Carlos sitting opposite him, still grinning inanely. Gripped in his hand was the pistol he had hit Jack with and it was pointed directly at his stomach.

They were no longer in the Range Rover and had switched vehicles. Jack had no idea how long he'd been knocked out cold for and could see that he was in the back of a van and, more worryingly, Carlos was not the only person pointing a gun at him. His heart missed a beat as he counted four other men sitting with them who were all dressed scruffily in jeans and t-shirts, which appeared to be their standard uniform, all of them heavily armed with semi-automatic weapons. They looked like they weren't going to be very interested in any complaints that he might want to make.

'Carlos, where the fuck are we going? Where's Malkie?' Jack demanded.

Carlos laughed and spat a soggy lump of coca leaf out of his mouth onto the floor and said, 'No hablo Inglés.' The other men in the van laughed.

'Bollocks. You dirty piece of shit you understood that perfectly,' Jack shouted at the grinning Peruvian. As he shouted, the other men in the van raised their rifles in unison and directed them straight at him. Carlos grinned even more and laughed loudly.

Inside the back of the van Jack could see that the four men were sitting in front of a huge pile of kilo slabs of coke. Jack estimated that there must have been at least half a tonne of powder in the van. The slabs had been pressed and cut into kilo sizes and then sealed up tightly in a clear vacuum plastic which had then been wrapped up tightly in brown insulating tape to protect them from any damage. Jack guessed that each kilo slab had been covered in a solution which would fool any customs dog anywhere in the world.

During his time working for the NCA he had learnt that the drug smugglers could easily evade the detection of a customs sniffer dog. It was an old wives' tale that the authorities liked to get across to 'Joe Public' that a dog's sense of smell was a thousand times stronger than a human's and that they couldn't be fooled by any substance.

In reality, dogs possess up to 300 million olfactory receptors in their noses, compared to about six million in humans and this means that the part of a dog's brain that is devoted to analysing smells is, proportionally speaking, forty times greater than that of a human. But their sense of smell can be massively reduced by certain chemicals and the smugglers use these chemicals to fool the sniffer dogs when transporting their cargo of drugs.

The van screeched to a stop and the rusty back door of the van was opened with a grating noise that set Jack's teeth on edge. As his eyes adjusted to the sudden sunlight which streamed into the van, he heard Malkie's voice barking out orders in what he guessed was Spanish.

Malkie appeared at the back of the van and said to Jack, 'Get your arse out of the van, laddie. You can take a stretch and have a piss but don't wander too far as my men are watching you and the little fuckers can be a bit trigger happy. They're very suspicious of any gringo as transporting this powder shit puts food in front of their children. I've been dealing with these people for three years and they still don't fucking trust me. It must be the Scottish in me; nay cunt trusts the bloody Scots.'

The four gunmen sprung out of the back of the van and Carlos followed them leaving Jack sitting there, unsure of his next move.

With the back of his hand, Malkie slowly wiped away the sweat which was dripping down his face in the blazing sunshine onto his moustache and said, 'Are you going to get out of the van, laddie, or do I have to drag you out myself? If you're wondering about Carlos whacking you around the head again with his favourite gun, don't. He just gets carried away sometimes. I give you my word that as long as you behave yourself you're safe whilst you're here as my guest. I apologise for the method of getting you here, but you must understand that there's a lot at risk here and this is a fucking dangerous country. If I wasn't here to protect you, you'd already be a dead man.'

Jack scrambled out of the van, dragging his injured leg. He stumbled, but Malkie grabbed him by the arm to hold him up and passed him his crutch.

'Right, let's go meet the main man then, laddie. I wouldn't want Mr Riordan to think I've been fucking anyone around and wasting his favourite employee's time now, would I?'

'Neither would I. Mr Riordan will be very interested to hear how helpful you've been,' Jack answered with a heavy hint of sarcasm. 'I hope we don't have to walk too far as my leg hurts like fuck after your toothless monkey kicked it.'

Blinded by the bright sunlight, Jack shielded his eyes with the palm of his hand and could see that the van had stopped on the edge of what appeared to be some sort of military compound. There were four large green camouflaged canvas tarps which had soldiers sitting under them idly shielding themselves from the hot sun. The tarps surrounded an enclosure which had been cut into the forest and about one hundred yards away from where Jack stood he could see the enclosure widened into a thin grassy clandestine airstrip which eventually fell off the edge of what looked dangerously like the precipice of the mountain.

Jack felt decidedly uneasy as he watched groups of heavily armed men loading large hessian sacks full of kilos of processed coke into trailers attached to quad bikes. The scale of Riordan and Malkie's operation was far bigger and appeared a lot more organised than the information gathered by the NCA and cross border services had suggested.

Malkie shouted to Jack above the noise of the quad bikes and trucks which were transporting the drugs towards a small twin-engine plane sitting on the airstrip, 'The coca paste is flown out from Colombia to here in Peru where it is manufactured into high grade cocaine and I have a little dabble with selling some of the paste on as Mr Riordan doesn't pay me enough to risk my balls every day. Okay, so I sell a little of the paste on the side to the Venezuelan's but every pound of coke Mr Riordan buys is accounted for and I guarantee safe delivery for him when the finished product is shifted out of here. I'm not a fucking idiot, laddie. I know that tight-arsed Mancunian bastard sent you out here to check up on me and you can go back home and report back to him that I'm not ripping him or anyone else off. It's just basic economics in this dangerous environment and if I add ten pounds of gear for myself to each flight out of this hell hole, so fucking what.'

Reynolds didn't have a chance to reply to Malkie, not that he wanted to after Malkie had seen through the reason why Riordan had wanted him in Peru. Malkie had already turned away and started walking towards the largest tarp closest to the airstrip and shouted over his shoulder, 'We haven't got much time so follow me, the gear has to be airborne in fifteen minutes and the army can't stay here too long protecting us from the other rebels. It doesn't matter what you pay them, they are only as corrupt as the next person. A mercenary is a mercenary but when you bribe the local army it's a whole different ball game, laddie.'

Following Malkie, Jack wished that he didn't still need the crutch. He limped painfully over the uneven ground as fast as his gammy leg would allow him. The pain was excruciating and he hoped that before he left Peru he would find a moment to explain to Carlos the art of breaking bones, and this time it would be Carlos that would feel the pain.

As they reached the camouflaged enclosure two of the soldiers guarding the entrance raised their rifles and shouted, 'Gringo, adónde vas?'

Malkie replied, 'Okay, laddies. Calm yourselves down, the man is with me and we have a meeting with Ramos.'

A spitting noise could be heard from inside the tarp and then a voice shouted something which Jack couldn't understand but he did catch some words, 'bastard' and 'Malkie' and then the two soldiers roughly pushed them both into the enclosure using the barrels of their rifles as persuasion.

Sitting opposite them behind a trestle table which had six large lines of coke laid out on a mirror was a man who, if Jack hadn't blinked twice, he would have thought was the reincarnation of Pablo Escobar, the notorious Colombian drug lord who, until his death in the early 90s, had supplied the United States with over eighty per cent of its cocaine.

The man in front of him was dressed smartly in light sandy trousers and a white cuff-linked shirt which was unbuttoned nearly all the way down his hairy chest which had shiny streaks of sweat dribbling down it in the ferocious heat. The man called 'Ramos' had a small but bushy moustache which was hidden behind a huge cigar. The polished look was neatly finished off with a pair of expensive Italian leather shoes and a large diamond encrusted Hublo watch dangled from his left wrist.

'Malkie, my good friend. Better late than never. I trust this man is a friend of yours and has something for me from our partner overseas in rainy England?'

Jack looked at Malkie who nodded his head at him and quietly hissed, 'Give the man the envelope then.'

Jack had decided earlier on the flight from England that he wasn't going to trust Malkie with the envelope that Riordan had given him and his instinct had proven him correct. He felt more in control of the situation dealing directly with this 'Ramos' character. He had a sneaking suspicion his cards may have been marked and he might have ended up dead if he'd given the envelope to Malkie at the airport. Gut instinct had told him he was more likely to stay alive if he personally dealt with the leader of the Shining Path. The envelope was his bargaining tool and he would hand it over when ready.

Jack said, 'Can I have a cigarette please?'

Ramos clicked his fingers. One of his uniformed bodyguards walked over and gave Jack a cigarette from a packet he had in his combat jacket pocket; the bodyguard then stood there waiting patiently whilst Jack also borrowed his lighter.

Malkie glared at Jack, thinking he was taking the piss and pushing things too far with Ramos.

Inhaling the smoke in a long deep breath, Jack winced as his lungs burnt in the high altitude before he said, 'My employer, Mr Riordan, has instructed me firstly to ensure the quality of the product, secondly he wants assurance that the route the product is transported through is completely safe and that all government agencies will turn a blind eye. He's not paying for the product until it arrives at the agreed destination safely. Mr Riordan is aware that the United States has reopened its friendship with Peru and any planes flying over unauthorised airspace will be shot down by government agencies. This is a major worry to him.'

Ramos flicked the tip of his cigar and some segments of the ash fell onto his shiny Italian shoes but he looked unconcerned. He smiled and said, 'Please, Mr Jack, you are a guest in my beautiful country and I welcome you. I want you to be assured that all government agencies have been taken good care of and the route the product will take is completely safe. I give you my personal guarantee that I will cover any loss should the product not reach the destination. Please enjoy a line of coke with me and then I will explain further my assurances and show you around just a small part of my operation which is hidden throughout the mountains of Peru.' Ramos then shot a look at Malkie and said, 'Malkie, please wait here whilst I show our guest around.'

Ramos stood up and as he did so his bodyguards raised their rifles, but with a wave of his hand they obediently lowered them again. Ramos leant over the table and using a rolled up 100 dollar note he loudly snorted a long line of the coke that was already chopped up on the table. He then snorted a second line before passing the note to Jack who quickly hoovered up the fattest line left on the table to help calm his frayed nerves. Before Jack had lifted his head up from the table he could feel the euphoria from the high purity coke rush around his body and his legs started to shake from its effect. He felt an indescribable rush which set him on edge leaving him with small goose pimples all over his skin. He had never snorted cocaine that pure before.

The rollercoaster of coke rushed through his brain sensors as he followed Ramos out of the enclosure. He tried to focus on Ramos explaining how he managed to move the coke to Puerto Limon on the Caribbean side of Costa Rica and then onto drop points like Pico Island in the Azores, where he then promised that he could guarantee the safe delivery of the product as far as Portugal, which was where Riordan had agreed it would be collected for onward transportation to Ireland and

England. Ramos appeared to take great pride in the scale of his operation and wasn't shy about explaining the intricacies of his wholesale global drug dealing network to Jack.

After they had walked to the airstrip Jack decided that in order to stay in favour with Ramos he should give him the envelope from Riordan which contained the missing bank numbers. Ramos gave him a big smile and said to him, 'My friend, not all of you gringos are what we call Gilipollas or I believe in your language the word is wankers. Unlike your associate Malkie. I tolerate him because of our mutual business interests but it has been a pleasure to meet you. Please give my best regards to Mr Riordan and reassure him that I am positive we can continue to do business together. Now, let's watch the plane take off adding more money to our off shore bank accounts and then I will arrange some safe transportation so that idiot Malkie can take you back to Cusco airport.'

Jack's spirits rose on hearing the word airport, he'd been in Peru long enough and was going to buy a flight to Dublin as soon as he got to the airport. He would call Riordan and tell him his flight back had been diverted or something.

Ramos walked to the edge of the airstrip followed by Jack who stood beside him watching the last of the coke being loaded onto the light twin-engine Piper Aztec airplane. He was surprised how large a load the airplane could take as he watched it turning around to get ready for take off.

Eventually, the plane's engines burst into a high-pitched roar and as the last sack of coke was loaded on, Jack watched a tall muscular man climb up into the plane and as he turned to pull the aircraft door shut Jack squinted his eyes and thought that he recognised him. He had seen the confident gait and stature before, but couldn't place it at first. His mind raced faster than the aircraft as it sped down the airstrip increasing speed by the second and then it hit him. All of his childhood memories came flooding back as he thought he recognised the passenger in the plane.

Luke Grainger, or 'Lanky' as he had known him.

CHAPTER 34

For once it was a bright sunny day in Dublin and even though there was a slight chill in the air Amy felt warm all over. She had managed to score a ten euro bag of heroin from a small-time dealer known as Shades. Shades lived in a squat on Bachelors Way, down beside the River Liffey, above what used to be an old plumbers merchants which had at some time been converted into flats.

Amy's life had spiralled completely out of control in the last couple of weeks. She'd lost her place on the law course at university shortly after losing her room in halls, she had no idea where Luke was, she wasn't sure if the Gardai had a warrant out for her arrest, and she was relying more and more on drugs to get her through each day. Reflecting back over the last few weeks, she really didn't think her life could get much worse.

Suddenly she felt a vibration in her pocket and took out her pay-as-you-go phone which was set to vibrate as well as ring when someone called or texted her. She saw Luke's name on the screen and paused a second before deciding to answer.

'Hi, babes, where are you?' Luke cheerfully asked before Amy's screaming voice interrupted him.

'Don't you *babes* me, you arsehole. Where the fuck have you been? I've really needed you and yet you just disappear without any explanation. What, now you think you can ring me up and act all casual as though nothing's happened.' It wasn't a question.

'Whoa, calm down, Amy. I had a little bit of business to attend to and I had to earn some cash to spend on my beautiful girl, didn't I? I wanna take you out, let's have a party.'

Amy felt her empty pockets and knew that she'd spent her last bit of money on the bag of smack that she had bought earlier that morning from Shades and now that was already nearly all gone.

'You'd better not be lying to me, Luke,' Amy warned him.

'I'm not, babes, but don't ask me how I got the cash,' Luke said shiftily.

Amy's resistance weakened and sighing she said, 'Alright, meet me opposite the Parnell monument on O'Connell Street in about an hour, say about one o'clock?'

'I'll be there waiting for you, I promise.'

Amy put her mobile back in her pocket and pulled up her parka hood to keep the freezing wind from numbing her ears, the wind chill factor making her feel cold even though the sun was shining.

Though she wouldn't let on to him, she was happy that Luke had come back. She felt safe when he was with her. She smiled as she thought how she could never stay angry with him for long.

Waiting near the Parnell monument an hour later, Amy finished her rollup and was feeling twitchy because the heroin she'd smoked that morning was beginning to wear off and it was also annoying her that Luke was late. If he didn't turn up soon she didn't know what she'd do. Her body was badly clucking for more smack.

She looked across the street and watched all the happy couples and families walking along the pavement wrapped up in their warm clothes and their warm lives. She felt jealous of them, and vulnerable. At the thought of one day being happy again, a small tear dropped out of the corner of her eye and slowly ran down the gaunt lines in her once youthful-looking face.

Her attention was broken by a voice she recognised shouting out at her. 'Do you want to get in or what?'

Amy looked up and saw Luke grinning like the cat who'd got the cream. He was sitting in the driver's seat of a silver Mercedes CLK with leather seats and a dark mahogany wood trim interior. Luke shouted, 'Hurry up or the coppers'll nick me for parking on a double yellow line.'

Amy rushed over and opening the passenger door jumped into the Mercedes and gave Luke a big hug as she strapped the seat belt across her skinny frame.

'Where the hell did you get the car from?' Amy asked, dreading the answer.

'I borrowed it, didn't I. Now stop all the questions will you, everything will be alright and I'm going to take my princess out for the day.'

Luke had his phone on bluetooth and was playing *Machine Gun Kelly* in the car. The song *TILL I DIE* pulsated through the top of the range quadrophonic speakers and the deep base sound began to float around the inside of the car. Amy leant over and nestled her head against Luke's shoulder as they drove across the O'Connell Bridge which took them across the River Liffey towards Trinity College and Temple Bar. The area they drove through was where the students in Dublin hung out and Amy felt a pang of regret as she knew that her student days were probably over for ever.

Amy asked Luke where they were driving to but he just smiled and passed her a joint from his shirt pocket saying, 'Light this, darling, and listen to the music, but go easy on the spliff as the weed's been soaked in a bit of ketamine and it'll spin you right out into a 'K hole' unless you're careful.' Amy couldn't believe how brilliant it was to be back with Luke and the weed and ketamine he had given her would keep her prayer bones from rattling too much from the smack with-drawal she was experiencing. She took a deep draw on the joint as she relaxed back into the folds of the luxurious leather seat of the Mercedes and closed her eyes. She started to drift off to sleep as she listened to the sound of the booming bass swirling around inside her head searching each emotional corner of her brain as the rap music complemented the weed.

They hadn't been driving for too long before the sound of a police siren disturbed the tranquility of the music playing through the expensive sound system in the Mercedes. Amy looked through the back window and assumed the Garda car with its siren on and lights flashing would overtake them and waited for Luke to pull the car over and let the police car pass. But she suddenly lurched back into her seat as Luke dropped the Mercedes down a gear and rammed the accelerator to the floor so that the car quickly started to speed away.

'What the fuck are you doing, Luke?' Amy screamed. 'I thought you said you'd borrowed the car?'

'Yeah, I had, but I didn't say who off, did I? I'm sorry, I nicked it this morning from down by the docklands.' Luke braked hard and took a sharp right hand turn hoping that the police car behind them would miss the turning. Unfortunately, he had completely misjudged the turning and as he put his foot on the brake the car lurched to one side, virtually taking off the ground, and careered across the road in a lift off oversteer. The music had stopped and Amy started to scream as almost in slow motion the back end of the Mercedes swung out and an oncoming taxi hit the left hand side full on, crushing the passenger door where Amy was sat strapped in.

Amy's head jerked backwards and then forwards, violently slamming into the windscreen. The force knocked her out cold as the car spun round again and then rolled over three times. The Mercedes eventually came to a stop embedded in the front wall of a pensioner's living room. The shocked pensioner was fortunately cooking his lunch in the kitchen at the time.

CHAPTER 35

Malkie had eventually driven Jack back to Cusco Airport and during the whole journey he'd tried to justify to Jack that ripping off Riordan was just a perk of the job. Jack had quite liked Malkie at first but after spending the last few hours with him he was glad to see the back of him.

Flying out of Cusco was a lottery as due to the altitude it was possible to be stuck there for days depending upon the fog. Jack's luck was in and he managed to get a flight which was leaving to the capital Lima in one hour, he also bought a connecting flight direct to Dublin.

He found a small bar with access to the internet and immediately emailed Stan asking him to meet him at Arrivals in Dublin. With the wind behind he reckoned the flight was around fifteen hours which meant he should be in Dublin by lunchtime the next day. Looking at his inbox he could see he'd received numerous emails from Sarah, he quickly scanned through them to see if Sarah had heard anything from Amy. No news; except Sarah was furious with him because he hadn't contacted her. As Jack heard the last call for his flight he quickly emailed Sarah saying he was in Ireland but hadn't found Amy yet. There was no need to add fuel to the fire by telling her he'd been delayed flying to Ireland and was actually in Peru.

Walking through Arrivals at Dublin Jack saw Stan's floppy blond hair and thought how little he had changed compared to Jack who nowadays was sporting a few wisps of grey hair.

'Thanks for meeting me,' Jack said, shaking Stan's hand which crushed his own in Stan's vice-like grip. Stan was a strong man and stood well over six feet tall.

'No problem, glad to be of help. The car's outside. I've taken the liberty of booking you a hotel, you must be shattered and need a clean up after the flight?'

'Cheers, but I probably won't need it. Let's get into Dublin and on the way you can fill me in on what you've found out.' Jack followed Stan towards the exit.

Stan's driving hadn't improved since his army days when he'd often accidentally crashed tanks through houses. Jack found himself gripping the dashboard each time the car braked. If Stan didn't pay more attention to the other cars on the road it would be a miracle if they stayed alive long enough to find Amy.

Whilst they drove towards Dublin Jack stared out of the misty car window and it struck him that Amy could be lying unconscious in any one of the houses they drove past, she could be being raped at this very moment or even worse, dead.

Turning to look at Stan he said, 'I want you to take me to every squat you know she's stayed in. We're going to kick some doors in and some fucker out there must know where she is. I've tried the Gardai but as she's over eighteen they're not interested, so it's up to us.'

'Okay, but be careful, some of these places are bloody dangerous and the last thing you need is some deranged junkie stabbing you with an infected needle,' Stan said looking at Jack and instantly regretting what he'd said. 'I didn't mean Amy,' he stammered.

'It's alright, no offence taken,' Jack replied returning to staring out of the window at the brightly painted weather beaten houses.

They drove along in silence for a short while. The quiet was a pleasant respite for Jack and it gave him time to gather his thoughts after what had been a whirlwind of a couple of days. The airport was north of the city centre and ten minutes later they turned off the M50 to head into Dublin. After another ten minutes Stan stopped the car outside a derelict pub which had been boarded up.

They got out of the car. Stan leant his elbows on the roof of the car and looked at Jack saying, 'According to my snitch this is the most recent squat Amy has been staying in. I can't say the information is one hundred per cent reliable but it's the best we've got.'

Around the back of the pub they found a door which had previously been forced open and went in, the place was a wreck. There was graffiti all over the walls and it smelt more like an abattoir than where people actually lived. They searched the downstairs but found nobody so they continued their search upstairs. This must have been where the owners once lived when the pub had been a thriving den of inequity.

Without any warning a scared voice shouted out from the dark, 'What the hell do you want?'

They peered down the darkened corridor and could see in the shadows the shape of a young junkie holding a broken pool cue as a weapon, he looked terrified.

'Don't worry, we're not Old Bill,' Stan lied. 'We won't hurt you, you can drop the pool cue. We're looking for a young girl, she's about the same age as you and might be in trouble. Her name's Amy, Amy Reynolds, do you know her?'

'I dunno, I might do but I ain't no grass,' the young junkie said shiftily sensing something in it for himself.

Jack took a step forwards towards the dubious young junkie and held out a twenty euro note.

'Listen, Amy is my daughter and she's in trouble, all I want to do is find her. No come backs on you. Freckles, mousey coloured hair, have you seen her?'

The young junkie snatched the note from Jack's hand saying, 'You might want to try Bachelors Way down by the river, I think she went there to score this morning.'

'Score off who?'

'Some dude called Shades or something, hey, have you got another twenty?'

Jack gave him a tenner saying, 'Don't spend it on any gear, go and get yourself a meal. Oh, and by the way, thanks.' He then nodded towards Stan and they rushed downstairs back to the car.

It didn't take long to drive down to the river. Stan knew where Bachelors Way was and more importantly he told Jack that he'd heard of this guy Shades and knew where he lived.

Stan parked the car a little down the road from where Shades lived. Jack explained to Stan that it wasn't his call and he'd done enough; he didn't want him to jeopardise his job any further so he would go up to Shades' flat by himself.

Jack found himself standing outside an old door with the paint peeling off it, he was sure from the information that Stan had given him that this was the flat. Stubbing out his cigarette on the floor with his foot he pressed the door buzzer. It didn't work so he knocked on the door with his knuckles.

A deep Irish voice emitted from behind the door, 'Yeah, coming, who is it?'

'Ah, come on Shades, open the door, I'm fucking desperate,' Jack shouted trying to imitate how a junkie might act.

The door opened ajar slightly and using the weight of his shoulder Jack forced it open. The man behind the door staggered back from the force but didn't fall over so Jack headbutted him and then kicked him in the groin.

'I'm only going to ask you once, is your name Shades?' Jack shouted at the man sprawled on the ground. The man had a cut across his nose from where Jack had butted him.

'You bastard, you've broken my nose.'

'That'll be the least of your worries unless you tell me what I want to know. Do you know a young girl called Amy, freckles, mousey hair?' The man gave a shriek as Jack kicked him in the stomach to stop him getting up.

'Probably, I think so. Is it that scrawny girl who got kicked out of uni?'

'Maybe,' Jack growled feeling his temper rising further.

'She was round here earlier, but from what I hear I won't be seeing her again as she died in a nicked car which demolished a house earlier this afternoon. Shame really, the bitch still owes me twenty euros.'

All of the colour drained out of Jack's face as he struggled to comprehend what he'd just heard. He leant over Shades and whispered in his ear, 'My daughter isn't a bitch,' he then punched Shades with all of his strength full in the face knocking the drug dealer out cold.

Jack fell against the wall with tears streaming down his face; wailing he slowly slid to his knees in despair crying his heart out.

CHAPTER 36

When Amy woke up she had a nasal oxygen tube strapped to her face and her left arm was raised in a sling. It didn't take her long to realise that she was in hospital again. The pain in her arm was excruciating and when she tried to cough her ribs stabbed her in her left lung and she screamed out from the pain.

A huge man with a friendly smile rushed into the room on hearing her shout out and said, 'Amy, try to keep calm. You've been in a bad car crash and are in St Vincent's Hospital.'

Amy looked at the big man with black platted hair and thought she recognised him, but couldn't remember where from. Then it came to her; he was the male nurse who looked after her when she'd been brought in after her overdose.

'Hello Johnny,' Amy said reading his name tag and attempting a smile. 'I can vaguely remember the car crash. How's Luke, my boyfriend, the guy I was with?'

Johnny grimaced and said, 'Whoever was in the car with you isn't a friend. When the ambulance crew got to you, your friend had scarpered and left you for dead.'

'What? I don't believe you. He wouldn't leave me.'

'Well, you were found alone in a crashed stolen car and the police will be wanting to speak to you about it.'

Amy struggled to comprehend what the nurse was saying, she couldn't believe that Luke would have run off and left her for dead.

'There must be some explanation, you're lying,' Amy shouted, not knowing whether she was trying to convince herself or the nurse. One thing was for sure she was angry with Luke and started to cry.

Johnny ignored Amy's petulant comment and in a monotone voice continued, 'You were bought into the hospital alone. You were in a terrible state with broken bones protruding from your forearm and suspected fractured ribs. As you had an open fracture we had to get you down to surgery immediately. You're lucky to be alive.'

Amy started to shake and tears streamed down her freckled cheeks as though they were in a race to drop off her small dimpled chin.

Johnny's face softened as he walked around the side of the bed to hand her a tissue from the box on the wooden side cabinet.

Suddenly the door to the room burst open and a stocky man in his early forties walking with a crutch rushed in. Johnny was just about to restrain the man and call security when Amy shouted, 'Dad!'

A nurse followed into the room quickly behind the man and looked at Johnny pleadingly saying, 'I tried to stop him, but he wouldn't listen.'

'It's alright; he's the patient's father. I think we should give them a few minutes alone.' Both nurses left the room closing the door behind them.

'Christ, Amy, I thought you were dead.'

Amy pulled the bed covers over her painfully fragile frame as her father leant over the bed attempting to give her a cuddle. She shook him off not wanting him to feel her skeletal frame. Rejected her father turned and slumped down on a chair beside the bed.

'Dad, I don't understand, how did you find me?'

Her father looked at her with tears in his eyes and started to explain. 'Your mother and I have been worried sick about you;

your mother contacted your tutor who told us he hadn't seen you in ages and that he had to exclude you from the course.'

Amy gasped and winced with the pain from her ribs at the same time. 'So you know about me losing my place...'

'I pretty well know everything, and the bits I don't know I can piece together. You're in a whole load of shit, young lady, but we will talk about that later. All that matters right now is that you're safe.'

'But how did you know I was in hospital?'

'Once I discovered you were in trouble I flew out to Dublin and went to some of the squats you've been staying in. What the hell were you thinking? You should've called us? Why didn't you answer our calls?'

'I, I .....' Amy stuttered.

'After visiting a few shitholes I tracked you down to some dealer's place, his name was Shades and he said you'd been killed in an accident.'

'Oh my God, really?'

'Yes, thank god you're alive. I didn't know how I was going to break it to your mother, not that this'll be easy either but it's better than telling her you're dead.'

'I'm so sorry, Dad. I never meant for any of this to happen.'

'Don't worry about that now, Amy. I'm just relieved you're alright. An old army mate who works with the security services over here has been helping me track you down. When we heard the Gardai had been chasing a stolen car which had crashed and the passenger fitted your description we rushed straight down here. I was a wreck. If it wasn't for him I would never have found you. He's outside now squaring your arrest warrant with the senior detective involved and hopefully he can persuade him to drop all the charges, including the theft and the assault from a few days ago.'

'Oh... You know about that as well.' Amy lowered her eyes from her father's face. She began to feel a little foolish thinking that she could have kept her problems hidden from her parents forever.

'I also know about the drugs. Your druggie mate Shades told me you were dead. How could you, Amy?'

'Everything just got on top of me.'

'Don't worry about it darling, we'll talk about this later. I'm going to see if the warrant has been dropped and I'll speak to the surgeon to see how long before you can be discharged.'

Amy's father stood up, he leant over the bed and gave Amy a kiss on the forehead and said, 'Get some rest, kitten. I love you.' He then walked out of the room.

Amy pulled her knees up to her stomach as far as her damaged ribs would allow and sobbed hysterically. She was so happy to see her father but she knew her mother wouldn't take it so well. She was likely to kill her.

CHAPTER 37

During Amy's stay in hospital Jack could have sworn that he'd seen a man lurking around near Amy's room but each time he'd tried to catch the man he'd disappear quickly down the corridor out of view. Jack's bad leg had stopped him from running after the man – he'd definitely recognised his gait though. He thought he might have been mistaken in Peru, but all of his NCA training and instinct had told him that he couldn't be mistaken. It was definitely Luke 'Lanky' Grainger. He wondered what Luke was doing in the hospital and why he kept his distance but Amy was his priority at the moment.

Three days later Amy was allowed to leave the hospital. Stan had somehow squared things with the Gardai and, in the interest of good cross-border relations, the warrant for Amy's arrest was rescinded. Stan had then driven Jack and Amy to the airport where they were fast tracked onto the plane and Jack had thanked Stan for all of his help, promising not to wait so long next time to get in touch.

After landing at Gatwick Airport, Jack paid for one of the extortionately expensive airport taxis to take them to Sarah's house where she was waiting expectantly to a give Amy a huge hug followed by a huge telling off. As the taxi drove up outside Sarah's house, the front door opened and Sarah came running out barely giving Amy a chance to get out of the car before she started to hug her and smother her with kisses.

'Careful, Mum,' Amy said as she tried to stop Sarah aggravating her injuries. The neighbours would almost certainly be watching Sarah crying and would be wondering what all the commotion was about. Amy's cast and bandaged head, together with her panda-like black eyes, would certainly give them something to gossip about.

'I'm sorry, darling,' Sarah said, letting Amy go. 'Come on, let's get your bags and get you inside.'

Jack put Amy's sparse belongings inside the front door of Sarah's house and gave Amy a kiss whilst whispering in her ear that he loved her as he started to get back in the taxi. Sarah looked at him and shouted, 'Where the fuck are you going? I need you here with me, we have a lot to discuss and we need to get to the bottom of what the hell Amy's been up to.'

Trying to calm Sarah down Jack looked at her and replied, 'Amy's been through a lot in the last few weeks and I think that right now she needs a little bit of time alone with her mother. She's very fragile and needs to know that we both love her. I have some things to sort out workwise but I'll be back later on this evening to see how you both are.'

The fight went out of Sarah's eyes as she wiped away a tear explaining, 'I didn't say it earlier, but thanks for finding Amy. I just wish your damned job didn't always have to come first.'

'I'll be back this evening, Sarah. Go easy on Amy.' Jack sighed as he closed the taxi door and gave the driver directions to his flat. As the taxi drove away Jack thought to himself that family life was never going to be the same again. Amy wasn't his little girl anymore, she was an adult and the big wide world could be a nasty place to live in sometimes. At least for now she was safe.

Jack arrived back at the flat and picked up the mail off the doormat, most of it bills, hate mail he called them. There was one thick envelope which drew his attention, he opened it and inside were his keys from the valet company together with a very expensive bill.

Jack limped towards the sofa suddenly realising he had left the crutch in the taxi, not that he cared as he hated using it anyway. He'd found leaving Sarah and Amy difficult but urgently needed to make some phone calls and the quicker he made them the sooner he could get back to looking after his family.

He decided that he would call Riordan first before he called Gazza or DI Rice because he knew that using his passport would have alerted the cover team to the fact that he was back in the country anyway, so they could wait a little longer before he contacted them.

The phone had only rung twice before Jack heard Riordan's strong Mancunian accent growl, 'Is that you, Jack?'

'Yes, Mr Riordan.'

'Where the fuck have you been? Malkie said that you left Cusco nearly a week ago.'

'I was delayed by fog for twenty-four hours and I had an infection in my leg from the stab wound. I've spent the last few days in hospital,' Jack lied, trying to cover his tracks about the last few days in Ireland.

'Well next time I send you on a job I want to be kept informed of your whereabouts otherwise you may find that you won't have the use of either leg for very long,' Riordan replied menacingly.

'I'll try to remember that, Mr Riordan.'

'Good. Have you spoken to Skeggsy at all?'

'No, not yet. I was going to give him a call shortly,' Jack replied, getting the feeling that Riordan had something on his mind and it involved Skeggsy.

'Don't call the idiot. Leave him to me. He's gone completely overboard this time. All that powder up his nose and the fucking steroids the nutter sticks in his arse have sent him crazy. That thieving toe rag Sean is dead and Skeggsy has gone and started a turf war with Big V who's after his blood. There used to be an understanding between myself and Big V that we leave each other's business interests alone, but recently his lads have been trying to tax my business interests. The word around South London is that if anyone does business with Skeggsy they're a dead man. So you can see why I have concerns, can't you?'

'He killed Sean?'

'It doesn't matter what he did. The prick went too far and is causing problems for some major families in London. He's out of control.'

'Is there anything you want me to do, Mr Riordan?'

'No. Just call me if you see or hear from him.'

The phone went dead and Jack limped to the toilet changed SIM cards in the phone and flushed the one he'd just used down the pan. Quickly returning he fell back on the sofa from the effort.

He couldn't believe his luck. Skeggsy's days in the gang looked like they were numbered and Riordan trusted him more than Skeggsy now. So even with all of the trouble that Amy was in, Jack felt his dampened spirits lifting slightly.

Time was of the essence, he had to call Gazza. He needed to arrange a meeting at one of the many NCA safe-houses. These nondescript flats or businesses were where runners met the undercover agents and debriefed them. The general public would never have guessed what was going on behind the doors of any of these premises.

Jack rang the number for Gazza and waited for him to answer.

'Hello, is that you, X4?'

'Have you missed me?'

'Don't take the piss. The Governor wants you in as soon as possible. He's annoyed with you jetting off abroad without the trip being sanctioned. He's ordered me to get you in for a debriefing on what the hell you've been up to.'

'I guessed as much. I can't wait,' Jack replied sarcastically. 'Where and when?'

'Just be at Wickes' car park in Dorking at ten o'clock tomorrow morning, we'll do the rest.'

Jack knew that meant they would sweep him up in a van and drive him to a safe-house but at least the meeting was tomorrow, which meant he could spend some quality time with Amy and Sarah beforehand.

CHAPTER 38

Jack's bringing Amy safely home had made Sarah ecstatically happily but he'd ruined the moment when he announced he was going back to the flat to make some phone calls. Sarah was seething with anger and frustrated that Jack couldn't understand his job was the biggest stumbling block in their relationship. She could just about put up with the drinking but each time he worked undercover his character changed and she couldn't live with him when he was acting like that. In her eyes she felt that his job always came first and his family second.

When they had first been married they were blissfully happy and Amy had been a doting little daddy's girl. Sarah couldn't put her finger on exactly how or when, but over the years the once happy family unit had somehow descended into the chaotic mess that it was today.

Sarah loved Amy, but as most of the time Jack had been away working it had fallen to Sarah to try to instill discipline in Amy whilst she was growing up. In this regard she felt a complete failure. She didn't know what she was going to with Amy but all that mattered was that she was safe.

Since Amy had come home she had been a virtual recluse and had stayed in her bedroom, only coming out to take H for a walk in the mornings. There were so many questions Sarah wanted to ask Amy when suddenly her thoughts were interrupted by the sound of Amy's footsteps coming down the stairs.

'Amy, you're awake, how do you feel darling?'

'How do you think I feel?' Amy said feeling tired and irritable from lack of sleep and needing a hit of smack as the drugs from the hospital to combat her heroin addiction had eased off.

'Amy, please don't be like that. We need to talk.'

'Don't go on Mum,' Amy moaned, turning back upstairs to her bedroom.

Sarah followed Amy up the stairs desperate to talk to her and this turned out to be a massive mistake.

Sarah's attempt at trying to stay calm had ended up in a furious shouting match with Amy who had told her to fuck off, saying that she hadn't come home to take all of this crap and Amy had grabbed H by the collar and said she was taking the dog for a walk to calm down.

Sarah was upset with herself for losing her temper. She poured herself a glass of white wine in the kitchen. She needed to calm down. She didn't usually drink during the day, but today was a little bit different and she persuaded herself that if Jack could drink during the day then why couldn't she? As she gulped instead of sipping the wine the phone in the front room began to ring. She put the glass down on the kitchen table and went over to answer it.

'Hello?'

A warm deliberate voice replied, 'Sarah, it's me.'

Sarah's legs went weak and she almost collapsed on to the sofa. It had been a long time since she'd last heard the voice on the phone and she'd honestly never thought that she would hear it again.

'Sarah, are you still there?'

Sarah hesitated for what seemed like an eternity before she bought the phone back up to her mouth and whispered, 'Yes, Luke.'

'I know I promised to never contact you again, but you must listen to what I have to say. It's important and it's about Jack.'

'What about Jack? You promised to leave us alone. Our affair was a stupid mistake and he must never know.' Sarah could hear the fear and agitation in her voice. 'I think he's had his suspicions and he often says to me it's strange how you just disappeared out of our lives without saying a word even though you two had been virtually glued together since you were kids. He's always said to me he believes there's more to your disappearance than meets the eye. It's almost as though he knows what we did and is giving me the opportunity to come clean. The guilt has nearly destroyed our relationship.'

'I know, Sarah, I'm really sorry for all the damage I've caused, but believe me I wouldn't have called unless I had a very good reason. Jack's in danger and I need to meet him.'

'Danger. What do you mean?'

'I know that he works for the NCA and he fucked up by going on an unsanctioned job abroad. I don't want to go into detail but I think he's seen me a couple of times which may have compromised us both. The people we're dealing with are extremely dangerous and would think nothing of putting a bullet in his brain if they discovered he was working as an undercover.'

'Oh Christ.' Sarah couldn't take it. Not now, not with Amy only just back safely. 'Not now, Luke. Please don't tell me this. It can't be true.'

'It is Sarah and I need him to meet me in Ireland otherwise we're both dead men. It won't take these guys long to look into our backgrounds and make a connection, however good our cover is. I'm probably a dead man anyway, but if I can, please let me save Jack's life.'

Sarah let out a small sob.

'Sarah, just tell him to meet me tomorrow at Durty Nelly's pub at one o'clock. Jack knows where it is. Our parents used to take us there in the summer holidays and get bladdered. Please, Sarah, you must understand this is a matter of life or death.'

The phone went click. The call ended just as the doorbell rang and the noise nearly made Sarah jump out of her skin. Sarah rushed to the door and opened it. Jack stopped her as she fell into his arms crying hysterically.

CHAPTER 39

Jack listened to the whirring noise as the flaps rose up from the plane's wings creating a vapour trail. Then there was a series of banging noises as the landing gear doors opened and finally the wheels were lowered and clicked into place. After circling Shannon Airport twice due to the backed up air traffic created by the dense fog, the plane eventually descended and there was a loud roar from the slowing engines as it landed with a jolt on the runway.

The day before, Jack had got the shock of his life when he'd rung Sarah's doorbell and she'd opened the door in floods of tears and rambling incoherently. Two large glasses of wine later, Sarah had calmed down enough for Jack to just about make sense over what she was repeating about Lanky's phone call.

Jack knew it had been him he'd seen. Until the other day, he hadn't seen Lanky for years. The last time was a year or so after they'd served together in Bosnia where Jack had been injured then medically discharged from active service.

It was all too much of a coincidence seeing Lanky twice in recent weeks. And now the guy had phoned Sarah out of the blue saying that he needed to meet Jack at Durty Nelly's.

He'd always had his suspicions about Lanky and Sarah, but this wasn't the time to dwell on it. Lanky was clearly involved somehow in Riordan's operations and who knew which side of the law he was on. But he'd said Jack's life was in danger and he believed that his old friend wasn't lying.

It must have been thirty years since Jack had last flown to Shannon Airport and he hardly recognised it as it had now expanded into a transatlantic gateway between Europe and America handling over 1.7 million people each year.

Jack was pleased to go back, but saddened at the reason for his return to Shannon. What did make him smile was the fact that DI Rice's sweep up team would be sitting in Wickes' car park for a long time waiting for him. Rice would throw a fit when he discovered that he'd flown back out to Ireland and chosen to ignore his order to be bought in for a debriefing.

Having passed through Customs without any interference, Jack was again greeted by the blond straggly mop of hair which covered Stan Wacameyer's head. Stan smiled and said, 'When you said let's get together soon, I didn't reckon on us meeting again quite this soon.'

Jack laughed replying, 'Neither did I, Stan. Thanks for coming.' He shook Stan's hand and said, 'Shall we get going then? I'll explain on the way.'

Stan drove down the N19 and then onto the N18 towards Bunratty which was about twelve kilometres from Shannon, situated between Limerick and Ennis. Jack looked out of the window and gazed at the unspoilt rolling green countryside of west Ireland. He cast his mind back to when his parents used to holiday in the area every year and Lanky's family used to tag along as well.

They used to visit beautiful places like Galway and the lakes of Killarney which were all an easy day trip from Bunratty. Their parents always rented a converted barn on Old Man Kelly's farm, a few kilometres outside of Bunratty. Old Man Kelly had lost his wife to cancer about fifteen years ago and then about five years ago he'd been diagnosed with cancer as well. After a long and painful illness he had also died and the farm had become an empty ruin.

As they drove, Jack explained to Stan why he'd returned to Ireland so quickly but was careful not to tell him too much as he didn't want to compromise Stan's safety. Stan turned his head whilst trying to keep one eye on the road and said, 'You always did like trouble. Even in Bosnia you were the one who went out looking for a firefight with the enemy and never waited for them to come to us.' Stan took one hand off the steering wheel and reached into the inside of his jacket. He tossed a pistol into Jack's lap saying, 'You might need this, just to be on the safe side.'

'Thanks, Stan. You're a fucking diamond,' Jack said, taking the Beretta M9 in his hand and checking it over.

'Don't worry, it's untraceable. I got it off a US army buddy of mine who has a small sideline in selling firearms.'

Jack quickly put the Beretta in his pocket. In the distance he could see the fifteenth century Castle of Bunratty looming at them over the brow of the hill. Lanky had said to meet him at Durty Nelly's which was a pub found next to the castle beside the banks of the River Raite. Durty Nelly's dated back to the 1620s when it had originally been built as a bar for the castle guards to use when they were not on duty.

Stan parked the car and Jack got out, dropped his cigarette on the ground and stamped his foot on the butt end. He stretched his arms out wide. It had been a long morning so far and his tired body was no longer the well-oiled fighting machine that it used to be. Stan locked the car and before they went in the pub they both stood still for a second looking at the impressive sandy yellow building which was famous throughout Ireland for its welcoming atmosphere.

The two men walked across the old stone floor which together with the naked wooden beams gave a timeless quality and feel to the pub. Stan found them a small wooden table in the corner of the main bar and Jack went to order some drinks at the bar. As he stood there, all of his childhood memories came rushing back to him and he could remember his father drunkenly singing along to the music played on the piano as they warmed themselves beside the log fire which roared with huge flames long into the night.

A stocky middle aged man with scroll tattoos on both arms and a long plaited ginger beard which nearly reached his belly button approached.

'Can I have two pints of Guinness please?' Jack asked, looking around the room for Lanky.

The man started to pour the drinks and Jack said, 'There's one thing you may be able to help me with. I'm meant to be meeting a friend from England but it doesn't look like he's here.'

'Jack Reynolds, is it?' The man interrupted in a subtle Irish accent inconsistent with his imposing appearance.

'Yes, that's right.'

'Thought so.' The man smiled, flashing some gold dentures. 'Your friend said you'd have a wobbly leg and that you were from across the water. He said to tell you to meet him at the farm at half-past one, nothing else, and you would know what he meant.'

'Cheers,' Jack said, picking up the pints and putting some money on the bar. 'Keep the change.'

Jack passed Stan his pint and sat down at the table. Neither man said anything for a while, they just looked around the pub and inconspicuously drank their pints whilst trying to blend into the atmosphere and look like two innocent tourists having a quick drink.

Jack broke the silence. 'I appreciate everything you've done for me Stan but I need one last favour. I need to borrow your car for an hour.'

'But—'

'But nothing, Stan. It's too dangerous for you to come along and you've risked enough for me already. If your bosses find out that you've been helping me you could lose your job – or worse.'

Stan took his car keys out of his pocket and slid them across the Guinness-slicked table. Jack downed the rest of his pint in one go and picked up the keys. He nodded at Stan saying, 'Lanky left a message at the bar to meet him at an old farm near here at half-past one and it's nearly that now. Stay here, I shouldn't be too long. If I don't come back or haven't rung you by three o'clock then the shit's hit the fan and you should get the hell out of here and forget you ever saw me.'

Jack put his empty pint glass on the table and walked quickly out of the pub before Stan could say anything that might make him change his mind.

Old Man Kelly's farm was only a ten minute drive and Jack parked the car outside the front gate and approached the farm entrance cautiously on foot. It was too late now but he realised that he was wearing his favourite expensive leather brogue shoes which weren't the sort of footwear to go trudging around a muddy wet farmyard in. He could see a new four wheel drive Jeep parked near the large farmhouse which was ramshackle with broken windows and half of the roof had caved in. It certainly didn't resemble anything that Jack could remember from his childhood. He hoped that the Jeep belonged to Lanky but as he crouched down and stealthily walked towards it, he slipped the Beretta from out of his pocket and felt the comforting cold firm steel in his hand. His eyes darted from side to side scanning the area for any movement.

Jack reached the Jeep and opened the passenger door. It was empty but still had the keys in the ignition. Using the Jeep as cover he shouted out, 'Lanky, it's me Jack.'

There was an eerie silence abounding the farm which was only broken by Jack's laboured breathing from having smoked too many cigarettes over the years, and there was no reply from Lanky.

Out of the corner of his eye Jack noticed that there were two dead dogs beside the tractor in the old cow barn and as he walked over he could tell that it wasn't malnourishment that had killed them. Their brains had been splattered around the barn by the velocity of the bullets pumped into them. He carefully sidestepped the pools of blood, trying not to stain his shoes.

When he came to the front of the tractor, he stopped in his tracks. His blood turned to ice and his stomach churned at the sight which confronted him.

The corpse was lashed with razor wire to one of the large wheels of the tractor with a pitchfork sticking out of its forehead. Where the eyes should have been there were gaping holes where they'd been gouged from their sockets. The face no longer resembled anything human and the jaw was locked in a final scream of pain as the last breath of life had finally left the agonised body.

There was a large wound stretching all the way down the sternum which exposed the inside of the ribcage into which there had been inserted an oxy-acetylene torch. The body had been disemboweled with the torch and the innards had spewed out all over the ground in a gruesome mosaic.

The body was mutilated almost beyond recognition, but Jack knew it was Lanky.

He reeled back in a state of shock and emptied the contents of his own stomach all over his leather shoes. His survival training skills brought him back to reality and he ran out of the farm, darting from side to side in case there were any snipers ready to take a shot at him. He vaulted the gate and falling hard on his bad leg he limped as fast as he could to Stan's car.

The car engine strained as Jack pushed the small 1.6L engine to its maximum. He drove with one hand on the steering wheel as he called Stan on his mobile with the other. He shouted, 'Stan, Lanky's dead, are you still at the pub?'

'Shit... I'll meet you outside.'

A few minutes later Jack came screeching into the car park with the wheels of the car on full lock and nearly ran Stan over as he braked hard.

Opening the passenger door Stan asked, 'Is anyone following you?'

'I don't think so.'

Stan looked straight at Jack and shouted, 'I don't know what sort of trouble you've got yourself into but get out; I'm driving.' Stan jumped in grabbing the steering wheel and drove whilst Jack tried to describe to him the horror that he had discovered back at the farm.

Stan said, 'I'm going to take you to a friend's house. He's an ex-mercenary and you'll be safe there. I'll get the mess at the farm cleaned up. There are loads of splinter terrorist groups killing each other all the time over here and the murder will be put down as tit-for-tat crap and all that. I just need you to stay low for a while until I can arrange to put you on a protected caveat list so you can get on and off a plane without any keen young copper or an immigration twat nicking you.'

'Cheers, Stan. I owe you one.'

Stan replied, 'You know when I said let's meet again soon? Well can I take that back? It's probably best we don't meet again for a very long time after this.'

Jack couldn't understand why someone would want to torture and murder Lanky, but he had a feeling that the trail led to his involvement with Riordan somehow. Had someone discovered that Lanky knew Jack from a past life?

As they drove, Jack scratched the scar on his left cheek which had been made by Lanky accidentally shooting him when they were kids. He racked his mind for a possible reason for the murder and the thought struck him that Riordan had used an oxy-acetylene torch to avenge the death of his brother, Big Dougie.

With a feeling of dread Jack knew that Lanky's death had put him in mortal danger but he didn't know who from.

CHAPTER 40

Skeggsy lit his tenth cigarette and it wasn't even ten o'clock in the morning. Every time he injected speed it made him smoke more than a bonfire did on Guy Fawkes' night. He'd been sat in the car for three hours and yet again he watched the young girl leave the house with the black dog at around the exactly the same time as she had done for the last two days. Each day he had followed her when she walked the dog. She was a pretty girl but too thin for Skeggsy's taste. He liked his women with a bit more meat on them and her breasts were far too small. He guessed that she was going to walk the same route with the dog as she had for the last couple of days. He started the car engine and watched as the girl disappeared down the road out of sight before he drove off.

It wasn't long before Skeggsy parked the car on the corner of Hampstead Road opposite the entrance to the Nower Heath and waited. On Tuesday he'd been in a pub near Dorking and couldn't believe his luck when a taxi driver he knew who occasionally delivered drug packages for him had told him he'd picked up a fare and surprisingly the fare had been Jack and a young girl. The taxi driver had told him that the girl looked as though she'd been beaten up or in a car crash as she had a cast on her arm and a bandage wrapped around her head. What was even more interesting was that he had said the young girl was Jack's daughter.

Amy sang to H as they walked up the steep road. She used to sing to H when she was a child and it was a habit she couldn't stop. She felt at peace when she was alone with H and even the craving for drugs went away for a while. As she reached the top of the road, a car door opened and a large man with short ginger hair got out and looked directly at her with his piercing blue eyes. H started to bark loudly and Amy shouted at him to be quiet and calm down.

Amy smiled at the man and said, 'I'm sorry, he isn't normally like this with strangers. He's quite friendly really.'

The man smiled flashing his yellow cigarette-stained teeth and said, 'Don't worry, Amy. All dogs seem to bark at me for some reason.'

Amy felt a spike of dread run down her spine. The man knew her name. With as much confidence as she could muster, she asked, 'I'm sorry, do I know you?'

Skeggsy punched Amy hard in the face and there was a crunching of bone as her nose splintered from the force of the punch and she was already unconscious before her head hit the ground. He picked up her limp body and kicked the barking dog out of his way as he threw Amy into the boot of the car. Looking around to make sure nobody was watching he took a syringe out of his pocket and, rolling Amy's sleeve up, quickly injected the needle's yellowish fluid into her already needle-ravaged arm before slamming the boot of the car shut on her motionless body.

He pulled a knife out of his pocket and turned towards the dog which was still barking loudly at him and was probably going to start attracting unwanted attention soon. But as he walked towards the animal with the intention of silencing it, the dog turned tail and ran off down the road.

The traffic hadn't been too bad and it had taken just over an hour for Skeggsy to reach Tower Hamlets. He'd wrapped Amy up in an old dust sheet and had carried her limp body up to his third floor flat which he'd kept on since the violent death of his mother. Nobody knew about the flat as far as he was aware and quite often he took solace in using the flat as a bolt hole to get away from all of the pressure that came with the violent world that he lived in.

Amy came to lying on a bed and immediately tried to scream but it was pointless. She had a gag tied around her mouth and her wrists and ankles had been secured with plastic ties.

'Stop struggling,' Skeggsy told her from across the room. 'You'll only make the ties hurt more and nobody can hear you. Even if someone heard you shouting they wouldn't do anything. In this area people know better than to butt into other people's business. You'll be safe as long as you behave yourself. I'm not interested in you; it's your scumbag copper of a father I want.'

At the mention of her father, Amy screamed a muffled obscenity through the gag and furiously tried to break free of the plastic cuffs. It was useless and after a few minutes she shrank back on the bed, sweating profusely from the effort she'd exerted.

Skeggsy laughed at her pathetic struggling and pulled the tourniquet tight around his arm before he injected another gram of speed mixed with a little coke to give him a stronger hit. As he injected himself, Amy whimpered in the corner watching him with fear and, he noted, a little envy.

Amy was looking around the bare room. Her eyes locked on the photo standing on the small antique cabinet in the corner.

'Beautiful isn't she?' Skeggsy said. 'She was my mother and she was raped and then brutally murdered. The police were useless and didn't even attempt to catch her killer. They thought that her death was just one less whore to worry about.'

Looking away from the photo, Skeggsy saw a large yellow stain spreading across the white bed sheet underneath Amy's shivering body. He jumped up and walked across the room towards her. He raised his hand and hit her with the back of his palm across the face shouting, 'You dirty bitch. Those sheets were clean on this morning especially for you.'

Amy shook with shame and fear but managed to shout through the gag a muffled, 'Fuck you.'

Skeggsy lit another cigarette and said, 'Calm down, Amy, I want you nice and relaxed whilst I explain what you are going to say to your father when we ring him in a minute.' Then, using the camera app on his phone, he took a photo of Amy tied up on the bed.

Jack had managed to fly back from Dublin two days later and had rushed straight to the mortuary. He breathed in the Trigene disinfectant and ignored the sound of Eddie, the young pathologist, chomping on his sandwich.

He looked down at Lanky's body on the mortuary slab and tears welled in his eyes. It hardly even resembled a human being. He was grateful to Stan who had managed to fly the body back to England almost straight away. Stan had used his police connections to cut through all of the usual red tape and Jack had used his NCA connections to gain access to the mortuary.

It was a murder enquiry and Jack couldn't get involved without blowing his cover, which grated on him as he had a good idea who murdered Lanky even if he didn't know why.

His phone bleeped and he could see that it was a picture message from Skeggsy. Opening it Jack froze and could hear his heart pumping the blood around the veins in his body. He stared in horror at a horrific photo of Amy tied up lying on a filthy bed when his phone suddenly rang - it was Skeggsy.

Before Jack could say anything Skeggsy said, 'Hello, Mr NCA. Don't bother denying it, you prick. I have someone here that I think you might want to speak to before I kill them and then come after you.'

Before Jack could say anything he heard the sound of a girl crying and Skeggsy shouting something, then a voice came on the phone. 'Dad? Please help me, I'm so scared.'

Jack felt a sharp pain in his heart as he listened to Amy's fearful voice pleading for help.

'Amy. Are you OK? Has he done anything to you?'

Amy whimpered in response.

'Don't worry. Just do whatever he says and I'll get you home safely as soon as possible.'

Skeggsy's snarling voice came back on the phone. 'Cute little thing your daughter, not really my type but I might just make an exception in her case.'

'If you touch her . . . If you harm one hair on her body, I'll fucking kill you, you ginger prick,' Jack shouted.

'There's no need to be rude, if you carry on like that she might just end up like your friend Luke,' Skeggsy said laughing. 'I'll call again tomorrow and let you know what I want. I've got to go as I've got a little party planned for tonight with your daughter.'

The phone went dead.

CHAPTER 41

The drive back from the mortuary to Dorking passed in a complete blur to Jack. All he could hear going over and over again in his mind was Amy's voice desperately begging him to help her. He'd only just got her back from Ireland in barely one piece and now this. The problem was that this time it was a lot worse than any filthy crack or smack den. It was Skeggsy calling the shots and calling him a loose cannon was an understatement.

The more Jack thought about it as he broke the speed limit racing down the A3 in his Audi, the more all of the pieces of the jigsaw started to fall into place. Jack had always thought Skeggsy had the potential to be a dangerous lunatic, but he had never thought that he would come up with the notion of kidnapping Amy and on the phone he'd also virtually admitted to murdering Lanky. The scaffolder turned coke thief, Sean, had also been murdered and Riordan was acting all cagey about needing to talk to Skeggsy.

It all started to make sense. Somehow Skeggsy had got to Lanky and in his crazy mind he'd added up two and two and it had come to eight. He'd discovered Jack was NCA and that Jack and Lanky knew each other, so he had needlessly murdered Lanky. Skeggsy was now completely out of control and was more than likely going to murder Amy unless Jack could find a way to stop him.

Everything was suddenly falling around Jack's ears like a game of Jenga when the loser's wooden blocks crash to the floor and the whole undercover operation stank of there being a leak in the NCA somewhere. Putting a leak from the NCA or any other security agency to the back of his mind, Jack knew his priority was to get Amy away from Skeggsy's clutches using whatever means he had to, legal or otherwise. Either way, Skeggsy had just signed his own death warrant as far as Jack was concerned.

Swearing at himself for forgetting to fill the car up with petrol Jack pulled into a petrol station beside the chicken roundabout. As he got out of the car a large van with blacked out windows pulled up beside him, before Jack had a chance to ask the driver to move the van a little the sliding door opened and two sets of arms roughly dragged him into the van.

Lying in the back of the van, Jack looked at Gazza, his cover officer, who was bent over double swearing.

'Bloody hell, Jack, there was no need to punch me in the bollocks.'

'Sorry, Gazza, but you should know better than to jump me without any warning. You're lucky I didn't do more damage.'

'I'll let my wife be the judge of that,' Gazza said starting to laugh through the pain.

'I haven't got time for this Gazza,' Jack shouted, as every minute wasted put Amy in more danger. 'Let me out, I'll report in tomorrow.'

'Sorry, no can do. My orders are to take you to a safe-house in Reigate. I think I'd better warn you that DI Rice is waiting to see you and he's spitting bullets. Whatever you've done, the shit's really hit the fan. I've never seen the DI so pissed off.'

'Well fucking hurry up then or else I'm going to kick off and God help you if you try to stop me.' Jack threatened menacingly and threw the Audi's keys at Gazza adding, 'Park my sodding car somewhere safe as well.'

Fifteen minutes later the van stopped in a small car park behind a newly decorated block of flats. Jack followed Gazza out of the van and into the flats where they took the lift to the third floor. As Gazza put a key in the lock of flat nine he looked at Jack and whispered, 'Good luck.'

The inside of the flat was a hive of activity, there were three plain clothes officers sitting at a large table with headphones on their heads. In front of them was a vast array of electronic surveillance equipment with a mass of dials and flashing lights which meant very little to Jack.

DI Rice was pacing up and down the room shouting loudly into a mobile phone which was stuck to his ear. He took one look at Jack and without stopping shouting into the phone he clicked his fingers loudly and pointed towards a sofa in the corner, indicating where he wanted Jack to sit.

After a couple of minutes, DI Rice ended his phone call and sat down in a chair opposite Jack. Rice stared at Jack for a few seconds without saying a word and then shouted, 'Who the fuck do you think you are, Robocop?'

Before Jack could answer the DI leapt out of the chair and leant over him. His face was so close to Jack that Jack could see the burst blood vessels in the whites of his eyes. 'You directly disobeyed an order to come in and have repeatedly not kept myself or your cover officer informed of the progress of this operation. You're a fucking liability.'

'Sir…'

'Don't bloody "Sir" me, you tosser.'

'Okay, I know I haven't reported in as often as I should've, but the shit has really hit the fan. It's a matter of life and death, I've got to get out of here. I'll explain everything later in my report.' Jack pleaded with his superior, desperate to try and find Amy. Out of the corner of his eye Jack could see Gazza sitting at the table with the other officers. He was smirking and whilst he was looking directly at Jack he made a slow cutting motion with his hand across his throat.

Rice shouted, 'I've got DCI Smith chasing my arse for a result and guess what? I can't even tell him where my undercover is as he's pissed off abroad without any sanction and I haven't got a fucking clue what he's doing. This whole operation has been jeopardized by your uncontrollable behaviour and probably illegal actions for all I know. I mean all I am is your DI, for fuck's sake.'

'But, sir…'

'Shut up, Jack, I haven't finished yet. There are other security agencies involved and I can't put the operation at risk with a jumped up out of control undercover acting like Rambo. From now you're suspended pending an enquiry from Internal Investigations.'

'You can't do that. I've spent more than three years of my life risking my balls for you and we're so close to busting Riordan.'

'I just have. Gazza please show Jack out.'

'Fuck you then,' Jack shouted at the DI and stormed out of the flat.

Jack didn't bother with the lift. He ran down the stairs as fast as his bad leg would allow. He was almost sliding down the bannisters in his hurry to get outside. Jack had already worked out that there was a leak from inside the NCA and with Rice pulling him off the job when they were so close to nailing Riordan's gang, it had really started to stink of some sort of a cover up. His mind was racing in overdrive and all of his senses told him that there was something seriously weird in his being pulled off the case just for acting out on a limb. He was meant to be undercover, for Christ's sake.

As Jack burst out of the back entrance to the flats, he saw Rice's silver Mercedes SLK. Jack glanced around and couldn't see anyone watching him so he quickly slid his body along the wet ground underneath the Mercedes and, pulling a black box nearly as small as a box of matches from his pocket, he attached it to the underneath of the car. The box bleeped once when

Jack turned the tracker on and he smiled knowing that the tracker was so advanced in technology that there was nowhere a slippery eel like Rice could go without Jack being able to know his every move.

After what seemed like an eternity Gazza came out of the lift. Jack was standing beside the van they had driven to the flats in. Scowling at Gazza as he unlocked the doors he said, 'You took your bloody time. I told you I've got to be somewhere.'

'Well, the DI hadn't finished throwing his toys out of the pram and wanted to have a go at me for letting you run around like a headless chicken. You might think it's funny but he's going to give me every shitty boring surveillance job he can think of for the next six months. My wife's going to kill me as that twat will have me working every evening and weekend that he can, just to massage his ego and to prove who's the boss. You don't have to work with him every day, Jack, he can be a real dickhead and he can really make your life hell if he wants to.'

'Fair point. Look, Gazza, for what it's worth I'm sorry if you feel that I've dicked you about and screwed up the job. Christ, nobody feels as bad as I do. I've spent a long time risking my prayer bones on this job and we're so close. It'll probably be back to traffic duty for me or, if Rice has his way, I'll be out of the NCA and sleeping with the drunks under some viaduct by the Thames Embankment. Problem is I haven't got time to fuck around with Rice's ego, just drop me off quick will you.'

As Gazza quickly drove Jack back to his Audi where they had swept him up, Jack lit a much needed cigarette and thought about what had just happened. Breaking the thought processes down in his head he reached the obvious conclusion that Rice pulling him off as an undercover was bullshit and there was more to it than just his erratic behaviour. Rice was hiding something from him and he was going to find out what it was. There was no way he was going to roll over and just forget the last three year's work infiltrating Riordan's criminal gang, especially since it had now put his family in mortal danger.

Jack was determined to use every NCA and police contact he knew to help him get Amy home safe and unharmed. It didn't concern him whether he was a serving NCA officer or not and he swore to himself that Rice had better watch his back. If he discovered that Rice's incompetence had resulted in just one tiny hair on Amy's head being out of place, Jack knew he would be adding Rice's name to the same list as Skeggsy's.

CHAPTER 42

The previous night Sarah had drunk nearly two bottles of wine, which was a lot more than she would normally drink. She'd been upset after arguing with Amy. Her emotions were all over the place at the moment and it wasn't due to the early onset of the menopause.

Sarah's earlier elation at Amy's return home hadn't lasted long and she had soon come crashing back down to earth with a bump after Amy had stormed out of the house taking H with her. She had waited all day for Amy to return. Sick with worry Sarah eventually fallen asleep drunk on the sofa.

A violent headache from the wine had woken her up and after quickly swallowing two headache tablets she'd rushed upstairs to see if Amy had come back whilst she'd been crashed out on the sofa. She looked in Amy's bedroom but wasn't sure whether her bed had been slept in and Amy was nowhere to be seen. Sarah was now frantic with worry and a hundred different thoughts raced through her mind. What if Amy had run away and bought some drugs? What if she had overdosed? She could be dead in a ditch for all she knew.

As she ran back down the stairs she could see a large black shape through the frosted glass in the front door. Her heart missed a beat thinking it could be Amy's body, cautiously opening the door she looked down and stared into the large eyes of H.

H barked and ran between her legs into the house, leaving a trail of muddy pawmarks on the clean hallway floor. Sarah looked all around outside, calling her name over and over, but there was no sign of Amy.

She had felt a cold shiver of fear run down her spine. H would never leave Amy's side unless there was a very good reason. He was an incredibly loyal dog and he had a strong bond with Amy.

Sarah rushed into the living room looking for her mobile. She grabbed her handbag and in her rush turned it upside emptying all of the contents over the floor. Amongst the useless clutter that she kept in her bag, she spotted her mobile and, picking it up, immediately rang Jack's number, praying that he would answer and it wouldn't go straight to voicemail.

Her prayers were answered when Jack's voice came on the phone.

'Jack, it's Amy. She's gone.'

Jack had dreaded Sarah ringing him. He knew he should have called her himself but he'd been putting it off, hoping that he could get Amy back safely before Sarah discovered she was missing. Well that plan had clearly gone completely tits up.

'Jack, I'm scared.' Sarah's voice sounded close to tears. 'I had an argument with Amy yesterday and she ran out of the house taking H with her and she hasn't come back yet. I know there's something wrong. This morning I found H sitting outside the front door and there's no way he would come home by himself.'

Sarah was crying openly now.

Jack had to think fast and said, 'Don't worry, Sarah. She isn't thinking rationally at the moment. She probably just needs a little space. There could be any number of reasons why she isn't at home. As you said, H wouldn't leave her side so maybe she bought him home and has gone out again.'

'Bollocks, Jack. I know my own daughter and I'm telling you something's wrong.'

'Okay, I hear you. I'll make a few calls and see if anyone has seen her. In the meantime it might be a good idea if you went to your parents for a while. She usually goes round there when you two have had a fight. I'll pop into the house in a few hours in case she turns up whilst you're at your parents.'

He'd guessed that Skeggsy must have been watching Sarah's house but at least he felt a little more at ease in the knowledge that Sarah would be out of the way at her parents.

Jack put the phone down and stared out of the car window wondering where Amy was. He had spent most of the night and morning driving around all of Skeggsy's haunts trying to dig up any information he could on where he might be hiding. He seemed to have hit a wall of silence as no one was prepared to grass against Skeggsy. It looked like he was going to have to crack a few heads against walls to get any information on his whereabouts. Thinking of how to track down Skeggsy and Amy posed one hell of a problem considering he was officially suspended.

Jack scrolled through the numbers in his phone hoping that he hadn't previously deleted the number he was looking for. It had been quite a while since he'd last rung it. His heart missed a beat as he found the number he was looking for and he immediately rang it. After a few moments the phone was answered and he heard a young sounding female voice say, 'Hello.'

At the sound of the woman's gentle voice, he said, 'It's Jack.'

'Jack Reynolds?'

'Yes. I really need your help. I wouldn't normally ask, but it's life or death. Can you meet me at the Kings Arms in Dorking as soon as possible?'

'This is against my better judgement, you know? Well, I'm not due on shift for another three hours, so okay. I can be there in twenty minutes.'

'Thanks. I really appreciate it.'

'Oh, and Jack?'

'Yes?'

'It's good to hear your voice.'

Twenty minutes later, Jack was sitting in his usual seat by the bay window when almost to the second on the appointed hour a pretty blonde woman walked into the pub. As her eyes set on him she smiled, flashing a perfect set of white teeth. Jack shouted over to Jim to bring a gin and tonic and she sat down in a chair opposite him.

'Hi, Julie. Thanks for coming.'

Jack looked at Julie and could see that she was still just as attractive as when he had first met her at Wandsworth nick fresh out of her training at Hendon. Her eyes glistened like uncut pure blue diamonds and she had a figure that would have made any catwalk model jealous.

When he'd first met her, Jack and Sarah had been going through a rough patch and, like a foolish young buck, Jack had embarked on a passionate affair with Julie. The stress of their jobs had pushed them together and the affair was based purely on sex. They'd used each other to satisfy their own needs and the affair had ended when Julie had decided to get married.

'Hello, Jack,' Julie said smiling at him. 'I've only come here out of curiosity. You know I'm a happily married woman still, don't you?'

'Yes. He's a lucky man.'

'So... What's the emergency?'

'I've heard on the grapevine that you're doing a bit of plain clothes work now and have been seconded to the drug squad.'

Julie hesitated before she answered. 'I've been doing a little bit but I won't say I enjoy it. Most of the squad is full of egotistical sexist male pigs who think I don't notice when they drool over me and make dirty comments behind my back.'

Before Jack continued he made Julie swear on her life that anything he told her would stay in complete confidence and would go no further. He skirted around the edges of the truth and explained to Julie that his daughter had got involved with drugs and that she'd been seen with Skeggsy and he needed to talk to him.

Julie said, 'So all you want to do is talk to this scumbag called Skeggsy, nothing else?

'That's right. There won't be any leads back to you if that's what you're worried about. I need to find an address for him. He must have a lock up or a bolthole somewhere and I know that your lot have had him on their radar for a while. All I need is for you to have a little root around on the quiet and see what you can come up with. But I need this information today.'

'Blimey. You don't ask for a lot, do you? I don't see or hear from you for a couple of years and then you ask me to put my career on the line.'

'Sorry but I wouldn't ask if it wasn't really important. Amy could be in real danger.' Jack slid across the table a photograph of Skeggsy's scarred face and said, 'All of the details that I know about him are written on the back. Destroy the photograph when you've finished with it.'

'Ugly looking ginger, isn't he,' Julie said, picking up the photograph and putting it in her handbag. Julie stood up, leant over the table and with her smooth lips she gave Jack a kiss on the cheek, lingering just long enough for the musky smell of her perfume to tickle his nostrils. She then left saying that she'd call him as soon as she could.

CHAPTER 43

DCI Peter Smith had requested Daryl to be in his office within the next ten minutes and had also asked, but his tone of voice suggested that it was blatantly an order, that he was brought up to speed on the Riordan case. Daryl knew that Smith was no fool and suspected that the DCI had found out that he'd suspended Jack from the operation and wanted to know the reasons behind that decision being made without his knowledge.

Any decision taken on an undercover assignment was usually made at the highest level. Daryl had probably overstepped the mark when he'd suspended Jack. The only thing in his favour was that Jack had been flagrantly disobeying orders and hadn't been reporting in, which was in strict contravention of undercover guidelines.

Daryl had been unsure of the reception he would receive in the DCI's office, but his expectations weren't let down. The DCI's face was glowing a strange shade of green and red with anger, and Daryl couldn't help but think that he resembled a Halloween pumpkin.

After two hours, Daryl left the DCI's office and after closing the door behind him could feel the clammy sweat patches from his shirt sticking under his armpits. The DCI had read him the riot act, but he smirked as he thought that he'd got away with just about saving his career.

Daryl decided against taking the lift after the claustrophobia of the DCI's office and calmly took the stairs to the ground floor reception where everyone who entered the building had to hand in their mobile phone and any weapons that they might have on their person. After handing over his receipt to the bored looking officer sitting behind the reception desk he smiled as graciously as he could as he holstered his firearm and pocketed his mobile phone. He only just managed to restrain himself from telling the bored officer that a smile wouldn't hurt anyone.

Daryl was in a good mood after the meeting with the DCI and switched his mobile phone on. Unfortunately for him his good mood wasn't about to last very long.

The message on his phone read, *Victoria Embankment Gardens. One o'clock.* The message didn't say anything else and Daryl didn't need to be a mind reader to know that the message had come from DI Steele. He thought that he'd got the bastard off his back after suspending Jack and smoothing the DCI out, but maybe he had misjudged Steele's tenacity for causing trouble. There was only one way to find out if he could ever get Steele to stop blackmailing him and that was to meet him face to face.

Feeling the weight of the firearm he had holstered under his jacket gave him some comfort. If it came to it he knew he wouldn't hesitate to use it. Anything was better than being locked up as an ex-copper and a convicted paedophile. That was a certain death warrant.

After Julie had left the pub, Jack stayed in the Kings Arms for a while listening to the antique dealers swapping stories about who had ripped off which tourist for the most amount of money. As Jim looked over at him giving him the *Do you want another pint?* kind of look, Jack's phone bleeped.

He opened the app which was set to warn him of any movement from the tracker device on Daryl Rice's car. The car was on the move.

The wait for information on Skeggsy and Amy was killing him. He needed to keep busy so he decided he would follow Rice's car and see where that might lead him. He had nothing to lose by following Rice and sitting in the pub getting drunk wasn't going to bring Amy back.

Jack drove with one eye on the road and the other on the tracker which showed him every movement Rice unwittingly took in his car.

He followed the tracker and before long the signal warned him that Rice's car had come to a stop near the Embankment. His heart missed a beat – he knew precisely where Rice was headed for.

The DI was heading for Victoria Gardens, a pleasant leafy area, open and fairly safe for any operative having a meeting. Jack was very aware from his previous covert experiences that many a dubious meeting had been held in Victoria Gardens by various personnel from different security agencies.

Jack illegally parked the car on a double yellow line and couldn't care less. The tracker indicated that Rice had stopped the car about a hundred yards further up the road, so Jack decided to walk to the gardens.

It didn't take him long before he saw Rice sitting on a wooden bench with a shiny brass plaque on it dedicated to some poor sod who died. Rice was sitting alone and was staring at the statue of the girl with a begging bowl. He was oblivious to everything and everyone around him. Rice didn't notice a man wearing a black knee-length raincoat and a flat cap until the last second before he sat on the bench beside Rice and spoke to him. Jack watched as Rice recoiled away from the man and it was clear that they knew each other and even more interestingly it was clear that there was some animosity between the two men.

Rice appeared terrified of the man as Jack concentrated his attention on watching the man's face and his body language.

By the way the man held himself Jack surmised that he was someone in authority. He could even be ex-military. He had a certain air of confidence about him. Jack was extremely good at putting names to faces but he didn't recognise the tall stranger in the flat cap.

For once the London rain had stopped and the late afternoon sun had come out; it was shining from behind Jack directly at the two men sat on the bench which meant that they had very little chance of seeing him.

Jack knew it was a calculated risk but took the chance. Using his phone he set the camera app to zoom and rattled off some photos of the two men as quickly as he could. After a couple of seconds Jack put his phone back in his pocket. He didn't want to risk the chance of Rice seeing him anymore than he had to and watched intrigued as the man suddenly grabbed Rice by the shoulders and shook him roughly. The man then shouted something at Rice who just sat on the bench looking like he'd seen a ghost. Unfortunately Jack was too far away to hear what was being said, but this meeting between Rice and the stranger had certainly aroused his curiosity. The man let go of Rice quickly and walked away. This was the signal for Jack to go too. He'd got everything he needed and all he wanted now was to rescue his daughter.

CHAPTER 44

It hadn't taken Jack long to drive back to his flat. He couldn't get the thought of Skeggsy hurting Amy out of his mind. Skeggsy was playing mind games with him and hadn't called him as he had said he would. He was an evil bastard and was probably enjoying every second of the mental pain he was inflicting on him.

Jack had been sat on the sofa for half an hour staring at his mobile phone willing it to ring when it suddenly did. It was Julie.

'Julie?' Jack shouted down the phone.

'Hi, Jack. Are you keeping yourself out of trouble?'

'Very funny. Have you got anything for me?'

'It took a while, but when I ran this Skeggsy character's name through the HOLMES computer - it didn't take long to find him. He's been quite busy and after a bit of digging it turns out that it's not only the NCA that are interested in him.'

'I know all of that. Have you got an address for me?' Jack could feel cold sweat running down his face and prayed that Julie had come up trumps.

'Yes. The drug squad have a file on him dating back to his childhood. It turns out that his mother was a prostitute and when he was a sprog he was abused by some of her punters. It gets worse though. His mother was brutally tortured and murdered by an unknown but presumed punter of hers.'

'The address, Julie?' Jack impatiently butted in.

'Okay. I'm getting to it. Well, it just so happens that when his mother was murdered Skeggsy was in prison but when he came out he inherited the council flat and it's still in his name today, even though he doesn't officially live there. The flat is on the Limehouse Fields Estate on the edge of Mile End.'

As Jack scribbled the address down on an old newspaper he had found on the table he said, 'Julie, I really owe you one. Thanks.'

'No problem. Just remember this didn't come from me. I know there's more to this than you're letting on. I hope whatever it is works out for you.'

'Oh, before you go there's just one more thing.'

'You're joking? I've already put my job on the line for you once.'

'Sorry. You won't get in any trouble with this one, I promise.'

Julie gave a soft laugh and Jack remembered how the sound used to melt his heart and turn his legs to jelly.

'DI Rice had a clandestine meeting in Victoria Gardens with someone and I think the guy he met is in the job. I'm just curious to know a little bit more about the person he met. I'll send over some photos I managed to take of the meeting to your mobile. Can you run them through personnel files and see what you can come up with?'

'You've just made my day. It would be a pleasure. Anything that involves that sleazeball Rice is bound to be dirty.'

Jack heard a dull tone signifying that Julie had ended the phone call and he sat down on the sofa holding his head in his hands trying to gather his thoughts which were all over the place. The flat must be where Amy was being held. Skeggsy was clever but not that clever and Jack needed to carefully plan his next move. What really scared Jack was that Skeggsy hadn't called him, any unthinkable horror could have happened to Amy in the last twenty-four hours. He knew Skeggsy was trying to wind him up by not calling him, but the wait was unbearable.

Jack grabbed his leather jacket off the back of the sofa and headed for his car. He knew what to do and needed to get to Cavendish Road fast.

A few moments later the silver garage doors clanged shut as Jack drove the Audi out of his garage and wheel spun up the slope before turning onto the bypass heading for the Dorking Cockerel roundabout and then Redhill. The traffic was as bad as usual due to the never ending road works but once he'd navigated the painfully slow one way system in Reigate it didn't take him long to reach Redhill and Cavendish Road.

Jack turned right into the cul-de-sac and the Audi bounced over the potholes sending shooting pain from his wounded leg. For once, he barely noticed. He had one thing on his mind and that was to get his baby girl back safely.

He jammed the key in the lock twisting it hard and pushed with his shoulder against the red wooden door to get into the bungalow, the door creaked as it had warped in the torrential rain they had been getting recently. He almost fell into the hallway as the door eventually opened and the musty smell of stale lager and out of date food took his breath away. Jack recognised the familiar smell; his own flat had the same foul aroma.

Without bothering to take his leather jacket off, Jack raced across the Alpine Lodge wooden flooring leaving a large snail trail of mud behind him in his rush and ran into the kitchen at the back of the bungalow. He pulled the drawer beside the larder cupboard out so hard that it came off its runners and four kilo bags of coke spilt out over the floor.

Bending down to pick up the bags, his left leg gave way and he collapsed in a heap on the floor almost blacking out with the pain. Unfortunately, he had fallen on top of one of the kilo bags which split and the powder burst out across the kitchen floor. He didn't have any choice so he left the burst bag on the floor. Picking up the other three bags, he stuffed them into his inside jacket pockets. Closing the front door behind him Jack ran back to the Audi and jumped in the driver's seat. It had been less than twenty minutes since he'd been sitting in his flat in Dorking when the idea of a plan to rescue Amy first started to form in his mind.

CHAPTER 45

The bluetooth music playing in the car was *Ace of Spades* by Motorhead and the insane guitar being thrashed out by Lemmy matched Jack's mood.

He tried to drive slowly but his anger was intensified by the music pounding full blast out of the Audi's top of the range stereo. If he played the music any louder he would probably blow the graphic equalizer or one of the speakers, but given the mood he was in he didn't give a fuck. He tried to stay calm as the thought of rescuing Amy was all consuming and the last thing he needed was some bored traffic cop pulling him over for speeding, searching the car and finding the three kilos of coke.

After what seemed like hours, but in reality was probably a drive of less than an hour, he indicated right and drove into the Limehouse Fields Estate where Julie had said Skeggsy possibly still had a flat. Jack parked the car outside a small row of shops which consisted of a bookies, a run-down off licence, a Chinese takeaway and a Bengali restaurant which had a large metal front covering where the front window used to be. Sprayed across it were various tags by the local kids and some racist graffiti.

Beside the off licence a group of hoodies on bikes were huddled smoking weed. He guessed that the average age of them couldn't have been more than fourteen and that their parents didn't have a clue where they were. The parents, or he presumed single parents, were probably just glad the little thugs were out of the house and not annoying them at home. It really pissed him off seeing these kids trying to act all hard when all they were doing was being used to run drugs around the estate by the elder gang members. They would eventually take the fall for those gang members and inevitably start the sad passage through prison life.

Their lives were already ruined and all their parents cared about was sending them down the shops to get them King Size Rizla so that they could smoke weed and drink cheap booze. If their kids robbed the shop it was probably a bonus to the parents as it meant they saved some money.

Jack got out of the Audi and walked towards the group of hoodies. As he approached them they started to circle him on their little bikes like a shoal of sharks preparing for the kill.

He shouted at the group of circling hoodies, 'There's twenty quid in it for you lot to make sure my motor isn't damaged, right?'

The biggest of the group cycled over and said, 'Sorted, bruv. You wanna buy any rocks or weed?'

'Just watch the car,' Jack said turning to walk away.

The hoodie pulled Jack's arm and demanded, 'Bruv? Aren't you forgetting something?'

Jack said, 'Before I give you the twenty do you know which block of flats a ginger meathead with a personalised BMW plate lives in? If you do I'll bump it up to a fifty and none of your little mates need know. Strictly between us, right?'

'Sound, bruv.' The elder boy grinned flashing a gold tooth which made him look older than he probably was. 'That ginger nonce has got it coming to him anyway, he's a freak. The creep beat up some of my crew the other day. The car's parked by the flats behind the off licence. Laters bruv.'

The gold-toothed wannabe gangster snatched the fifty pound note out of Jack's hand, then he bashed his knuckles against Jack's fist and faded off into the shadows with his crew following in his wake.

Jack walked behind the off licence and down a small alleyway which was littered with discarded needles from the druggies on benefits. The alleyway opened up into a large square with a small playground with swings where mothers still wearing their pyjamas watched overweight children play on the swings.

Opposite the swings stood two imposing high rise tower blocks. They reminded Jack of 'The Twin Towers', a pair of equally unpleasant blocks on one of the local estates in Dorking. His eyes caught sight of Skeggsy's BMW with its distinctive number plate parked outside the tower block on the left.

Jack took his mobile out of his pocket and used it to rub against the ever increasing pain in his left leg as his adrenalin started to peak at the sight of Skeggsy's car. He then quickly scrolled through the names on his mobile and finding the name he wanted he sent a short text message.

Looking around him to see if anyone was watching him he strolled towards the car as inconspicuously as he could, which wasn't difficult on a crime riddled estate such as Limehouse Fields as everyone kept themselves to themselves and tried not to look anyone in the eye inviting unwanted attention or violence.

He reached the BMW which Skeggsy had helpfully reversed parked against the wall of the tower block which meant Jack could duck down behind the boot where it was less likely that anybody looking would be able to see him. Reaching into the pocket of his leather jacket he took out a small box and attached it to the boot of the car. He pressed the small switch on the side of the box and a green light started to flash and a series of numbers scrolled horizontally across a tiny LED screen in a blur.

Jack waited impatiently. His leg was killing him crouched down in such an uncomfortable position. Suddenly the green light switched to a red colour and the numbers stopped scrolling across the screen.

Jack carefully removed the device which had silenced the alarm and unlocked the car. Putting a handkerchief over his hand he quickly opened the boot and took one last quick look around him before ripping open the side panel inside. Wiping the plastic clean of finger prints he stuffed the three kilos of coke hidden in his inside jacket pockets down the inside of the panel. He clicked the side panel back into place, slammed the car boot shut and casually strolled away. The whole procedure had taken less than thirty seconds.

Jack walked back down the filthy alleyway heading towards his car when his mobile started to ring in his pocket. Swearing under his breath he took the mobile out and as soon as he saw the name on the screen he answered the call immediately.

'How's my favourite NCA officer?' Skeggsy asked, sounding as high as a kite.

'Don't piss me around, Skeggsy. Where's Amy? If you harm just one hair on her head, then by God I swear I will fucking kill you.'

'Now, now. There's no need to be like that, Jack. You'll be glad to hear that I'm going on a little holiday but first there's something I want you to do for me. If you do this one small thing for me I might let you have your little bitch back in one piece.'

'What guarantee do I have that she's still alive?' Jack shouted, feeling as though his head was going to explode at the thought of Skeggsy being anywhere near Amy.

'You'll just have to trust me for the moment but I'll bring proof before the exchange,' Skeggsy said cackling dementedly down the phone.

'What exchange?'

'Shut the fuck up and listen. I want you to go to Cavendish Road and clear out all of the product – the weed, coke, cash, everything. I then want you to drive to the car park beside the lookout post on Box Hill where I'll meet you in one hour.'

'You're crazier than I thought,' Jack said. 'If I don't kill you first then Riordan will.'

'Fuck Riordan. I haven't spoken to the northern prat in days and before he finds out I've ripped him off I'll be sitting on a beach in the sunshine having my balls massaged by some cheap whore. Anyway his days are numbered. Word on the street is that Big V is making moves to take over the whole show and Riordan will be taken out permanently, if you get my drift. You've got one hour, Jack.'

The phone went dead.

CHAPTER 46

Jack stood standing in the alleyway for a few seconds before he scrolled down to the same number he'd texted earlier, but this time he rang it. After one ring a voice answered it.

'Yeah?'

'Are you where we agreed?'

'Yeah.'

'Good. Everything is set and that prick Skeggsy is leaving now so I'm going in. Let's just pray my hunch is right and Amy is in the flat, otherwise I could be signing her death warrant.'

Jack stuffed the mobile back into his pocket and started to walk back towards the tower block. As he neared the end of the alleyway he stopped and lit a cigarette using his gold Zippo lighter. As the warm smoke enveloped his lungs he began to feel calmer. He'd learnt in his training in different war zones that when he needed to get his emotions in check, smoking definitely helped.

Inhaling the last drag deeply he watched as a figure appeared from the doorway of the left tower block. Jack could immediately tell that the figure was Skeggsy by the ginger hair and the huge ape-like frame. Skeggsy got into the BMW and Jack watched the car drive away and disappear out of sight before he started to casually walk back towards the tower block.

Jack reached the graffiti-covered front door and opened it. There was a vandalised lock system which looked like it had probably been broken for a long time. The entry hall was empty but the walls were covered in graffiti just like the door and it also stank of urine. Jack wondered what it was that made people piss in hallways and lifts. He blamed the government and the schools for not teaching any discipline or respect anymore. The country needed National Service like a lot of the European countries. He thought the whole structure and fabric of the country was falling into disarray and nobody seemed to give a fuck.

Jack decided against using the urine scented lift and painfully limped up the stairs. He reached the third floor and took a second or two to get his breath back before he opened the door. The door had a smashed window and led out onto the third floor landing. The landing was empty apart from a few bulging black bin liners full of rubbish which had been left outside some of the flats. Most of the bags were over-spilling with empty bottles and take-away cartons and some idiot had kicked over some of the bags so that the contents were littered all the way across the landing.

Jack stood outside one particular flat and, putting his ear to the door, he listened intently to see if he could hear the sound of voices coming from inside. He suspected that Skeggsy was working alone but he couldn't be too careful.

He couldn't hear any voices coming from the flat but thought that he could hear the muffled noise of what sounded like a girl crying. Wasting no time at all he pulled a small pistol with a long silencer on the end out of his jacket pocket and shot the feeble lock which held the door shut. Jack then took a couple of steps back and ran at the door and using all of his weight with his shoulder he smashed it open.

He immediately ducked down rolling across the floor before coming to a stop in a kneeling prone position, clenching the pistol tightly between both hands he moved his arms in a sweeping arc covering all of the angles of the room.

The room was badly lit but the sight that greeted him almost stopped him in his tracks. Empty beer cans littered the floor and in one corner stood a large table with a photo of a pretty young girl who couldn't have been older than twenty. Surrounding the photo were lots of lit candles giving off that strange smell which only burning wax gives. The smell reminded Jack of when he used to go with his parents to Christmas Mass but this was not Christmas. The photo could only be of Skeggsy's murdered mother and the whole set up represented some kind of weird mausoleum to her, giving a clear indication about the state of Skeggsy's sanity.

In the other corner of the room was a bed covered with a stained sheet and sitting on it, leaning against a radiator, was Amy. She was crying and she was handcuffed to the radiator with plastic cuffs similar to the ones used by the police.

Jack rushed over to her and pulled the loosened gag away from her mouth. He held her tightly to his chest.

Amy leant into him whimpering, 'Dad, thank God. Please help me.'

Jack took out a pocket knife and sawed through the ties which cuffed Amy to the radiator. He finally cut through them as Amy fell into a whimpering heap in his arms.

'Amy, don't talk, save your strength. We have to get out of here quickly but tell me one thing. Did you see anyone else or was it just that ginger man with you?'

'I didn't see anyone else. I'm so scared....'

'I know. Now come on, let's go.'

Lifting Amy up with one arm he dragged her to her feet and as quickly as he could he led her out of the flat. With the state Amy was in he decided to use the lift as it would be quicker and the fewer people who saw them the better.

In a matter of minutes they were rushing back down the needle-strewn alleyway that Jack had previously walked down and reached the parade of shops. Thankfully the gold-toothed hoodie was true to his word and the Audi was still there and didn't look damaged.

Jack carefully put Amy in the passenger seat. She was in a state of shock and mumbling to herself. He tried to talk to her but couldn't be sure that she was even listening to him. The Audi engine roared into life and the car wheel-spun as Jack rammed his foot on the accelerator driving them both out of the estate.

'Amy, I need you to listen to me carefully. Okay?'

After a few seconds Amy turned her head and looked at Jack with her eyes which were red raw from crying and nodded her head a couple of times. She had the thousand yard stare on her face which soldiers had after they returned from battle, but Jack had to take a chance and prayed that she understood what he was about to say to her.

'I'm going to leave you with an old friend of mine. He's ex-army and we served together. You can trust him completely. He'll take you to the nearest hospital to get you checked out and then back to my flat in Dorking where you'll be safe. He'll look after you and I'll come back in less than a couple of hours okay, but first I have to deal with the man who kidnapped you.'

Amy nodded, saying, 'Please don't leave me?'

'I know, honey, but I have to. It won't be for long and then all of this will be over.'

Jack slammed on the brakes and turned left into a large pub car park. He pulled up beside an old blue Volvo and turned the engine off. As he got out of the car a tall man with a shaggy mop of blond hair got out of the Volvo and they shook hands.

Jack smiled at Stan Wacameyer and said, 'Thanks, Stan. I owe you one.'

'Actually, you owe me two, but who's counting.'

Jack helped Amy out of the car and gently ushered her into the front passenger seat of the Volvo.

'Amy, don't worry. This is Stan who will look after you. He helped you when you were in trouble in Ireland. I'll meet you at the flat as soon as I can, okay?'

Amy nodded whilst using the back of her hand to wipe away the tears which were streaming down her freckled face. It broke his heart to leave her but there were loose ends to tie up so he jumped back into the Audi and without looking back he drove out of the car park back towards the Limehouse Fields Estate.

Jack had parked the Audi down a small residential road half a mile away from the estate and chain smoked whilst waiting impatiently for Skeggsy to call him.

After nearly an hour his mobile rang. Jack looked at the screen and saw Skeggsy's name. He threw the mobile onto the passenger seat and ignored it, smiling to himself he lit another cigarette. His plan was coming together nicely, especially now that Amy was safe.

The phone rang continuously for fifteen minutes and then went silent.

Jack drove back to the estate where he was careful to hide his car behind the off licence and walked back down needle alleyway again. There was no sign of Skeggsy's BMW so Jack walked over to the left tower block and crouched down beside the fire escape so that he was hidden from view and waited.

Whilst waiting the weather had turned colder so Jack zipped up his leather jacket and turned the collar up to try and keep himself warm. After twenty minutes he noticed a car speeding quickly towards the tower block and as it got closer he could see the distinctive number plate of Skeggsy's BMW. He crouched down as far as his painful leg would allow and watched as Skeggsy carefully reverse parked his pride and joy outside the front of the tower block.

Jack walked up to the car and drawing the pistol with the silencer from his pocket he pointed the pistol at the driver's window and tapped on the glass using the end of the silencer. The driver turned his face towards him and Jack stared at Skeggsy, revelling in the shock that suddenly appeared in in Skeggsy's eyes as he realised that it was Jack standing out there in the rain pointing a gun directly at him.

Before Skeggsy had time to move, Jack shot him through the glass straight between the eyes. The bullet had been hollowed out in order to maximise the damage that it would do on entry and especially exit. Skeggsy's brain erupted into small pieces as the bullet smashed its way through his skull and the passenger side window turned a thick red colour. The small pieces of blasted brain matter were weighted down with shattered tiny pieces of Skeggsy's skull and quickly poured down the window like racing speed boats on a river of fast moving blood.

Jack opened the car door and looked at the pathetic sight of Skeggsy's body, lying across the passenger seat in an array of thick red blood mixed with a hint of ginger. Smiling, Jack popped another bullet into his stomach for good measure whilst saying, 'Good riddance to bad rubbish.'

CHAPTER 47

Rushing back to Dorking to see Amy, Jack started to feel a sense of relief overwhelm him but there was one more thing he needed to do.

He quickly pulled the car over to the side of the road when he reached a local beauty spot called 'The Stepping Stones'. This was a man-made crossing stretching over a shallow part of the River Mole made of large stones which ramblers used to cross the river on their nature walks. Jack hurried along the bank of the river and came to a stop where the river deepened. He broke the pistol down into its individual components, as he had been taught to do in the army, then he tossed the pieces into the river.

Ten minutes later Jack opened the door to his flat and walked into the messy living room. In hindsight he should have cleaned the flat up a little from the night before, but it was too late now. Amy was in shock and would be too distracted to notice the mess or the aroma of last night's kebab, and Stan had lived in army billets in war zones all over the world so he was unlikely to worry about any mess or discom fort.

Amy was curled up on the sofa with a thick tartan blanket wrapped around her. She was watching television and Stan was making a cup of tea in the kitchen so he walked into the kitchen and asked, 'How's she been?'

'The hospital gave her the okay but she's in shock and hasn't said a word since you put her in my car, poor girl. Don't worry though. Give it time and she'll come round. I've dealt with kidnap victims back in Ireland during the troubles and you just have to let them open up to you in their own time. The worst thing you can do is start pushing them for answers.'

'Did the hospital say if that scumbag had--'

'No, she wasn't raped,' Stan cut in before Jack could say the dreaded word.

'Thanks, Stan.'

'No problem, mate. Did you sort out your little problem?'

'Yes, thanks. When the police find Skeggsy dead they'll search the car and find the coke. They'll come to one conclusion – that it must've been a drug deal gone wrong. It'll barely be investigated and after a few days the file will be lost deep in some police cabinet somewhere. By the way, Stan, you can say thanks to your army buddy and tell him that the gun has gone for a swim where nobody will find it.'

'Good. I'd better get going anyway, unless there's anything else you'd like me to do?'

'I don't know how I'll ever repay you, but one day I will,' Jack said, shaking Stan's hand and then grabbing him in a big bear hug. 'We've got to go too. I rang Sarah and she's expecting us at her place. I'd better not keep her waiting any longer.'

Two minutes later Jack and Amy watched as Stan drove away and then Jack started the Audi's engine and slowly drove off in the direction of Sarah's house. Jack didn't bother playing any music and quietly drove along in silence until they reached Sarah's house.

Before he'd even parked the car Sarah came running out of the house. She opened the passenger door and Amy collapsed in her arms sobbing and Sarah helped Amy walk slowly into the house. A few minutes later Sarah had run Amy a hot bath and had given her a clean towel and laid some fresh clothes out on her bed in the bedroom she'd used when she was a child.

When Amy was asleep, Sarah came downstairs and poured Jack a glass of wine. Jack refused the glass, saying to Sarah, 'No thanks, I think that you and Amy both need a sober Jack around.' Sarah sat down beside him on the sofa. Neither of them said anything for a few seconds and you could have cut the air in the room with a knife. Suddenly Jack broke the silence, saying, 'She's in shock so go easy on her. It'll take time.'

Sarah looked at Jack with tears in her eyes. 'You and your bloody job. It's never put us in danger before. We could have lost our daughter.' Sarah let out a sob, lashing out at him with her fists. Jack grabbed her wrists and held her tightly in his arms. He could feel her body shaking uncontrollably against his chest as she cried.

'I'm so sorry, Sarah. It will never happen again but Amy is back safe and sound now and she's our priority. The last thing she needs to see is us two arguing,' Jack said, gently kissing her on the forehead.

Suddenly the moment was broken by the noise of Jack's mobile ringing. 'Shit. Sorry, Sarah, but I have to take this.' Jack walked into the kitchen before he answered the phone.

'Jack?'

'Hi, Julie. What have you got for me?'

'You were right about Rice and that stranger. What I've got for you is dynamite. It's too explosive to talk over the phone. Can I meet you in the same pub we met in last time? Say in half an hour?'

'Okay. I'll see you there.'

Jack walked back into the living room and said to Sarah, 'I'm really sorry but I've got to go. I'll call you and come over later so that we can talk things over properly. I'll explain everything I know to you then.' Jack picked up his leather jacket and kissed Sarah on the cheek before stepping over H who was asleep on the floor.

Ten minutes later Jack was sitting at the round table in the King's Arms watching Jim trying to impress his new bar girl, a pretty brunette who had just started working at the pub whilst on a break from university. In Jack's hand was a small glass of diet coke. After a short while the door opened and the distinctive smell of Julie's perfume enveloped his nostrils as she walked through the door and sat down at the table.

'Hi, Julie. Do you want a drink?'

'No thanks. I haven't got long,' Julie said, flashing Jack one of her beautiful wide smiles.

'So… What is it that's so explosive you can't talk about it on the phone?'

'Well, I don't really know where to start.'

'Try the beginning.'

'Shut up, Jack. Sarcasm never suited you,' Julie said, laughing.

'Sorry.'

'Anyway. You were right about the man in the photo; he is in the job. He's attached to MI6 to be precise. His name is DI Peter Steele and he's under covert investigation for corruption on a large scale. He's suspected of being involved in the drugs trade and has links to organised crime. Now here's the real biggie which I think will really interest you.'

'What is it?'

'Well, looking at his family history, he has a half-brother, same father but different mother. Guess who?'

'Don't play games, Julie, just spit it out,' Jack growled.

'Mick Riordan.'

'Bloody hell. Really?' Jack was stunned.

'I told you it was dynamite. I reckon this MI6 chap has some dirt on Rice as he's also under investigation for blackmailing fellow officers. Oh by the way, Rice has gone off on extended sick leave and nobody knows the reason why.'

'That slimy prick. I wonder what Steele has on him?'

Julie slid a paper file across the table and said, 'I copied as much as I could and it's all in the file. Hopefully some of it makes some sense to you.'

'You're a star, Julie. This explains a lot of things.' It all started to become clear to Jack. This Steele guy had something on Rice and somehow must have forced Rice to suspend Jack from duty. It also explained how Riordan always managed to keep one step ahead of the NCA.

Julie smiled again at Jack and then her mood changed and she said, 'A strange thing happened today, the whole office is buzzing with the news. Your ginger friend was found in his car with his brains blown out and three kilos of coke were discovered hidden in the boot of the car. You wouldn't happen to know anything about this would you Jack?'

'No... Sounds a bit like a drug deal gone wrong to me.'

Julie laughed and said, 'It'll probably get logged as that but you wouldn't tell me either way, would you?'

Jack held up his hand and said, 'Scout's honour, I didn't have anything to do with it.'

'Anyway I've got to go. Take care of yourself, Jack, and please destroy that file once you have read it,' Julie said before she got up and left the pub.

Jack went to the bar and asked Jim for another for another glass of diet coke.

'I bet you can't keep this no alcohol up for long?' Jim sniggered.

Ignoring him Jack went back to the round table and opened the document that Julie had given to him. The file certainly made interesting reading and it looked like Peter Steele was up to his neck in corruption. Riordan's criminal activities were prolific as well – drugs, prostitution, extortion, you name it and he had his hand in it. But there was nothing concrete as he was slipperier than a snake covered in butter. The file was interesting reading but the information was useless to him. There was little he could do whilst he was still suspended from duty.

The song 'Diamonds' erupted from his pocket suddenly breaking his concentration whilst he read the file so quickly fumbling in his pocket he answered the mobile.

'Jack?'

He instantly recognised the gruff voice – it was Riordan and he sounded angry.

'Yes, Mr Riordan.'

'Have you heard the news? Skeggsy's been shot. He's fucking dead.'

'Bloody hell. It's the first I've heard of it. How? When?' Jack lied.

'I don't know all the fucking details but I can bet you that prick Big V has something to do with it. He's been trying to muscle in on my operations for a while now. I want you to get out there and find out what the word on the street is. Some cunt must know who did this and you can tell them there's ten grand in it for anyone who can tell me who did it. I'm not having people think I'm a fucking pushover.'

The phone went dead. Jack couldn't believe his luck. Riordan didn't know that Skeggsy had ripped him off and was blaming Big V for his murder and to top it all his cover hadn't been blown now that Skeggsy was dead. He finished his drink and thought that he had better go and check on how Sarah and Amy were doing.

As he walked across the car park beside the Kings Arms he noticed a van with its side door open and the smiling face of Gazza was staring out at him.

'Get in.'

Jack climbed into the van, pleased with himself that at least this time they weren't going to try to physically drag him into the van. That kick he had given Gazza in the bollocks the last time they had tried to sweep him off the street must have hurt him more than he had thought.

'What is it? I'm suspended from duty....'

'Not anymore,' Gazza said. 'Welcome back. DCI Smith wants you back on operational duty as DI Rice overstepped his authority and he's gone on extended sick leave.'

'It couldn't happen to a nicer person,' Jack replied sarcastically.

He then jumped out of the van and got into his Audi. Leaning slowly back into the comfortable seat he lit a cigarette and thought to himself that it had been one hell of a day and yet lady luck had shone on him and everything seemed to have turned out quite well. Amy was safe, Sarah was still talking to him, he wasn't suspended from his job anymore and his cover hadn't been blown.

There was still one missing piece to the jigsaw. Now that he was back on operational duty he was determined to unravel the web of deceit which had led to his suspension. He knew that somehow Rice was involved with DI Peter Steele and that all roads led to Steele's half-brother Riordan, the main kingpin. He hadn't quite worked out how he was going to prove it - but Steele was a marked man.

CHAPTER 48

Jack watched the bus come to a stop near Peter Steele's flat in Kings Cross where Steele got off, Jack then turned and headed in the opposite direction. It was a nice day and he decided to walk as he had half an hour before he was meant to meet Julie at the Dublin Castle pub in Camden. Jack had spent the last two weeks watching Steele's movements.

He entered the pub and after ordering a diet coke sat down on a rickety wooden chair opposite Julie. The subtle smell of Julie's perfume swept over him.

'Hi Julie.'

'Hello Jack. I see you're still drinking diet coke then?'

'Yes and it's the only coke I do nowadays,' Jack replied laughing.

'You do know I'm seconded to the drug squad?' Julie joked, smoothing her hair back with her hand as she laughed. 'So why did you call? I'm not going to discover another dead drug dealer friend of yours with his brains blown out shortly after this meeting am I?' Julie asked, with a heavy hint of sarcasm.

'I need you to do a little digging for me,' Jack said, choosing to ignore Julie's little niggle at him. 'I need to know who owns a warehouse in Pimlico. If I start asking questions it could jeopardise my cover but I think I'm onto something and it could bust this whole case wide open.'

'What, Riordan?'

Jack had told Julie the case he was working on as he needed her on side; it was against protocol but that was the way Jack worked, rules were made to be broken.

'The whole pack of cards – Riordan, Steele maybe even Rice, the whole lot.' Jack passed Julie a piece of paper with an address scrawled on it. 'I can't say too much at the moment but I'll let you in on the bust when it happens and you'll probably end up with a commendation or even a promotion.'

'I'll hold you to that promise,' Julie smiled taking a small sip of her gin and tonic.

'If possible, can you send me a photo showing the proof of ownership?'

'Shouldn't be a problem. Just give me an hour or two.'

'Great, thanks Julie.'

As Jack got up to leave Julie suddenly asked, 'How's your family?'

'They're good, Julie.' Jack left the pub as he felt a little uncomfortable talking about his personal life as he felt guilty about making such a mess of it recently.

He walked back to Kings Cross to collect his car and twenty minutes later his phone bleeped. It was a text from Julie with a picture attached. He read the text: *You won't believe this? Steele's wife is a director of various small companies and the warehouse is registered to a small subsidiary called Gateway Electronics.* Attached was a photo of a registry at Companies House confirming DI Steele's wife as the owner.

This was explosive news to Jack. He had suspected for a while the warehouse was used as a safe-house for the distribution of drugs and had photos of Riordan entering the warehouse. With the photos of Riordan and the warehouse connection to his half-brother Steele, they'd got him. It had taken him three years but now he felt confident he could put Riordan way for a long time. Also, thrown into the mix was the bent MI6 agent Steele which was a real bonus.

Less than an hour later Jack was seated in DCI Smith's office trying hard not to stare at his unusually globe-shaped head. Jack explained everything including the photo evidence.

DCI Smith commented, 'It's tenuous, we might not be able to nail Riordan in the act but I agree it's the best evidence yet. Whatever happens we'll blow his whole distribution network apart and he won't have the protection of MI6.'

'Exactly sir. The photo evidence links Riordan to the warehouse and the drugs. All I need is an armed team ready to go in at a moment's notice when I give the word. I'll give the word when I'm sure the warehouse is full of drugs.'

DCI Smith scratched his balding head and pushed his last few wisps of greying hair across globe-shaped head. There was a short silence whilst the DCI considered what Jack had told him. He stood up and walked over to the window which looked out across the London skyline. After a few seconds he turned round saying, 'Let's do it.'

Jack smiled broadly. 'One thing sir?'

'Yes?'

'You let me take Steele down. There's one thing I can't stand and it's dirty coppers.' Jack was sure that it was Steele who in some way was responsible for Lanky's death and it was probably his deception that led to Skeggsy discovering he worked for the NCA; without Steele's involvement Amy would never have been kidnapped and Jack wanted revenge.

'I don't see why not,' DCI Smith replied nodding at Jack, his few wisps of combed across hair falling across his shiny forehead into his eyes.

'Thank you, sir.'

'I haven't finished yet, Jack. I have a lot of political pressure to get a result on this one and I want it done today. This guy Steele has upset a lot of people in high places and if we can upset Riordan as well and the CPS go for it, then all the better. Two hours, then we hit the bastards.'

Leaving the DCI's office Jack felt the last three years' work was finally coming together when unexpectedly his phone rang. It was Gazza, he was doing Jack a favour by helping to watch Steele, ensuring he was under surveillance round the clock.

'Yeah, what have you got for me?'

'You'd better get down here Jack. The little shit is on the move and something seems to have spooked him, he seems well jumpy.'

'What the fuck do you mean – spooked?'

'I don't know but he's outside the flat putting suitcases in the car. I think he's arguing with his wife about the amount of suitcases but it's hard to hear without getting too close. I'm going to follow them.'

Steele's wife, Tatyana, came from Bulgaria and alarm bells rang in Jack's head. Maybe Steele's wife was involved with the Bulgarian mafia? Had he made a huge mistake thinking Riordan was the one in charge? He didn't know what to think!

'Okay, follow them discreetly. I reckon they're going to the airport and I'll check on flights. Stay in contact.'

'Yes, guv.'

It was a race against time if Steele was leaving the country and was it coincidental considering Jack's conversation with the DCI? It didn't take too many phone calls to find out that Steele was on the next flight from Heathrow to Bulgaria. Jack rang Gazza and told him to ask Special Branch to detain Steele and his wife at all costs. It left Jack less than an hour to get to Heathrow.

Jack's leg ached as he drove through the London traffic but he forced himself through the pain barrier. Once out of London it was a quick drive to Heathrow. He parked the Audi in the short term car park across the ramp from Terminal Five and leapt out.

Running into the airport as fast as his leg would allow he rang Gazza.

'Yes, Jack.'

Jack could hardly hear Gazza's Brummie voice above the din of the airport. 'Where are you?'

'They're just about to check-in at desk number 19, I'm with the SB guys near the trolley stand.'

'Well done. I can see you and I'll be behind them in less than a minute. When you see me standing behind them I want SB to pull the bastards.' Jack jumped the queue, flashing his rarely used NCA identification card, and stood directly behind Steele and his wife. Tatyana was at least fifteen years younger than Steele and her taste in clothing revolted Jack. She was wearing an ankle length real fur coat.

Jack watched as four SB men from airport security approached Steele and his wife. One of the men asked Steele to follow them but Steele turned and attempted to run. In a moment of desperation Jack stuck out his left leg and tripped Steele over. The pain in Jack's leg was excruciating but Steele fell to the ground dragging his wife tumbling over with him. The couple lay in a heap on the floor trapped amongst their suitcases and Tatyana's vile fur coat.

A few minutes later Jack was sat in a small square shaped room with only the noise of the CCTV filming him to keep him company. The door opened and Steele entered the room followed by two burly uniformed policemen. Jack motioned to him to sit down on the chair opposite him.

Steele looked at him and shouted, 'Where's my wife and why the fuck have I been dragged in here? Steele's eyes widened as he recognised Jack. 'Hang on a minute, aren't you the prick who tripped me over?'

Without saying a word Jack slid a thick file across the table.

Steele slowly flicked through the file then losing some of his earlier air of confidence quietly asked, 'What's this all about? I have a plane to catch.'

'That file is the end of your career and I'm your worst nightmare come true. Come to think of it, your half-brother Riordan's as well. Times, dates, photos, they're all in there.' Jack smiled at Steele as he pressed a buzzer and the door opened.

A pretty blond woman walked in. The smell of her perfume tickled Jack's nostrils, her musky perfume usually had that effect.

'Thanks, I'll take it from here,' Julie said, with a large grin across her face smelling a long overdue promotion in the air.

THE END

28240040R00142

Printed in Great Britain
by Amazon